It's In His Kiss

EVE DEVON

A division of HarperCollins*Publishers*
www.harpercollins.co.uk

Harper
An imprint of HarperCollins*Publishers* Ltd
The News Building
1 London Bridge Street
London SE1 9GF

www.harpercollins.co.uk

A paperback original 2016
1

A catalogue record for this book
is available from the British Library

ISBN: 9780008114930

Set in Minion by Palimpsest Book Production Limited, Falkirk, Stirlingshire

Printed and bound in Great Britain

MIX
Paper from
responsible sources
FSC™ C007454

FSC™ is a non-profit international organisation established to promote
the responsible management of the world's forests. Products carrying the
FSC label are independently certified to assure consumers that they come
from forests that are managed to meet the social, economic and
ecological needs of present and future generations,
and other controlled sources.

Find out more about HarperCollins and the environment at
www.harpercollins.co.uk/green

For Lana and the oodles of joyful 'Darth Daisy' inspiration you supply and because one day you will be old enough to know what your 'Mad Auntie Eve' does for a living!

CHAPTER ONE

'Wait – what? Did you just ask me to sell sex at the launch party for your lingerie line?'

Luke Jackson's usually reserved tone had taken on a new, gruff edge that trickled over Sephy King's senses, making her heartbeat spike alarmingly. As if her heart needed any more of a workout.

Standing on the newly constructed catwalk in the large ballroom of the King's family estate, it turned out that T minus two weeks to the launch of her new lingerie collection, Seraphic, and with her stress levels higher than the Shard with the Cheese Grater building stuck on top of it, Sephy's heart was skipping, dipping and nose-diving quite enough, thank you very much.

Lord, could this go more spectacularly wrong? She should never have attempted to ask him without first practising. She already found his rock-solid approach to their friendship way hotter than she should, without introducing words like 'sex' to their banter.

She flicked a look to Luke and saw that her friend had gone from slouching in one of the two hundred gilt-framed chairs surrounding the catwalk, to sitting up a little more straight and a lot more alert.

Damn. There was now no way to retract her garbled plea.

Sephy tried to remind herself that she was good at thinking on her feet. That she excelled at rolling with the punches. But this was Luke she had just made a fool of herself in front of and embarrassment was brought to her on a whiff of defeat that had her shoulders dipping a little.

Clearing her throat she went with a lame, 'It's not that I want you to sell,' she paused and flapped a hand about, creating a new and interesting gesture to indicate the word 'sex', 'specifically – it's more, the idea of it.'

'The idea of it?' Luke's eyebrows remained in the region of his hairline. 'I thought you asked me over here to check out how well it was all coming together before getting around to asking me to hand out a few catalogues on the night?'

'Actually, I have someone for that. What I'm asking for involves a more,' she licked her lips and searched her head for a tactful phrase, 'hands-on approach.'

'Hands-on?'

'Uh-huh.'

'Okay. So, then, you're going to have to be more explicit about the sex thing.'

Sephy blinked as Luke relaxed back against the chair he was sitting on, his arms stretching out to rest against the backs of the chairs either side of him in a pose that practically shouted, 'and Honey, I'm all ears.'

She forbade herself to drop her gaze to where his olive-green tee now stretched across his impressively honed chest. Friends weren't supposed to notice things like that and it was bad enough that the tips of her ears had grown hot at hearing the words 'explicit' and 'sex' coming out of his mouth. No way did she need her eyes getting in on his act.

And it had to be an act, didn't it? How could Luke not be as mortified as she to be having this conversation? But as her eyes disobeyed her, and tracked back from their circuit around the vaulted-ceilinged room to land on his face, she caught the unmistakable edge of a grin creeping on to his expression.

Double-triple-quadruple damn.

This had to mean the dimples were about to make an appearance.

Sephy steeled herself for their impact.

Mortification wasn't even on his radar, was it?

Figured.

Okay, so she was going to have to pull on her big-girl panties and get explicit.

She could do that, right?

She'd already had to employ her most fierce expression while using words of one syllable to get the printer to correct all the signage she wanted for the launch party. Then, in order to get the contractor to finish the catwalk ahead of schedule so that she could see how it all looked and make any changes to the layout in good time, she'd had to go from a winning smile and cajoling tone to being downright expletively explicit.

Neither experience had made Sephy feel great. She didn't usually have to operate by getting all up in a person's face. Usually all she had to do was smile. She tried one out for Luke, now.

Just ask him, her sister Nora had calmly advised her when Sephy had told her that she had figured out what would absolutely fix the problem she had with her advertising campaign.

Sephy wanted to roll her eyes as she remembered exactly how many times Nora had thought her sage 'just ask him' advice bore repeating. It was at least once every time Sephy tried to think what else she could do to get around the fact that the problem with her marketing campaign was now perfectly encapsulated in the sleek banners that draped down from the ceiling either side of the catwalk and against the walls of the room.

She glanced at the banners now, hoping against hope that what she'd see would somehow have changed.

But no. The models on them, while looking gorgeously every-woman, like she had insisted upon, all made her lingerie look… okay.

Just – okay.

Sephy's head dropped to her chest.

She wanted – needed the artwork to scream 'Crave Me'.

Because although she believed in her designs, what she really needed, above everything, was to *sell* her designs.

In two weeks' time she needed to be able to look herself in the eye and know that she had given her absolute all to secure the best-possible start for her business and Nora's whole grinning-like-a-Cheshire-cat thing that had accompanied every one of her 'just ask hims' had made Sephy want to sock her in both eyes.

Like it was that easy to ask someone to do some modelling for you.

Like it was that easy to ask *Luke*.

What she should have done was phone her brother Jared for another business opinion. He could probably have convinced her that all the doubts plaguing her over how non-effective the advertising campaign she'd signed off on was, were all simply down to nerves.

Jared, though, was weeks away from marrying his fiancée Amanda and displaying all the signs of being so in love she wouldn't have been surprised if he'd just grinned like a buffoon and offered up the same unhelpful advice as Nora.

Huh.

Now she came to think of it, Nora's grinning was probably down to the fact that she had recently got engaged to Ethan Love.

Marriage.

Nuptials.

Weddings.

Sephy shuddered.

It was like some giant conspiracy.

She didn't begrudge Jared and Nora finding their soul-mates, but she much preferred it when her brother and sister had been completely focused on their businesses. What she wouldn't do now to go back and spend halcyon days soaking up their knowledge.

Not that she'd had the slightest interest in running a business then. She'd had other priorities. Namely: raising her daughter, Daisy.

Sephy felt a cramp forming in her shoulders and as her hands came up to knead the tight muscle and encourage them to decamp from the vicinity of her ears, she sighed.

Could she really do this?

Could she still devote the time and attention her precocious five-year-old needed, *and* make Seraphic a success?

Of course she could, she repeated to herself. She'd had clients come to her for couture lingerie for the past six months and she'd managed. She could step it up and expand.

She could.

She had to.

'Hey, not to pressure you,' Luke chimed in helpfully, 'but how much longer are you planning on stalling explaining how I fit into this sex-plan thing of yours, because don't you need to go pick Daisy up in an hour or so?'

'It would only be your hands,' Sephy blurted out.

Luke lifted his hands for inspection and as he held them up, Sephy sucked on her bottom lip.

Last night, in a mind-blowing turn of events, Sephy had learned that Luke Jackson had *the* most amazing, incredible, beautiful hands.

The discovery had taken place in her living room. A room she'd walked into every day for the last five years. But when she had entered her living room last night, it was to find Luke holding up one of her scarlet satin bras. Instead of looking bashful that he'd been caught trying to put it back into the bag it had fallen out of, Luke had looked…hot and maybe a little bit bothered.

To be fair, Sephy probably could have explained that she had stashed some of her more colourful bras into her bag to bring over here and see if a splash of colour might be the missing ingredient in the banners.

But she had been too busy zeroing in on the way his hands had held the bra, making it look like one of the sexiest garments she had ever designed.

Snapshot after snapshot had flooded her imagination.

Male hands on a female body, highlighting and showcasing the lingerie the model was wearing.

Luke's hands.

'I'm going to need more information,' Luke said, his deep, rough voice exuding patience.

Dark-brown eyes met his moss-green ones.

'More?' Really, was it so difficult to understand? 'I'm talking a few photographs of your hands…and your torso. Sans shirt.' That last bit had totally been said under her breath because her eyes had taken another peek at the way that soft cotton pulled across hard muscle and more images had flooded her brain so that she was suddenly one-hundred-per-cent sure that what would make her collection fly off the shelf was if Luke's upper body… his upper *naked* body was also somehow in the photos.

In desperation she looked around for her usually ever-present coffee. She needed a drink. Stat.

The next thing she knew Luke was fishing his phone out of his pocket.

'What are you doing?' she asked.

'I'm making a doctor's appointment,' he said matter-of-factly, 'because one of us definitely needs some help. Either my ears need syringing or you really did ask me to take off my clothes so that you could use my body to sell sex at the opening of your lingerie line – in which case it's you who needs the help.'

'That's exactly what I'm trying to ask you for, idiot – some help.' He knew she wasn't any good at this; couldn't he at least cut her a little slack?

'I'm thinking the kind of help you need comes more under the heading of–'

'Hey,' Sephy cocked a hip in indignation, 'if you're sitting there thinking this is a "men-in- white-coats job", then it's on you to help me sort out childcare.'

Luke's head snapped up from his phone. 'I'm sorry, but did

you ask me for help. Again. As in twice in one day? Once for,' Luke paused and gave his head a quick shake, as if even his massive brain couldn't quite compute what she was asking him to do. 'And then, again, just now?'

'Oh, forget it,' Sephy said, walking to the edge of the catwalk and hopping down. Normally she could stand a little being laughed at. She had learnt that getting over herself allowed her to concentrate on making sure Daisy's needs came first. But, honestly, if she had known starting a business was going to turn her inside out like this...

She still would have done it, she thought on an inward sigh. She didn't have any other choice. Waiting until she finished her degree in fashion and then trying to get an internship somewhere wasn't going to cut it. Not now she needed funds for her and Daisy to live on.

Marching towards the heavy wooden double doors of the ballroom, she heard the scrape of a chair being pushed back.

'Hey, wait up.'

'Look, it was a dumb idea,' Sephy said, shoving her long hair behind her ears before reaching out to grab the door handle. 'Way too left-field.' She tried out a light laugh to show it was no big deal, but when Luke didn't murmur in acknowledgement, she added, 'Put it down to me being so tired I can hardly think straight.'

When he stepped up behind her she nearly let out a squeal. They didn't do getting in each other's personal body space. But then, maybe the part where she tried asking him to pose semi-nude and model for her kind of switched things up.

'Look, left field or not, at least explain why for me,' Luke said, his voice now gentle and she hated that she had brought that out in him. She could not remember the last time someone had felt the need to treat her with kid gloves.

'Come on, what's the worst that could happen?' he added.

Sephy swallowed and continued to stare at the century-old patina on the oak doors in front of her.

What was the worst that could happen?

The worst that could happen was that he would see her as needy.

As less than she wanted to be.

Then he would say 'no' anyway and it would be always there between them. She didn't have time to then be worrying if he'd said 'no' because she had finally crossed that invisible line she'd so carefully carved into the sand between them.

'Why is it you Kings have such a problem with asking for help?' Luke said, stepping back and showing the first sign of impatience with her.

'Just lucky, I guess,' Sephy whispered and turned around to face him, still feeling that the only way to save her ad campaign was to have a proper shot at asking Luke to model for her.

'Cursed, more like,' Luke muttered and shoved his hands into the back pockets of his jeans.

He was right.

It was a curse of sorts.

The competitive streak that ran through the Kings bordered on the ridiculous. The fact that she and her siblings never wanted to appear like they couldn't achieve whatever they set out to achieve was arrogant beyond belief, and the blame lay squarely at the feet of their father, Jeremy King.

Bracing automatically, she felt the wave of grief rise up to take a hefty swipe at her. The emotional maelstrom her father's death had brought was in such opposition to the studied passivity she had strived for while he was alive that sometimes she wondered if he was up there just to punish her.

But because life was better when she wasn't feeling angry or negative, she deliberately stepped away from her thoughts and concentrated on her current problem instead.

The difficulty in asking Luke for help really had little to do with wanting to achieve things herself and everything to do with how good he was at helping.

There was this remarkable generosity within him and Sephy was finding it harder and harder to keep the score of who helped who balanced.

He had already helped her develop a storefront for her website and made sure it could handle the extra traffic she hoped for. Now here she was, two weeks to the launch of Seraphic and he'd had to go and inspire her to come up with the perfect solution to her latest problem.

Trying to gather up her thoughts she side-stepped Luke, chose a chair at random, sat down and stared up at the banners.

'What do you see when you look at these?' she asked, gesturing to them.

Luke walked up to her and sat down on the chair next to hers, his head tipped up to the life-sized models staring back down at him.

'I see underwear models.'

'Exactly.'

'Surely that's the point,' he said.

'No. That is so *not* the point.' Frustrated, Sephy twisted in her seat to look at him while she tried to explain. 'I need you to see "I want you".'

Luke went absolutely still.

The ballroom felt like it had shrunk to the size of a steam-room for two, and suddenly Sephy really wanted to play with her hair, or lick her lips, or meet Luke's quiet and intense gaze with one of her own.

Wow. Okay. Of all the Freudian slip-ups, in all the world…

Dragging in a breath she tore her gaze away to face forward again and said, 'I mean, if you were a woman looking at this banner,' she opened her mouth to force in a little more oxygen, 'nothing about this advert makes you drool or reach for your credit card, does it?'

For a moment, Sephy thought Luke wasn't going to move, but then slowly he turned his head to look back at the banners.

'Try to think about it from a female's perspective,' she urged. 'And then think about all the other designer labels out there who sell lingerie.'

'Okay,' Luke conceded. 'Maybe they don't stand out as much as some of the big names, but those big names have a budget a quadrillion times larger than yours.'

'You're right about budget and I'm not looking to compete in that way yet, but tell me you don't see that I could have made more of an impact with these banners.'

Luke frowned. 'When the live models come down the catwalk–'

'That'll help, sure,' she said, cutting him off. 'But the guest list Nora helped me come up with would make London Fashion Week weep with jealousy and I need every single guest to be wowed from the moment they walk in.'

'So where does sex come into play?' Luke asked and Sephy tried not to blow her second chance by getting caught up in a game of how many times she could get him to say 'sex' and survive it.

'You have to understand that achieving sales starts way before a buyer even gets their hands on the product. It starts with selling an experience. The most effective way to do that is to either tap into the lifestyle they already live and make the buyer associate your product with it, or, provide a snapshot of a lifestyle they want to aspire to. A lifestyle that they'll fantasise about so much that they'll buy my lingerie to get a step closer to it.'

Luke let out a low whistle. 'You know, any lack of confidence you had about your ability to understand business and marketing is a crock. You have this stuff nailed.'

Sephy felt his quiet compliment warm her through. 'Um, thank you.'

Luke shrugged like he was simply speaking the truth and cocked his head to the banners again. 'So what is it you want these banners to sell to the women seeing them?'

'Yeah, so, um…sex.'

'O-kay.'

'That's putting it too basically.' How could she explain that last night when she had seen him holding her bra it was as if the bra was saying 'You want to buy me so that a guy with hands like the one holding me can take me off you,' without, you know, having to actually say that to him?

'Sex can be basic all the way through to advanced,' Luke said drily, 'I'm pretty sure I understand all the levels.'

Sephy's stomach bounced up to meet her heart. 'I know you do. I mean,' she licked her lips and went for broke. 'I can see that you could sell...that experience. That's why, and here comes the left-field part, I really need you to be in these shots with the models.'

Silence while Luke's eyes sought out, and then searched, hers.

Then, finally, 'Look, I'm flattered that you feel that these,' Luke held out his hands, 'and this,' he said, pointing to his upper body, 'fit the bill, but this isn't something you fix on the cheap. You need to hire a professional male model.'

Sephy winced. 'I don't have the money to do that.'

'I'll give you the money.'

Damn it, she didn't want him to think this was some long-winded game of getting him to help her out with money. If she hadn't accepted any from her brother or sister, there was absolutely, positively, no way, she was going to take it from Luke.

'I don't want your money, I want you.'

Luke's square jaw went into granite mode and Sephy decided that what would help is if she quit saying she wanted him like that. It would definitely help *her*, because maybe deep, deep, deepest-down she could acknowledge wanting Luke, but she was never going to bring that up to a level where Luke gained first-hand knowledge of how rubbish she was at romantic entanglements. She valued the relationship they had too much.

'All you'd need to do,' she said, aiming for a no-big-deal tone as she steered determinedly away from a suggestion of 'them', 'is stand behind the model and maybe put your hands on her hips, or something.'

'You really think me simply standing shirtless with my hands on her body is going to sex up your lingerie shoot?'

Sephy swallowed. 'Yes.'

Luke looked at her like she had lost it. Was it possible he spent so much time on his computer as creative director of his Zombie Freedom Fighter games that he had forgotten what he looked like?

'Please don't be insulted or freaked out,' she begged. 'Please, just think about it. I really don't have time to source a professional model and Nora has a photographer lined up who will do the work ASAP at cost, to add to their portfolio of work.'

Sephy could feel herself coming very close to batting her eyelashes or laying a hand on his and letting it linger, but she would absolutely not use her femininity to get this from him.

'I can give you the money you need to sort this problem,' Luke said slowly. 'I can *loan* you the money if it makes you feel better, but get my kit off, put my hands on these models and sell a sexier image of your lingerie? No.'

'Why not?'

'And the fact that you even have to ask,' Luke said, running a hand through his hair in frustration.

Wait. Luke was now staring at her mouth. Had she just pouted? Oh God. She had. Pouting and Luke were verboten. Gentle flirting she could cope with, but she was always so careful not to let it become overt with him. His friendship was too important to her.

'I'm a game designer, not a model,' he reminded her.

'If it's your work you're worried about, we could crop your head out of the shots.'

'Sephy. Stop. You're starting to sound desperate.'

'I am desperate.' Sephy mentally gave herself a slow hand-clap because that statement was hardly going to make Luke feel special.

'You're not desperate. You only think you are because you've got a quick fix in mind and you're too tired to look at it with your business head on.

'I am totally looking at this with my business head on. I admit it, okay? I got it wrong with this advertising campaign. Played it too safe. I should never have signed off on it.' She shook her head slightly, as if to reject how overwhelmed, how under pressure, she felt to get this all right. 'I can't afford not to correct this mistake.'

'Everyone who launches a business makes mistakes.'

'Absolutely, but the ones who survive do so because they fix their mistakes. Come on, a couple of hours in the company of beautiful women. What's not to like?'

'No.'

Sephy stared at him as the simple word dropped from his lips to land between them like a boulder.

'Wow,' she whispered. He wasn't even wavering? 'I thought that last bit would tempt you, at least.'

'Don't make me feel bad about this,' Luke said, standing up.

'No. Absolutely not. Sorry.'

Luke stared down at her for a moment before turning to walk towards the ballroom's double doors.

All of Nora's 'just ask hims' must have sunk in deeper than she suspected. She had really thought, after explaining it all properly to him, he would agree.

His emphatic refusal had her reacting childishly. So childishly that as he reached the doors she heard herself emit a clucking sound.

Luke turned around, his expression a mixture of thunder and incredulity. 'Oh, you did not just make the sound of a chicken.'

CHAPTER TWO

Seraphina King had put *sex* and *nakedness* and '*I Want You*' into spoken-out-loud sentences and quite frankly, even days later and watching Daisy for her in an effort to feel less bad about turning her down, Luke was still a little pissed off.

What the hell had she been thinking? Did she really not have any idea how long it took a guy to scour those kinds of words from his mind so that he got to enjoy a platonic friendship with someone like her?

He didn't care how stressed she was over the launch of her business.

Okay.

He did.

He knew she had been finding it tough ever since her father died. Jeremy King's reputation in business had to have her stressing over every decision, wondering what he would have thought. Or wondering what her brother, who ran a large property-acquisition company in New York and what her sister, who ran the family King Property Corporation, did think.

Plus, Luke knew her mother going to New York meant Sephy not only had to keep an eye on the estate, she also lost out on guaranteed childcare help, which meant fewer hours to sew and work on the launch.

Even so…

How did she not see that asking him to sex up her ad campaign was crossing a line?

And when he'd said no, like any sane non-professional-model *friend* would have, she had clucked at him like a chicken.

As if basically calling him a coward was going to help.

'I now pronounce you husband and wife.'

Luke looked over the top of his laptop screen to where a half-pint Darth Vader was busy playing marriage celebrant to Princess Belle and a slightly dazed-looking Woody from *Toy Story*.

His smile reflex kicked in as Darth Vader, aka five-year-old Daisy King, decided the only obvious way to mark the end of the ceremony was to knight her newly married toys with her lightsaber.

Not quite what it had been designed for, but she definitely got points for imagination.

Bringing his gaze back to his laptop screen, Luke settled back against the sofa cushions and stared at his new computer-game project brief he'd helpfully titled: What Happens After All The Zombies Are Slain???

Two seconds into staring at it and his concentration wandered.

Helping out with Daisy was the kind of thing friends did for friends.

Helping out with that other thing? Insanity.

Thanks to Lily and Steve Jackson, Luke might not be the same shadow of a kid he had been under his biological mother's roof, or all the other foster homes he had been placed in, but that didn't mean he was happy being put on display.

He really had *nothing* to feel guilty about.

Daisy picked up Woody and Princess Belle and started walking them down the makeshift aisle she had created out of flowers pulled from the garden behind the row of garages that formed the ground floor of the apartment she and Sephy lived in on the King estate.

What he wouldn't give right now for a dose of Daisy's unfiltered imagination so that he could crack on with some work.

Actually, scratch that.

He had enough unfiltered, left-field, downright distracting imagination coming from her mother.

Luke stared at his screen and re-doubled his efforts to think about what types of challenges he wanted the users of his new world-building game to have to overcome, because his latest zombie evolution wasn't cutting it for him any more. Lately, he'd get so far on development before hitting a brick wall, but he had to keep faith that the online multi-platform role-playing gaming community would love his new game as much as the Zombie Freedom Fighter series he had created.

He didn't get why he was finding it so hard to create this new game. It wasn't as if he was in the 'second album' slump of despair. He had managed to navigate that scary time by gritting his teeth and being so determined to succeed – to better the success of his first game even, that nothing could have stopped him.

So why the problem? This getting to the edge of a precipice and staring into the void beyond had started even before Sephy had thrown him a curve ball.

He tracked the mouse pad with his finger and clicked on his email inbox. If he couldn't get into the design groove while Daisy was happy playing with her toys, he could at least deal with a few emails.

'Traitor,' he muttered under his breath when the arrow cursor on his screen bypassed the fresh batch of business emails and went straight to the middle of his inbox list.

Luke stared hard at the screen.

So, yeah, he thought he might know what had him so distracted from his work, and it all started and finished with the subject line: *Get the cleaner in lad…Lily and I are coming for a visit!*

It had to be the first time Steve and Lily Jackson had taken a break from fostering, and how had they chosen to celebrate that break? By visiting each of the brood that had flown the coop over the years, so that they could see them in their own habitats and check for themselves that they were all right.

Luke had taken great care over the years to assure them he was absolutely fine. Right up to the inclusion earlier this year of a little white lie that had put paid to the ever-increasing fretting that he was focusing way too much on work and not nearly enough on a personal life.

His fingers rubbed over his chest to ease the stab of guilt.

Yeah. Totally shouldn't have lied like that.

Because now, if he didn't come up with a plan and his lie was exposed, he was going to have to endure the unspoken lecture about how they had taught him differently. But worse than that, he would witness their disappointment morph into worry that they'd somehow failed him, and they deserved so much better than that.

'Mummy!' Daisy suddenly observed, at the sound of the front door opening, and Luke was saved from thinking about what he was going to do about the email and white-lie situation.

A couple of seconds later and Sephy King walked into her lounge.

Damn, but it was hard to stay mad at her, Luke thought, aware of his eyelids performing the slow-blink thing that they always did when he saw her.

He let the gesture slide because you couldn't look at Sephy, register all the siren-like qualities – the oval-shaped face, almond-shaped eyes, bow-shaped lips, long jet-black silky hair, and a body that could, and probably had, made more than one man beg, and not react a little.

He was just lucky he had got it down to that small betraying tick.

Especially after what she'd so recently placed front and centre in his imagination.

'Hey you,' he greeted, as she came to a stop behind the sofa.

Swinging from her shoulder was the same huge soft brown leather tote exploding with vibrant-coloured interesting froufrou that had got him into trouble the other day. One of her hands clutched a tablet and large sketchbook and the other was wrapped around a travel mug. From the way she was white-knuckling the coffee receptacle, Luke guessed she was on at least her fifth refill of the day.

Dumping the tablet and sketchbook onto the sofa next to him, she let her shoulder slump so that the heavy bag could slip down to the cushions as well. With a hand now free she took the keys that she'd been gripping in her mouth, tossed them into the bowl on the coffee table and moved to flick her long hair over her shoulder with a grace that had absolutely no business beguiling him.

'Hey you,' she said on a long sigh, raising her ever-present drink to her lips to sip, before hesitating and obviously thinking better of it.

Definitely for the best, he thought. The snap and sizzle of energy barely kept in check was tangible from this proximity. Or was that the uneasy undercurrent running between them?

'Did you find a model?' he asked, really, really, hoping that she had.

'That would be a negative,' she said, glancing over at her daughter and taking in the Darth Vader helmet and cape with a slight shake of her head, before sliding her gaze back to Luke. 'Was she all right for you?'

'Yep,' he replied, thinking they obviously weren't at the laughing about him saying 'no' stage yet, then. 'We went out for the Sunday papers and then she insisted on watching a DVD with me, before getting out every single one of her toys to perform multiple marriage ceremonies.'

'God, don't tell me,' Sephy moaned, 'Woody has committed bigamy again?' There was an accompanying and exasperated shudder that had Luke grinning in spite of the new wariness between them.

'You'd think Buzz would help a buddy out, but he's obviously seeking out infinity and beyond,' he said.

'Actually he's in my bag,' Sephy confessed in a whisper. A smile chased out some of the stress as she looked again at her daughter. 'I found him earlier when I was looking for my tape measure.

Luke wanted to ask her what the hell she had been measuring, given that she was supposed to be looking for a male model to re-shoot her ad campaign.

'So,' Sephy made a circling motion with her hand, as if to encompass Daisy's Weddings R Us setup. 'Is it only Woody who's off to jail as soon as the honeymoon's over, or did my daughter rope you in for a little bigamy too?'

'Nope. No bigamy here.'

'Phew,' she said, blowing out an oversized breath of relief. 'Not that I'm looking to get married.'

'And not that I'm asking,' he countered.

Sephy looked as if she was going to say something, but in a majestic show of self control, she walked around to the squashy armchair and plonked herself down instead.

'Mummy,' Daisy announced, 'I think Luke will come back tomorrow and then you and he can get married like Belle and Woody.'

An interesting sensation spread under Luke's chest wall as his gaze whipped to Sephy.

Her expression said it all. Comical horror that said in equal measures: 'What the hell?' and 'We so need to remember my daughter has the hearing of a bat.'

Luke wondered if Sephy even realised her hand was rubbing unconsciously over her sternum, as if to chase away her instinctive recoil at the mere mention of a make-believe marriage.

Disappointment ditched its cloak and streaked naked through his head and Luke needed a couple of seconds to work out that Sephy's reaction should mean nothing to him personally.

He was no longer a young boy facing rejection after rejection and she wasn't rejecting him for real or otherwise.

The whole world knew Sephy King was marriage-phobic.

He didn't know why, and probably never would. They weren't the kind of friends to focus on their pasts and make that about who they were now. They were the kind of friends who bantered, supported and championed each other – but only with the lightest of touches.

All of which was fine by him.

At least it had been, until Sephy had had to go and break the rule she had put in place the first time they had met.

Luke cast his mind back to seeing Sephy for the first time. She had been sitting alone in their local college canteen one summer evening and instantly caught up in the pull of her, he had ended up performing a move so completely uncool, it was only sheer dumb luck no one had whipped out their phone, filmed it and stuck it up on YouTube.

One moment he had been Mr Jackson, after-school coding-club mentor, giving a little back to the community. The next, in an actual tripping-over-a-chair-leg, tray-flying-up-in-the-air moment, he had managed to recreate every teen-movie pastiche of the geek falling for the popular girl. The fact that he and Sephy were both a good few years past their teen incarnation hadn't, in any way, made the move look ironic.

She had been so sweet about the coffee splash-landing against her portfolio and he had felt like such a schmuck when he had discovered she was waiting to interview for a place as a mature student on a degree course in fashion design. But as if used to men making an absolute fool of themselves in her vicinity, she had calmly mopped up the mess and offered to buy him a replacement after her interview.

Used to having way better game, Luke had spent the wait working out how to charm her into exchanging coffee for dinner. But when she had met with him thirty-five minutes later she'd had a determined look in her eyes that said she had cast their roles the moment of his initial bungled approach. They were going to be friends, nothing more.

Over that coffee, looking into eyes the colour of dark, good-for-your-heart chocolate, he had learnt that once Sephy King made her mind up about something that was that.

So friendship it was, and a year on neither of them had ever overstepped the terms Sephy had set out. Until she had asked him to be in her lingerie ad and he'd had to tamp down the spike of adrenalin that came with being reminded she had the power to surprise him.

'Daisy,' Sephy said mock-sternly and pulling Luke's focus back to the present. 'I know you know tomorrow is a school day. Stop fishing for more playtime.'

Daisy giggled.

'Uh-huh,' Sephy nodded. 'Knew it. Besides, I really think I'm going to have to limit you on how many marriage ceremonies you perform a week. Your toys must be exhausted.'

'No, Mummy, they love it,' came the confident reply as Daisy promptly started preparing to marry another set of toys.

Luke could tell Sephy was chewing the inside of her cheeks to stop herself laughing and as she turned her attention back to him and he mentally took his cue to put her back into the friend box, he knew that aside from the unconscious sexuality she exuded, what really drew her to him, and had him accepting her boundaries, was simple. Put her daughter anywhere in her sightline and the softness that washed over her expression merged with a sort of defiant warrior-like strength that reminded him of the way Lily and Steve Jackson went about loving their kids.

Even him, which he knew he hadn't made easy.

'I'm sorry,' Sephy said, flicking her gaze apologetically to his laptop, 'I was much longer than I said I'd be and I know it's impossible to work with Daisy running around.'

'Relax. I wouldn't have offered if I wasn't happy to help out,' *and if I didn't feel guilty as hell for not helping you with the other thing.* 'Besides, it wasn't Daisy who stopped me working. It was me.' He glanced down at his laptop and closed the lid. 'I'll get there.' At least he would as soon as he 'fessed up his white lie to his foster parents and dealt with the fallout.

'So are you staying for take-out, or is this a date-night for you?' Sephy asked.

Luke's gaze was drawn to the silks and satins and frothy laces hanging out of the leather bag next to him on the sofa and he remembered he hadn't had a date in...quite a while.

Damn.

No wonder he was focusing so much on Sephy and her out-there request.

Maybe he ought to go home, grab a shower and give the woman from the gaming convention he had attended in London last week a call.

Amy, he thought her name was. Or was it Laney? Jamie?

His gaze slid to Sephy, who was looking at where he had been staring. He caught the tinge of pink high on her cheekbones and noticed she wouldn't quite look at him as she stood back up and went to give Daisy a quick hug before wandering out to the kitchen, where he could hear her filling the kettle.

When he'd picked up the bra that had fallen out of her bag the other night, he hadn't liked that his first thought – his only thought – had been that she must have been wearing the bra... and then she wasn't.

Immediately that had expanded into wondering if it was because someone had taken it off her.

Ryan maybe?

Daisy's father hadn't been back on the scene for long, but Luke knew the man was busy trying to lay down all sorts of good impressions along with his good intentions.

A dart of jealousy had hit Luke clear between the eyes and he'd had to convince himself that Sephy was perfectly entitled to do whatever she wanted with whomever she wanted.

Except for with Ryan, he had thought, as his gut had tightened painfully.

Ryan would mean it was serious. She wouldn't go there again, otherwise. She wouldn't risk Daisy's happiness if it didn't work out.

Luke could still remember the feel of the satin between his fingertips, even as he'd scolded himself that he really did not need to be thinking about Sephy and sex.

With anyone.

'No, no date tonight,' Luke said now, ignoring the voice in his head telling him he really ought to go home and force himself to put in a few hours' work. He wandered into the kitchen and added, 'Take-out would be great.'

Sephy stared at him for a second longer than he was comfortable with and then, with a brisk nod, walked over to the dresser drawer, where she kept all the local take-out menus.

'What do you feel like having?' she asked, tucking a strand of hair back behind her ear.

You.

Luke balked and shoved his hands into his jeans back pockets. Crap. He had to nip this in the bud. Now, indeed *ever*, was not the time to be taking himself off the leash where he and Sephy were concerned. 'I'm easy,' he said and then cursed inwardly when she whipped around from the dresser, a teasing note lighting her eyes.

A heartbeat later and it was gone.

Like she too couldn't get her head around how asking him to model had created this awkwardness between them.

He should have left while he'd had the chance. Now, tonight – later, when he was supposed to be thinking about work, he was going to be thinking about how he hated saying 'no' to people he cared about; hated being the bad guy.

Hated that her asking him to help her had made him think about all those times the car had come to pick him up from where he was living and take him to someone else's home, where he'd been looked at and assessed for fitting in, and found wanting. Or rather…unwanted.

Luke knew his jaw had tightened when he felt the roots of his teeth protest. Deliberately he faked a yawn to try and relax and then tipped his head one way and then the other to try and release some of the built-up tension in his neck.

'Why don't I order while you get Daisy ready for bed?' he asked, taking out his wallet to check what cash he had.

'I can pay for a take-out, Luke.'

Luke studiously ignored the note of censure in her voice. 'Does it matter who pays for it?'

There was a moment's silence and then, 'I take it you were the one who bought Daisy that Darth Vader outfit?'

Luke caught the catch of chastisement in her voice and wished he could decipher whether it was down to the fact that he'd spent money on Daisy when Sephy was touchy about money, or whether it was because he wasn't Daisy's dad.

'I guess I should have run it past you, first.' Feeling sheepish, he thought he might as well confess all. 'I also bought her a lightsaber.'

Sephy reached over with a mug of coffee for him and Luke winced as the chunky porcelain landed extra hard on the large wooden kitchen table. The bee in her bonnet was definitely more about the money, then.

'In my defence,' he said lightly, 'you were only saying the other day that you really hoped she got over her sickly pink phase soon.'

He risked a glance, caught the twitch of her lips and thought a smile might be in the offing.

'So what you're saying,' Sephy said, 'is that I should be thanking you for helping her transition from Princess to Sith?'

'You're welcome,' he grinned.

Sephy rolled her eyes. 'And you let her watch *Star Wars* again, didn't you?'

Oops. 'Have some pity. There are really only so many times a guy can watch *Frozen*.'

Now Sephy's grin spread across her face as she lowered her

mug to the table and said, 'But Luke – don't you know? Love is an open –'

'Argh,' Luke stuck his fingers in his ears as Sephy started singing a tune from the film. When she saw him cross his eyes in pain, she laughed and sang louder until he was forced to start humming the theme tune to *Star Wars* to drown her out.

The louder she sang, the louder he hummed, until Daisy walked in, dragged off her helmet and in solidarity with her mum performed her own ear-splittingly loud rendition of 'Love is an Open Door'.

Luke and Sephy grinned at each other like big kids, near-argument over money and over-stepping the boundaries of friendship totally forgotten in the moment.

'Right then, Darth Daisy,' Sephy said once Daisy had completed every verse and chorus, 'say goodnight to Luke while I get you a quick drink. Then its bath time, followed by bed.'

''Night Luke,' Daisy said, making him proud when she started singing the theme tune to *Star Wars*.

'You,' Sephy said, pointing to him as she ushered Daisy out of the kitchen, drink in hand, 'order take-out and don't for one minute think that I'm not paying. If the food comes before I finish putting this one to bed, my purse is in my bag.'

Luke watched them depart the kitchen.

In their wake, the sudden silence reminded him of being in his own place and how he tried to avoid that as often as possible. Ears straining, he could just about make out Sephy and Daisy chatting away about their day. Glad of the background noise but needing more, Luke picked up his coffee and wandered back into the lounge to switch on the TV. He knew to leave at least fifteen minutes before he ordered food or it would be cold by the time Sephy got to it.

His gaze was drawn to where Daisy had set up her wedding chapel. With an amused shake of his head he tore his gaze away and made a grab for the TV remote control. Flicking through the channels to get the first station playing any kind of sport, he settled on the sofa and reached for his laptop again.

Opening up the email from his foster parents, he turned his head again towards 'wedding central', and damned if it didn't get him thinking.

And then he did some thinking about Sephy's predicament.

And then he started smiling.

He might just have come up with a genius idea.

CHAPTER THREE

Sephy pulled the door of her daughter's bedroom gently shut and turned to follow the scent of double pepperoni pizza.

At the top of the stairs, she stopped to drag a hand through her hair and then, instead of descending downstairs, backtracked down the corridor to her bedroom with its en suite, to freshen up.

'Not for Luke's benefit,' she whispered to herself, mentally flicking the ears of the little devil she imagined perched on her shoulder, holding its belly to try and contain its peal of laughter.

No, all she was going to do was splash some cold water on her face, because, wow, was she tired.

The amount of work she still had to do to get Seraphic under way meant that even her check list had check lists, but the tiredness wasn't going to magically disappear after the launch, so her only option was to suck it up and keep going.

In the mirror over the en suite vanity, Sephy peered at her reflection and took stock. Okay. It wasn't too bad.

But she was definitely going to get rid of the smudge of hours-old eyeliner, and maybe swipe on some lip-gloss. *What?* she asked her reflection. It was important to keep your lips hydrated. Everyone knew that.

Reaching out she plucked a face-wipe from the pack and let out the breath she'd been holding, hoping that along with it would come the release of at least some of the stress of the day.

But all she felt was a grinding pain in her stomach.

It wasn't hunger that was producing the sensation.

It was the certain knowledge that if she didn't get some more money coming in soon, she and Daisy were going to have nothing left to live on. By her calculations they had enough for two months. Depending on orders for Seraphic, three months absolute tops.

God, she must have been mad to think launching Seraphic would make all her money problems disappear, but it had been the only way she could think of bypassing asking her mum or Jared or Nora for help.

Sephy stretched to try and ease the tension in her belly.

If it came down to it, she would forsake pride and go to them. No way was Daisy going to go without.

But she wasn't quite there yet. First, she was going to try to fix things by herself.

It would work, she tried to reassure herself. It had to.

She wasn't sure she could endure the look on the faces of her family if she had to go to them for funds. Not after spending month after month turning them all down so vociferously.

Jeremy King had done what he'd done. Arguing about how archaic the terms of his will were, or how they didn't understand how he could have hurt her this way, wasn't going to change anything.

Sephy needed her family to be able to love him, not spend more time resenting him. Leading by example was the only way they would all heal from the giant hole his passing had left.

She knew why he'd done what he'd done.

Putting Sephy's inheritance into a trust fund for Daisy – making it so Daisy couldn't access it until she turned twenty-one – wasn't really as disrespectful to Sephy as the family thought.

Looking at things longterm, she even agreed with what he had done.

It was just this massive short-term problem it had created that she had to deal with.

Sephy looked at her reflection and reached for her lip-gloss. Slicking the wand over her lips, she supposed she could take on a few more couture clients.

But creating couture lingerie couldn't be rushed and the only uninterrupted time she had was when Daisy was at school or asleep.

She was already maxing out those hours as it was.

Finding another seamstress who took as much care as she did over putting her designs together, again, took time and money she didn't have.

No, the completely outside-of-her-comfort-zone forecasts and charts she had made herself do all told her the same thing. She needed the Seraphic ready-to-wear line to sell in volume.

Which brought her back to Luke.

Sort of.

She was a little mad at him still.

Not for saying no to her, although, yes, that did smart! It was more that as well as the shock on his face, she had glimpsed how difficult he'd found it to say no and had seen in the darkening of his eyes the temptation to say yes.

She was mad to be wondering what had made him say no. She didn't have time to indulge an overactive imagination. Luke had said no and that was that. She only had time to move on and keep focusing on the launch.

Casting one last look at what she saw in the mirror, she left her room and jogged down the stairs.

Having set out the pizza box, plates and kitchen roll on her coffee table, Luke was on his knees picking up the wild flowers Daisy had pulled up from the garden. Next to him was a plastic beaker that he had filled up with water.

Bugger.

How could you stay mad at a man who put wilting wild flowers into water after your daughter had finished trampling her toys all over them?

He looked up as she entered the room and she could feel his eyes on her as she snagged herself a slice of pizza and a plate to put it on.

With her hands full she realised he had moved her bag, complete with all the underwear samples she carried around with her, to her favourite chair and the only place left to sit would be on the sofa next to him.

'I see you've been checking out my underwear again,' she said as she yanked off a piece of kitchen roll to use as a napkin.

'Of course,' Luke grinned, 'but only as a way of getting into your purse. I had to take it all out to find your money for the pizza guy.'

'Was there enough in there?'

'Sure,' Luke said, and the way he turned from her to put the bunch of flowers into the beaker and set them on the windowsill, Sephy knew that there hadn't been.

'How much do I owe you?'

'Forget it,' he said, walking over to open the pizza box.

'No, I will not forget it. I said I'd pay. I'm paying. How much did you have to put in to make up the difference?'

'Ten.'

Sephy reached over, set down her pizza and rose to her feet at the same instant Luke tried to walk past her and take his seat on the sofa. Their eyes locked as they brushed up against each other and when she pushed her hand into the pocket of her skinny jeans, Luke seemed to press closer, bringing with him a sizzling heat that had all her thought processes scattering.

Sephy's insides felt as if they were tied to a bungee rope and were hurtling towards the ground before being yanked back up, and then Luke was springing backwards and she was finally remembering why her hand was in her pocket and withdrawing some notes.

Silently she passed him a ten.

Silently he took it from her and shoved it into his jeans

pocket before snapping up the control to mute the volume on the TV.

'I don't mind if you wanted to watch that,' Sephy said, glad her voice sounded normal, while everything else inside of her was screaming 'how do I make it go back to the way it was before I asked him to model for me?'

As if Luke was thinking the exact same thing, he grabbed up his plate and said calmly, 'You don't think we ought to try and get past this new weirdness between us?'

'Weirdness?' she stalled, her mouth going dry. 'What weirdness?'

'The, "you asking me to pose nude in photos to sex up your ad campaign, and me saying no" weirdness.'

'Oh, that,' Sephy forced a grin. 'I'm over that. Although, for the record, I did not ask you to pose *in the nude*. At least, not entirely,' she added.

'So even though you don't have a model booked and the launch is in less than two weeks, you're completely okay with how things are?'

Aiming for nonchalance, Sephy waved the hand holding the slice of pizza. 'Everything will work out,' she said.

'You're not even looking for a model, are you?' Luke said on a huff of breath.

She stared at the silent TV. 'I told you – I can't afford one.'

'And I told you I'm perfectly happy to help you out with that.'

'No thanks,' she said, shoving in a huge mouthful of delicious hot pizza in a bid to keep from following up with a lecture on how she didn't need anyone's money.

'Have you come up with an alternative?'

'I have chosen to let the banners stand as they are.'

'And you're completely happy to do that?' he pressed.

'No Mr Spanish Inquisitor,' she said, with a roll of her eyes, 'but I have to work with what I have. And what I have is a professionally shot ad campaign that I paid a lot of money for.'

'Sephy –'

'What?' Sephy whipped her head around to look at him, 'I asked you for help, but you said "no".' There was a flash of guilt that dulled the green of his eyes and she really didn't like how that made her feel, so she added, 'which you were perfectly entitled to do. I'm a big girl, Luke. I'm not going to hold that against you.'

'Right. You've decided not to resent that the one time you asked me outright for something, I said no?'

'That's right, because the last time I checked, I wasn't a child.'

'Ha. Let's put the clucking like a chicken on the evidence table.'

Sephy blushed. 'That was a mistake.' She took another bite of food and, after swallowing, said softly, 'I really don't resent you for saying no.'

Luke turned back to the TV and lifted the pizza to his mouth before dropping a casual, 'You know, you could ask Ryan to be your model.'

Sephy snorted and lowered her plate to her lap in shock. 'I am *not* asking Ryan.'

'Why not?'

'Because.'

Luke turned his head to watch her closely. 'Because…?'

Because he's not you.

Sephy was very afraid her eyes had become rather round and large as the realisation that she hadn't even considered asking Ryan, or anyone else, took proper hold.

Ryan may still have his bad-boy, wild-child looks, but his previous lifestyle had added a tired and jaded edge and, if anything, he now looked like a man who simply wanted peace in his life.

Luke, on the other hand, looked…

Sephy fiddled with the crust of her pizza.

Luke looked like still waters ran deep.

Luke had this quiet, serious and confident, can-take-care-of-himself presence.

But then those dimples would come out to play and that automatically translated as 'and-I-am-more-than-capable-of-taking-care-of-a-woman's-needs-at-the-same-time'.

The moment she'd seen Luke holding her bra, she'd known unequivocally the response images of him would evoke. No, she couldn't afford a professional model, but the truth was she didn't want a professional model. She wanted Luke.

Not for herself. *Obviously.* She already knew that kind of complication would lead to her losing his friendship.

Picking off a piece of pepperoni she popped it into her mouth, curled her tongue around it and then said, 'I'm only just getting to know Ryan again. We're,' she broke off to search for the right words, 'we're both somehow the complete opposite of how we were when we knew each other the first time round.'

Luke said nothing and, after a moment, reached past her for another slice of pizza.

Sephy's gaze fixed on his sinewy forearm and the twist of brown leather cord that wrapped around his wrist and rubbed up alongside his chunky, masculine watch. She wondered if the leather had been a gift. God, his hands and arms really would have looked so wonderfully sexy in those photographs.

'So how is it all going, with Ryan?'

'Huh?' She really, really had to snap out of sinking herself into the mental images she kept dreaming up to re-shoot her ad campaign.

'I was asking about Ryan. It's all going well?'

'I guess,' she answered and then frowned. 'At least I thought it was.'

'Why, what's happened?'

Sephy didn't know whether to tell him. She was probably worrying about nothing.

'Seph,' Luke pushed and the hint of protectiveness in his tone made her smile.

'He broke up with his girlfriend.'

'I see.' Luke finished off the last bite of his pizza, tore off a piece of kitchen roll, rubbed it between his hands until it formed a ball and tossed it onto his plate. 'And that's your problem because?'

'It's not really,' she answered, telling him what he wanted to hear and wondering if anyone would ever believe she could care about Ryan simply because he was the father of her child and not because she was starting to develop feelings for him again.

If there was one thing Sephy could rely on about herself it was that a lesson learned was a lesson learned. She didn't do repeat mistakes. Years of trying to get her father to notice her had taught her that life was too short to keep banging your head against a brick wall.

'You're worried Ryan's going to relapse?' Luke asked.

'Maybe.' It was a distinct possibility. Breaking up with his girlfriend was Ryan's first real test after coming out of rehab four months ago. What if the upset made him start gambling again?

Her sister Nora was engaged to Ryan's brother Ethan and Sephy had been dithering over whether she should ring Ethan and let him know. She kind of hoped Ryan had already told him and had been leaning on him for support, but Nora hadn't said anything and that made her question what shape Ryan was really in.

'Haven't you got enough to be worrying about at the minute?' Luke prompted. 'Ryan Love is not your responsibility.'

'I know. I just want him to be the best version of himself. You know? For Daisy. She deserves to have a decent father figure in her life.'

'She was doing okay before he came along.'

Sephy's heart dipped at Luke's automatic defence of her, and then dipped again because she knew that Daisy had already lost her granddad and the special bond the two of them had developed. Then, just as they were all getting to know Jared again, he'd had to return to his own life in New York.

The only constant male figure in Daisy's life was Luke and in those hours before dawn when Sephy did most of her waking-up-in-a-cold-sweat-parental-worrying, she acknowledged her friendship with Luke was getting to be dangerously close to something she counted on. What if Daisy became too attached to Luke and Luke finally found someone to get serious with and drifted out of their lives?

'All I really want is for Daisy to get to have that balanced parenting that Ryan could add,' she admitted to Luke. Before Ryan had broken up with his girlfriend, Sephy had only allowed a few short visits so Daisy could start getting to know him. She hadn't wanted to force too much contact until she could trust Ryan to stay in the area and want a relationship with his daughter. Now, she worried that if Ryan was struggling and needed to concentrate on himself for a while, and Daisy noticed, things were going to get messy.

'I'm already dreading how to handle the teenage years,' Sephy continued. 'It'll be just my luck if she ends up like I was at that age.'

'And how were you when you were that age?'

'I was –' Sephy broke off as memories flooded her of all the times she hadn't so much as snuck back into the house late at night as deliberately announced her return as loudly as possible. Back then she had seen any attention as good attention. She cleared her throat and finished with, 'Let's simply say I was not the best version of myself that I could have been.'

Luke looked like he wanted to know more, but she was suddenly filled with the need for a little reciprocation. 'What were you like as a teenager?' she asked.

He hesitated, as if quickly weighing up what to go with before finally responding with a one word answer of, 'Shy.'

Sephy blinked. 'Shy?'

'Yep,' he confirmed, staring down at his hands and flexing his fingers, as if he was deliberately trying to remain relaxed.

'You?' Sephy repeated, dumbfounded. 'You were shy?'

'I know.' He flicked a quick glance at her. 'I guess you can't even imagine what that would be like, can you?'

'Guess not.' There had never been any room for shyness in the King household. 'Is that why you wouldn't entertain the idea of doing the photo shoot?'

'Little bit, yeah.'

Sephy couldn't believe the quietness she'd always appreciated in him might stem from shyness.

'I guess I forget that because you don't look like your typical geek. That doesn't mean you're not more comfortable surrounded by and communicating via a bank of computers, but you're not shy around me,' she added, thinking aloud.

'You're right, I'm not.'

Sephy was still trying to work out a way of asking him precisely what he meant by that when he sat back against the sofa cushions, reminding her how close they were and forcing her to appreciate that it wasn't that her sofa was miniscule, it was that Luke could hold his own in the large-male-presence stakes.

'Tell me about why you chose to specialise in underwear rather than outerwear,' he asked in a fast-and-smooth change of subject that had Sephy needing a moment to catch up.

She stared fixedly at the lingerie on the armchair she usually sat on and decided to accept his change of subject on account of it meaning she could talk about something she understood, as opposed to what might or might not be going on under the surface of their friendship.

'Why did I choose lingerie? I guess underwear is all about foundation.'

'Not sexiness?'

Sephy's nose wrinkled as she smiled, because what woman didn't like to wear something that made her feel feminine, pretty, seductive and hot? 'That too – but mostly designing lingerie is about getting the structure right.'

Luke appeared to think for a moment. 'Feeling rock solid underneath equals feeling invincible on the outside?'

'Um, yeah.' Wow. Sephy let her breath out softly. He got it. She tried not to be too impressed.

'What if someone prefers going commando?' Luke asked.

'Huh?' Why had she thought this conversation would be safer again? And why, for the love of God, was she suddenly thinking about Luke and the way his jeans fit him and whether or not he preferred to go commando?

'You know – someone who prefers not to wear any underwear.'

'Yes. Thank you. I do know what going commando means.' She would not look at him. *She would not.* Reaching forward she put her plate carefully back on the coffee table and tried to surreptitiously add another one or two millimetres of breathing space between them as she tucked a leg under her and eased back against the back of the sofa.

'I guess,' she said, as casually as she could manage, 'if a person prefers not to wear underwear, well then I guess they're not my customer.'

'Oh, I don't know,' Luke said with a quiet intensity that had her breath coming shorter. 'I think your designs could convince them.'

'I *know* you could,' she whipped back.

Luke grinned. 'And that's absolutely all you're asking me to do by posing in those photos? You really think I could help you sell more lingerie?'

'Of course.'

'And my head would be cropped from all the shots?'

Sephy felt the leap of excitement and tried not to get carried away. Slowly, she turned to face him more fully. 'What exactly are you saying, here?'

'I'm saying okay.'

'Okay...?' She had to have this wrong, didn't she? Somehow the combination of pheromones and heat caused by her proximity to him had jumbled up the connections in her brain. He wasn't really saying…

'Okay, I will be your model.'

Sephy's hand came up to her mouth. Oh. My. God.

She could kiss him.

Wait – no.

She really couldn't.

A huge weight felt as if it had been lifted off her shoulders, making her want to jump up and happy-dance all over the living room.

'On two conditions,' Luke said.

The carousel of joy inside of her wound down and came to an abrupt halt.

'What are your conditions?' she made herself ask because, suddenly, with what she had asked for within touching distance, she realised she needed to keep her business head-on.

'First condition: you are the model in the photographs with me.'

Sephy snorted. 'Very funny. What's your real condition?'

'I mean it, Sephy. You are the model I model with. They're your designs. You shouldn't really have a problem with that.'

'Don't be ridiculous. I'm not a –' she stopped because Luke was looking at her like he was about to say touché. 'What's your second condition?' she asked, needing something to take her mind off what it would feel like to have Luke see her in her underwear, because telling herself it would be like posing in a bikini wasn't in any way having a dousing-with-cold-water effect.

Luke looked her calmly in the eye and said, 'My second condition is that you agree to pose as my fiancée when my parents show up for a visit in a couple of weeks.'

CHAPTER FOUR

It was crazy, Sephy thought, upping the intensity level of the elliptical she was on at Heathstead's branch of Love Leisure.

'Stupid', she muttered under her breath, determined to work up a sweat and work off some of her feelings.

In fact, what it was – was crazy-stupid.

And she was certifiably both of those things to be even considering agreeing to Luke Jackson's *ridiculous* conditions.

Sephy's finger stabbed at the volume button on the MP3 player attached to her arm. Heavy dance beats dropped through her ear-buds, helping her push her body harder, faster. She only wished they were loud enough to completely drown out thoughts of Luke and how much she really wanted him to model in her lingerie shoot and what she would have to do in return.

Last night, when he had named his second condition, it was as if someone had opened up the cabinet of emotions inside of her, chosen the bottle marked hysteria, taken out its stopper and upended its contents.

She had totally misunderstood and had heard 'actual fiancée' instead of 'fake fiancée'.

Scary-quick, she had jumped in her head from fiancée to wife to *married*. To Luke Jackson. All the while hysteria had bubbled and fizzed under her skin. Had Luke somehow got wind of her financial situation and concocted a convoluted plan to provide her with financial assistance? She wouldn't totally put it past his level of generosity.

But thankfully Luke had kept talking as she had stared at him dumbfounded. Finally his continued explanation about how helping him out with his little white lie would be fair exchange for him helping her out had filtered through.

There was no way Luke could have found out about her father's letter. The only people who knew its contents were Jared and Nora and they would never betray her like that.

She was safe from screaming from the rooftops that she wasn't living in a Jane Austen novel and that she was more than capable of providing for Daisy without having to resort to marriage. Getting mixed up in a kind of fixed arrangement that elevated her out of a bad situation smacked of what her father had assumed she would do when he had tied up her inheritance.

A hand brushed against her arm and Sephy let out a squeal. Turning, she saw her ex and Daisy's father, Ryan Love, standing beside her. Reaching up she pulled out her ear-buds and turned down the music.

'Want to tell me what this machine has ever done to you?' Ryan asked her with a grin.

'Sorry,' her breath came out in a rush and she realised she'd been pressing every button on the darned thing in her quest to exhaust her overactive imagination and beat it back into submission.

Ryan reached out and re-set the pace on the machine, and Sephy started to feel like she wasn't going to have a heart attack after all.

'You okay?' he asked, running his gaze over her. 'Only Ethan will kill me if I let one of our clients get injured.'

Ethan Love was the founder and CEO of the chain of deluxe gyms that made up Love Leisure. When Ryan had gone to him for help with his gambling addiction, Ethan had wanted to ensure his brother had a place to live and a place to work when he got out of rehab, so he had bought and refurbished this building, turned it into a branch of Love Leisure, and had then trained Ryan to manage it for him.

'Actually, it's good you came along,' Sephy admitted. 'I guess I got a little carried away trying to work through my –' she stopped. She definitely didn't need to be telling Ryan what was going on with her.

'Frustrations?' Ryan quipped.

Sephy felt herself blush as she heard the sexual connotation in the word. 'Er, yes.' Good grief, what was the matter with her? This was testament to how shaken up she was after Luke's proposal. *Non-proposal* proposal, she reminded herself. She really was going to have to do better at remembering the fake part.

The fake part, after all, was probably what was going to allow her to agree to it.

Sephy's stomach lurched – *was* she going to agree to it, then?

'So you want to tell me what has you so frustrated, over a coffee?' Ryan invited, thankfully interrupting her tracking mentally back to the one person she'd come in here to get a break from. 'I seem to remember that was your drink of choice.'

Sephy stepped off the machine. 'Can't think of a better legally addictive stimulant, can you? Oh, crap,' she put a hand up to her mouth, feeling all kinds of stupid. 'Sorry. I didn't mean to –'

'Use the "A" word?' Ryan shrugged. 'An addict is what I am – what I'll always be.'

'Put a "recovering" in front of it and we're all good here,' Sephy said, and then was immediately worried. Aside from having Daisy's best interests at heart, she wasn't sure she should be telling Ryan how to talk about, or deal with, his problems. 'Okay,' she muttered, 'Not my place, so sorry again.'

'Relax. No offense taken. Come on. I know a great place around the corner that's opened up. Or did you come in here for a quick workout before needing to be somewhere else?'

As Sephy eased into a couple of light stretches to cool down she determined to ignore the fact that she could feel Ryan's eyes making a slow sweep of her again. Straightening up she confessed,

'Actually I came in here hoping you would be around so that I could talk to you.'

The smile that lit up his face held such a potent reminder of the charming bad-boy she used to know that Sephy caught her lip between her teeth. She was under enough stress to be feeling like one sharp shock away from a meltdown as it was, so she pushed down the fear he was flirting with her.

As his eyes came up to meet hers she returned his stare steadily. Ryan's old modus operandi had been to hide pain under slow, sure, wicked smiles and easy flirtation, so maybe that was what he was doing now.

'I wanted to see how you were,' she said, hoping her serious tone would cut through the mask.

'Me? I'm fine.'

'You are?' Sephy searched his face for signs, but found it hard to get past that swagger of his. 'Look, Heathstead is a small town. I heard about the breakup with Michelle and so I wanted to check. But if you say you're fine…'

Ryan simply shrugged and went with, 'Her loss, isn't it?'

'I guess.' She supposed these days she didn't deserve more than the 'nothing touches me' casual approach from him, but it irked that she recognised the attitude as one she had once mimicked to the max. 'It must be hard, though,' she pushed.

Ryan looked around the gym and then brought his gaze back to hers and lowered his voice. 'You think I'm about to head for the nearest betting shop to numb the pain?'

'Am I being silly? Do you really have this locked down?' she pressed.

That slow grin teased as he leaned in and whispered, 'How about if I admit that I'm going to extra meetings at the moment?'

'Good.' She took a subtle step back because it had been a long time since Ryan had whispered into her ear and it felt weird. 'Is it helping?'

'Well it's certainly helping me not to gamble, at any rate.'

'Great.' Sephy pointed to the changing rooms. She could see she wasn't going to get anywhere checking up on him in his place of work. 'I'll go grab my bag and we can head out for that coffee.'

Twenty minutes later Sephy peered over the top of her latte at Ryan and realised that agreeing to have coffee with him had upped the level of complication between them. Until now she had only met with him while Michelle, who had seemed nice enough, was there, or, with Daisy.

She decided he was going to have to put up with her butting in and came right out with, 'Have you told Ethan about what's happened?'

There was a flash of surprise in his eyes, but she couldn't afford to let this go. Not if there was a chance he was struggling and had no one else to lean on. If Sephy had to step up and be there for him, well, hadn't she had already implied she would, by agreeing to Ethan's plan to help his brother all those months ago?

'Ethan trusts me,' Ryan said. He took a sip of his cappuccino, set it down on the hammered aluminium surface of the café table and added sombrely, 'I understand why you might not.'

'I'll admit that this isn't entirely comfortable territory for me.'

'Trust me, it's no picnic for me either. You think I want my ex stopping by to check I'm getting over a breakup simply because she doesn't know me well enough to know whether or not I'll relapse?'

'Do you know yourself well enough to know whether or not you'll relapse?' she shot back.

Ryan laughed and the laughter seemed to relax something in him. 'You know, I really never imagined you acting as my conscience. Although I admit you're much prettier than the one I have.'

Again with the flirting and again she hoped it was simply a defence mechanism.

'How about instead of seeing me as your conscience,' she asked carefully, 'you see me as a friend who has a vested interest in making sure you're okay?'

'How about you let me take you to dinner tonight and we discuss further how okay I am?' Ryan replied, without missing a beat.

Sephy's latte went down the wrong way. She hadn't got this wrong. He was totally flirting with her. As she grabbed the napkin he held out to her, she blinked back her watering eyes, took in his giant grin and dragged in a steadying breath.

'Ryan, I didn't come here for a date. I came to check you were okay. For Daisy.'

At the mention of their daughter his face turned serious. 'I'm not going to mess that up.'

'Okay. Well, that's good, then.'

'So it's a "no" to dinner?'

'You've only just stopped seeing Michelle.'

'Usually a woman thinks it's a bonus when the man she accepts a dinner invitation from is single.'

'I am not going to go out to dinner with you.'

She tried not to worry that she was making things harder for him, not easier. Luke had told her Ryan wasn't her responsibility, but if she wanted him to have a good relationship with Daisy, he kind of was.

Sephy glanced to his hands holding his cup and making it look small. They were nice hands. They were hands that had travelled over every inch of her body, she remembered, taking a quick sip of coffee.

But they weren't *Luke's* hands, is that what it came down to?

Surreptitiously she swept her gaze over Ryan. The man managed a gym. He worked out. What was the matter with her that when she looked objectively at his body she didn't see it in those banners sexing up her lingerie line?

'You know, I thought it would be hard to see you like this,' Ryan said, breaking into her inventory of his model looks.

'This?' she asked, hoping he wasn't about to call her on her looking him over and use it to up the flirting.

'You're so different from how you were when we were –'

Oh. She couldn't help the smile. 'You mean when we were the ultimate cliché?'

He laughed. 'I guess we were. The poor little rich kids running around town partying.'

'It would be easier to look back on and not cringe if we had been much younger than we were.' Sephy cleared her throat and raised her gaze to his. 'We stayed with each other longer than we should have, Ryan. We fell into a lifestyle and had no one to pull us out of it.'

'I guess having Daisy finally pulled you out of it,' he said, nodding as he stared down at his coffee.

'Having her made me grow up, yes.'

'I wish I could tell you that if I'd stuck around I'd have grown up too.'

'Forget it; it's all in the past.'

This time Ryan's smile was wry. 'You always were quick to forgive people their sins.'

She'd had to be. How else would she have survived being the one King who showed no aptitude for the family company KPC? She'd had to understand her father and how his emotional connection to the business translated to those who didn't share that, in order to forgive him enough to have any kind of relationship with him at all.

'If it makes you feel better, I didn't forgive you overnight,' she told Ryan, her voice gentle.

'It does. And who knows, maybe you're starting to see how much I've changed.'

'You don't have to show me. You have to show Daisy.'

'I will. But maybe I want to show you too.'

'Ryan –'

'What?' His eyes searched hers. 'That ship has sailed?'

'I don't want there to be any confusion.' Getting mixed up with Ryan would massively complicate the relationship she wanted him to have with Daisy.

'Is there someone in your life at the moment?'

She closed her eyes and saw Luke and felt the shock of that right down to her toes.

That was so completely messed up she didn't even know what to do with it.

When she opened her eyes it was to see Ryan staring at her with a tenacity that she remembered.

Without thinking it through, other than to realise that Ryan believing she was already involved with someone would help make things less messy, she answered, 'Yes.'

'Is he good with Daisy?' he asked.

Sephy grasped her glass of coffee and let the residual warmth steady her. 'You haven't yet earned the right to ask that question.'

'That's fair. Is he good for you?'

'He's – yes.'

'You don't sound too sure.'

'I am sure.' The last thing she needed was for Ryan to see her as a project to take on, to help keep his addiction at bay, or otherwise.

'Is it Luke Jackson?'

Sephy's latte glass clattered back down to the table. 'I –' She tried again, 'what makes you think that?'

'He came into the gym soon after it opened. Got the feeling he wasn't checking out the premises so much as checking on the manager.'

She would kill Luke. 'Did he say something to you?'

'We exchanged a few pleasantries.'

'A few...What the hell does that mean?'

'It means he was being a good friend to you and Daisy.'

Sephy didn't know what to say.

Ryan folded his arms and leaned forward. 'Don't tell me you're still not used to people paying attention and looking out for you?'

'Something like that,' she cleared her throat. 'It must be a novelty for you too.'

He seemed to be lost in thought for a moment and Sephy wondered if he was thinking about his parents and how ill equipped they were to deal with his gambling addiction – to deal with their sons in any way. Ryan was lucky he had his brother, Ethan, on his side.

'I guess we'll both have to try and get used to it,' Ryan murmured.

'I guess we will,' Sephy answered.

'So *is* it Luke?'

Maybe she should have listened to Nora all those months ago when her sister had told her to, for once, take having Ryan back living near her and Daisy to its worst-case scenario and properly decide if that was something she could handle before she said yes to Ethan helping him relocate.

Because what she couldn't handle was Ryan deciding he wanted back into her life in any other capacity than being Daisy's dad. He'd left her when she was at her most vulnerable, and even though she had truly forgiven him, she wasn't about to forget all the small-town whisperings she had endured, or how he had made her feel like she sucked at relationships and wasn't a safe bet as a partner in life.

Ryan was going to get swept up in learning to be a dad, and if he was going to be around her while he did that, she didn't want him confusing matters and blurring the lines in his head.

It was better if he thought she and Luke were together, so she looked him straight in the eye and told her own little white lie. 'It is Luke, yes.'

Sephy sat surrounded by signature antique gold-coloured tissue paper, rolls of sticky labels with the Seraphic emblem on, and different-sized samples from her lingerie collection. As she wrapped each sample in the beautiful paper, ready to place in goodie-bags for the buyers at her launch party, she was already starting to feel guilty about lying to Ryan.

It was for the good of their future relationship as Daisy's parents, she told herself as her phone rang. Now all she had to do was tell Luke she was agreeing to his conditions and they could get the photo shoot under way and that would be one more thing checked off her endless list.

Ignoring the lick of fire igniting in her belly at the thought of telling Luke, she lifted up a pile of tissue paper and found her phone. Glancing at the screen to see who the caller was, she answered with a, 'Hi, Sis,' and tucking the phone between ear and shoulder, laid out another sheet of tissue paper and pulled matching camisole and French knickers in champagne-coloured silk off the pile.

'I'm pulling rank,' Nora said, without preamble. 'You are coming into London this week and I'm taking you out for lunch and then we're going shopping for shoes for the launch and that is all there is to it.'

'I don't have time,' Sephy said automatically. Not being as obsessed with shoes as her sister was, she was pretty sure she could find a pair in her wardrobe that matched the LBD she had elected to wear.

'Make the time. You know there won't be any immediately following the launch.'

'There might be,' Sephy swallowed as her voice got small, 'if no one places an order.'

'That's the way, keep talking positively like that and the sky's the limit.'

'Okay. Okay. I'll try and free up some time.'

'Great. So did you do it?'

'What?' Sephy had reached out to grab a goodie-bag, but stopped at the question.

'Did you ask Luke *The* Question?'

'I did.' She snatched up a bag and shook it open.

'And…?'

'He has a couple of conditions.'

'Oh my God, he's actually going to do it?'

'If I agree to his terms.'

'Huh?'

Sephy stopped assembling samples and said into her phone, 'He wants me to model with him.'

'Delicious.'

'Nora,' Sephy warned.

'I can't help it.'

'Yes, because you've never got yourself into a fix at all have you?' Sephy muttered, thinking about the time Nora had superglued her shoe to her hand in front of Ethan.

'But mine worked out so well for me in the end. Maybe yours will as well.'

'You didn't have a daughter or your daughter's dad come back onto the scene.'

'What?' Nora gasped. 'You're seeing Ryan?'

'No. Of course not.'

'Good. Because there's complicating your life and then there's complicating your life.'

Sephy agreed. That was why she had lied and told Ryan she was seeing Luke.

'I'll get in touch with Frazer today and set up the shoot,' Nora said.

'I haven't exactly said yes, yet.'

'Why not?'

'Probably because of the other condition.'

'Intriguing. Ooh,' Nora said sounding excited, 'does he want to do a private set of photos?'

'Oh, would you please stop. There's nothing tawdry going on here.'

Nora laughed. 'Did you just use the word tawdry?'

'Okay, I really need you to focus.'

'But did you, though?'

'You know, I think I'm too busy to come to London after all.'

'Okay, okay, I'm sorry. So what's his other condition?'

Sephy dragged in a breath. 'He wants me to pretend to be his fiancée for a few weeks.'

There was a long pause and then, 'Sephy that's not even remotely a good idea.'

'I know,' Sephy said, immediately heading her sister off at the pass.

'I mean, you just got through telling me you understood about not complicating your life.'

'I know.'

'It's only that these things have a way of getting out of control.'

'I know,' Sephy repeated for the umpteenth time. What if she had to touch him in front of his parents? Kiss him, even? What if she forgot how playing with fire got your fingers burned?

'Why does he want you to pose as his fiancée anyway?'

Sephy peeled off a Seraphic label and sealed the ends of the tissue-paper parcel of lingerie together.

'Seph?'

'Something to do with his parents visiting.'

'What? He's told his parents he's engaged, when he isn't?'

'Apparently, yes.'

More silence, followed by, 'You can't worry about losing his friendship if you say no, and, Sephy, you should say no to this.'

'If I say no, he won't hold it against me. You know he's not like that,' she responded. She popped the lingerie into a bag and reached for another sheet of tissue paper. 'He's helped me out so many times.'

'Don't make it sound tit for tat. Friends don't keep score.'

'If I say no I don't get my photo shoot.'

Sephy ran her gaze over her little production line of goodie bags. The boutique factory she had signed an agreement with had done an outstanding job of the samples. She didn't want to even think about the debt she would incur if she didn't get to place that first large order.

'Is this about saving money?' Nora surmised. 'Damn it, you know I'll cover it.'

Sephy winced. 'It really isn't only about the money.'

'Then you lied to me when you told me you were over what Dad wrote to you in his last letter,' Nora accused.

'I really didn't. Not completely or intentionally, anyway.' This time the silence from Nora screamed at her. Sephy pushed out the breath stuck in her windpipe. 'Okay. Yes, of course I was never going to be able to start a business and not think about Dad and what he would have thought.'

'I can tell you what he would have thought,' Nora interrupted indignantly. 'I can tell you what he's thinking right now as he's looking down at you. He's thinking, that's my youngest girl and she's doing everything I knew she could do in life – and more.'

Sephy's vision blurred as she silently asked herself if her father might also be thinking, 'Of course, she's only doing it because I gave her that final push.'

'Why can't this be about two friends helping each other out?' she whispered into her phone.

'Sephy –'

'I know. I know.' Sephy sniffed and pulled herself upright. 'I'll let you know what I decided when I see you on Friday.'

'Wow. You're giving yourself a whole two days to think this through.'

'Progress huh? A whole forty-eight hours longer than I usually give myself to make a decision. See you Friday.'

She ended the call, but kept the phone in her hand as she ran her gaze over the goodie-bags she was assembling.

Her gut said the women receiving those goodie-bags were going to be delighted after seeing Luke Jackson with his hands on the contents!

Her gut said getting to help Luke in return was all the justification she needed.

She looked down at her phone and before the butterflies swirling in her belly managed to break through her stomach lining and invade every part of her, she scrolled through her contacts list and found the entry she wanted.

'Hey you,' Luke greeted as he picked up.

'I accept your conditions,' said Sephy in a rush.

There was a fraction of a pause and then Luke said, 'Great. My place. Tomorrow.'

'What?' She felt kind of breathy and on the back foot. He was talking like he was taking the lead in this, like it was his situation to control.

'I thought time was of the essence,' Luke said, when she ran out of words as quickly as she'd rushed them out.

'I'm not sure I can get Frazer – that's the name of the photographer, to make tomorrow.' Not that she would necessarily be able to make it, either, because surely Nora was going to kill her for not even sleeping on her decision.

'No problem. We'll use tomorrow only for practising.'

'Practising?' Sephy's voice went all high.

'The more comfortable we are with each other, the better and quicker the shoot will go.'

'I guess,' Sephy said realising that was probably true. 'But why your place?'

'It's less distracting than yours and afterwards you can tell me what I need to buy to make my place look more lived-in for when the parents visit.'

'Oh. Okay. You want me to bring anything?' Sephy rolled her eyes. God, what, like she should turn up with cake or something?

'Just bring yourself. And your lingerie. Pop over once you've dropped Daisy off at school.'

'Right. Me. Lingerie. Your place. Tomorrow.' Sephy swallowed.

'You okay?'

'Sure,' she said, thinking, of course she bloody well wasn't okay. Otherwise her voice wouldn't be all high and scratchy, while Luke's voice in her ear sounded all deep and confident and…

'See you tomorrow,' she muttered into the phone before ending the call.

She dropped the phone into her lap like it was on fire and stared again at the line of goodie-bags.

Tomorrow was a business thing.

That was all.

CHAPTER FIVE

'It's me.'

Luke heard Sephy's voice over the intercom. He pressed the buzzer to open the gates that led to the sweeping driveway and newly built Georgian-styled house he had moved into on the success of *Zombie Freedom Fighters I, II,* and *III.*

Was it his imagination or had Sephy's voice sounded all breathy?

He shoved his hand through his hair before heading for the imposing double doors in the entrance hall.

About to open them, he hesitated. It would probably look weird if he was standing at the front door waiting for her to drive up, wouldn't it?

Like he couldn't wait to see her in her underwear, or something?

You know what, mate? This might not be the brightest idea you've ever had.

In fact, Luke thought, as he hovered uncertainly in his own hallway, he could hardly believe he had thought the idea genius in the first place.

In his head, he had glossed over the finer points in order to get to the part where he could help her and help himself at the same time. At heart, he had never really expected her to agree.

But then she had and when she had his first reaction hadn't been relief he was going to get to allay his foster parents' fears for him. No, his first reaction had been to feel as if he was falling off the top of a very tall building, and hurtling, eyes wide open, towards the ultimate face-plant.

He heard the crunch of gravel and made himself return his mug to the kitchen before he wandered back out to throw the door open wide.

'Hey you,' Sephy greeted, with her usual, full-on, no-artifice smile.

Luke was still trying to form actual words of welcome when he saw Sephy's smile falter a little and a frown form over her brow-line.

She jerked her thumbs in the direction of her car and said, 'I'll, um, bring a couple of bags I brought with me in from the car.'

''Course,' Luke said belatedly. 'I'll give you a hand.' Christ. Was that even his voice coming out of his mouth? She had done something to her hair that caused it to fall in thick, touchable waves. He shoved his hands into his jeans pockets to keep from reaching out.

'I've got it,' Sephy declared. Pivoting, she walked back to the car, throwing over her shoulder, 'there's only two bags.'

Luke wasn't completely sure he could have got his feet to move anyway. They seemed rooted to the spot as he stared in fascination at that waterfall of black just-tumbled-out-of-bed hair, bouncing a little as she walked, making the waves ripple up and down.

She opened up the driver's door, knelt one knee on the driver's seat and reached in to bring out the bags she had stored in the passenger-seat foot-well and the air squeezed out of his lungs as his gaze dragged over the soft white denim of her skinny-jeaned derriere.

He didn't get it.

She had always worn her hair long and he knew he'd seen her in those exact-same jeans before and not felt this wall of lust rise up to block his every attempt to find his way back to platonic.

Was this to be his punishment, then?

One white lie and his friend was his friend no more. Instead she was an accessory to the crime. One who got his pulse racing and his blood thickening so that it pounded in his ears, while his body hardened to the point where surely she would notice?

All this and she hadn't even taken her clothes off yet.

Maybe he wouldn't let her take them off after all, because it now seemed as if situation- helpful was turning into situation-most-dangerous-ever.

'So, I brought a few different sets with me,' Sephy was saying, as she walked towards him with the Seraphic bags swinging from one hand and her car keys clutched in her other, along with her travel mug. 'I'm nearly sure which ones I want photos of. I guess it depends which suit me better. I'm not exactly model material.'

He begged to differ and immediately made an exerted effort to stop his thoughts straying down the path clearly marked 'trouble'. Neither of them needed this backfiring on them.

'I guess if we try lots of different things,' she hurried on, walking past him into his house, 'then we can run it all past Frazer when he does the shoot proper. If it goes well today, I'll get Nora to ring him and set things up for Monday. Would that work for you? Wow,' she came to an abrupt stop and turned in a slow circle. 'I can't believe I haven't been here before. It's really big.' She turned to face him as she said the last words, her eyes looking him up and down and snagging on his jeans zipper before she flushed scarlet.

Luke shoved his hands deeper into his pockets and prayed to God he wasn't doing the same.

Sephy turned away to take in the carved wooden staircase and started rambling like she was on the ultimate caffeine high again. 'I was thinking on the drive over how strange it was that I'd never actually been here before. I think that's strange. Don't you think that's strange? I guess it's always been easier to meet at mine because of D –'

'You want to take a breath?' Luke interrupted, deliberately making his voice as moderate as he thought he could get away with.

He knew that Sephy hated feeling like she was being manoeuvred, but he figured she was about two steps away from hyperventilating and although he was kind of pleased to see her so unsure of her footing, he knew she would bolt if panic hit full on, and then blame herself for ruining her opportunity to fix her ad campaign.

'What are you talking about?' Sephy said, turning back to face him. 'I'm breathing. I'm totally breathing. I'm –'

'How many of those have you had?' Luke asked, dragging his hand out of his pocket to point at her giant travel mug.

'Oh. This is my first one. I didn't want to be too, you know.' She flapped a hand about between them, rolled her eyes and shrugged, and as easy as that they were both smiling at each other.

'Okay. Well, given that I never ask guests to bring their own coffee, shall we go into the kitchen and I'll make us a fresh batch. We can talk.'

'Talk?' Sephy asked.

'Catch ourselves up.' Tell her about his family situation, he thought, deliberately ignoring the flash flood of trepidation he felt.

'Oh. Okay. Good idea. We could do the house stuff first and the other stuff…after.'

'Drop the bags here, then, and we'll take them up to my bedroom later.'

'Bedroom?' Suspicion hit her huge brown eyes.

'You can get changed up there and I've got full-length mirrors. I thought you'd want to see –'

'Of course. That's fine. So are you going to show me this kitchen of yours, then?'

Luke stepped to the side and gestured for her to precede him into the room off to the right.

They were friends who were helping each other out.

That was all.

So they'd talk, have a little lunch and then by the time it came to 'practice' they would both feel more like what they were doing really wasn't such a big deal.

Which it wasn't, he counselled.

He couldn't help wishing he had never thought practicing first would be a good idea, though. In his mind he had associated non-professional models with awkwardness and that, coupled with the very real worry he was going to feel as if the photographer was exposing his soul for others to gawk at, or something, had him suggesting rehearsing. But now he wished for the sterile white lights of the photographer's studio. The flash and noise of photographer and camera. Keeping it all professional would have had the distancing effect that it turned out he really needed.

Instead it was now all about his house, his bedroom with its super-king-sized bed, full- length mirrors…and Sephy with a bag full of stunning lingerie she was going to play dress-up in.

Luke walked into his kitchen, releasing the air from his lungs in a long, slow, meant-to-be-stress-releasing breath.

There was no way he could back out now. Sephy was counting on him and he wasn't a person who let people down.

Besides, it wasn't like he wasn't getting anything out of the deal.

As if she had read his mind, Sephy walked into the large kitchen, and disregarding all the mod-cons, granite work surfaces and glossy oyster-white units, she headed straight for the rogue's gallery on the far kitchen wall.

Luke deliberately turned his attention to organising coffee, feeling his shoulders creep upwards as he braced for the obvious question.

'Who are all these kids?' Sephy asked, getting right to the inevitable.

Luke flicked on the coffee machine and turned around to lean against the island unit.

It wasn't like he hadn't spent last night knowing that inviting Sephy into his home was also to invite a whole host of questions he usually avoided answering. But if she was really going to be his pretend fiancée, he was going to have to tell her everything.

'Those are my brothers and sisters,' he answered, his tone suggesting a matter-of-factness he would really appreciate being reciprocated.

No deal. Sephy simply shot a shocked look at him. 'All of these kids?'

He nodded and she looked like she couldn't decide whether to keep her eyes trained on him or turn back to the photos taking up the whole wall.

In the end the photographs won out.

He watched her look at the centre photograph of Steve and Lily Jackson and then he watched her count under her breath every one of the different faces in the photographs surrounding them.

'You have seven brothers and nine sisters?' she asked in wonder.

'Yep.'

'Well, how the hell did I not know this about you?' Now there was pure disbelief and a trace of anger in her voice.

Luke had expected that, had prepared himself. Yet, still, the accusation at the heart of her question cut deep.

'Luke?'

He moved to retrieve two mugs from an overhead cupboard and the hard-fought-for lightness he had worked on simply disappeared. 'What was I supposed to do? Introduce myself with, "Hi I'm Luke, I'm one of seventeen kids?" all so that you could then say, "Hi, I'm Sephy and I'm one of three, I have a daughter called Daisy and, oh, my father is living out his last days with cancer, so life is pretty unbearable at the moment".'

In the heavy silence Luke reached for the sugar he knew she

liked in her coffee and stole a quick glance at her. She had turned to face the rogue's gallery once more, her arms folded tightly in front of her, her back ramrod straight.

'The difference, Luke,' he heard her say stiltedly, 'is that I did tell you all of those things over time.'

Shit. He wasn't used to being the one who caused any hurt. Grabbing the coffees, he walked over to the large kitchen table and set them down. 'Coffee's up,' he said lightly. When she didn't turn around, his hand went to the back of his neck to knead the tight muscle there. 'I'm sorry,' he said. 'I shouldn't have said that about your father like it was something light and in any way the same.'

She looked at him over her shoulder, her gaze flicking down to the coffee, as if he had only conjured it up as a peace offering before she turned fully to face him and inhaled deeply.

'Did you get this brand of coffee in just for me?' she asked softly as the aroma wafted in the air.

'I might have.'

'Because you knew I would ask you about this,' she said jerking her thumb behind her to the picture wall. In answer to her own question, her gaze narrowed and she refolded her arms. 'You know, it's not nice to enable someone's addiction in a bid to get out of answering some difficult questions.'

'Yeah? Ryan tell you that, did he?'

Sephy's mouth dropped open in shock and Luke could have bitten off his tongue. He had never envisaged this conversation turning flippant or insulting – or that he would get so defensive. Not when he had gone through it all in his head and made himself okay with telling her.

He waited for her to announce she was leaving because she had come here to practise a photo shoot, not wander into some weird family issues. But once again, as if she was reading his mind, she said, 'I'll give you the benefit of the doubt for throwing Ryan in my face like that.'

She shouldn't.

It made him want to warn her not to be too nice to him in case all she got back was even more bad attitude.

'Everyone has a few landmines buried amongst their family terrain,' Sephy said, carefully. 'I guess one just exploded in our faces.'

Luke watched her walk slowly over to the table, pull out a chair and sit down. She didn't seem scared at all that there might be more landmines, or fallout from the one that had already detonated.

In unison they raised coffee mugs to their mouths, but just before Sephy would have taken a sip of hers he saw her shake her head slightly and lower the mug back down to the table.

'I guess what I'm struggling with, is that not once, during any of the many, *many* times I've moaned to you about Jared or Nora, have you said anything remotely like, "Siblings. It's hell on earth – I get it".'

'I didn't deliberately not tell you.'

Sephy leaned her elbows on the table, stared him straight in the eye and said, 'Bollocks.'

He had always admired Sephy's ability to cut through and face things head-on. But having that directed specifically at him packed quite the punch.

'You're sitting in my home,' he said, leaning back against his chair, though the effort to appear relaxed had no effect on his abs, which he could still feel contracting under his shirt. 'I'm not hiding anything from you now.'

'Only because you need my help,' Sephy surmised.

And because he wanted to prolong for as long as possible her looking at him differently, because as soon as she found out why he had sixteen brothers and sisters, she would. Everyone did. 'So I guess we are where we are,' he admitted.

Sephy stared into her coffee. 'Do you remember when I told you how disorienting it was when Jared absented himself from our family? I know I mentioned some of the knock-on issues it created between my father and me.'

He remembered. He remembered thinking he had no frame of reference to draw on and how that had made him feel kind of helpless and somewhat not good enough.

A feeling he wasn't altogether unfamiliar with.

'You didn't say one thing, Luke. You simply listened. And I can remember thinking this is why we work as friends. Because you don't judge. You just listen.' She took a quick sip of coffee. 'I also remember thinking you never talked about your family. I thought that and I let it go.' Her button nose wrinkled. 'I don't know why I let it go like that!'

There was confusion and regret in her voice and he wanted to reassure her that she had let it go, not because she was at fault but because he had made it easy for her to do so.

He hadn't changed the conversation in an obvious way, but he had done what he had learnt to do from a very young age. He had shifted the angle of the conversation slightly, so that the focus turned back to her.

'Being one of seventeen kids is a pretty big thing not to ever mention, Luke. In fact it's huge.'

He knew it. Knew that some of this was about him deliberately holding back from her and her having to make an adjustment for that, so he simply nodded.

'Is the reason you don't talk about your family because you did what Jared did and walked away for a while?'

'No.' He had never walked away willingly. He had always been sent away or taken away. Well, until that last time, he thought, drowning in guilt.

He watched as Sephy got up from the table and walked back over to the wall of photographs once more. As if she had to double-check the evidence before her.

'You're the only one who looks like them,' Sephy turned, her hand outstretched to the picture of Steve and Lily Jackson.

Luke ground down on his molars. 'I know. It's ironic, really.'

'Why?' Sephy licked her lips. 'Is it because,' she stopped and Luke braced himself for the rest of the sentence at the same time as willing her to say what was before her eyes. 'Is it because you are adopted?'

Here it was, then. The moment where context shifted ever so slightly on its axis, and their friendship either deepened respectfully, or she did what others had done to him and made it into an issue. Blowing out a short breath, Luke said, 'Two are their birth children. The rest of us are fostered.'

Sephy nodded and looked briefly back at the wall and then at him. 'What age were you when you were fostered?'

Luke took a gulp of his coffee. 'The first time or the last time?'

'I – either. Both.'

'The first time I was three. The last time, when I was placed with Steve and Lily, I was fourteen. I stayed with them until I left to go to university.'

'Okay, that's –' Sephy stopped and this time turned to stare out of the kitchen patio doors to his garden beyond, as if she didn't want him to see the pity in her eyes. 'Okay.'

Luke drained his coffee and got up to take it to the kitchen sink while he waited for her to ask the next inevitable questions.

The ones that stemmed from ever mentioning having sixteen brothers and sisters.

The: what-happened-to-your-biological-parents-and-why-were-you-put-into-the-care-system question. The: why-weren't-you-ever-adopted question.

Of course that all led to the ultimate question. The one that wasn't really a question – so much as an observation, followed by a judgement.

The one that went: what was wrong with you that your mother couldn't cope with you?

He told himself the cold hard facts were nothing to be ashamed of, that there never had been anything wrong with him.

He told himself that he was comfortable with the story of him.

But as Sephy stood silently staring out into his garden, the shame started to creep in and all he could think was: what a bunch of crap.

'So why did you feel the need to tell your…foster parents?' Sephy asked. 'You called them your parents when you asked me to pretend to be your fiancée.'

'They respond to either,' Luke said, remembering the first time he had called Lily Jackson his mum. It had been such an unconscious thing, yet he had felt so incredibly divided as soon as it had slipped out. But Lily Jackson had known that and she hadn't blinked an eye. And when he had gone straight back to calling her Lily for months afterwards, she still hadn't blinked an eye. Eventually he'd matched the thinking of them as parents with calling them parents because parenting was exactly the right word to describe what they had done for him. With patience and love they had guided, listened and protected. Without them, he would never have experienced what it was to be part of stable family environment. As mad as it was when the house was full, Steve and Lily had steered them all through safely.

'So why did you feel you needed to tell them you had got engaged?' Sephy finished asking.

For a minute he was so caught up in figuring out the first few words that would lead to the rest of the story that he didn't compute that Sephy hadn't asked any one of those inevitable questions he hated so much.

She was the first person *not* to have asked what he had expected.

He turned from the sink, a wry smile on his face. Why had he thought for one minute that Sephy King was like every other woman he'd told?

Perversely it made him want to tell her the whole story in one fell swoop. Push the envelope and stand in the face of what he knew would be her very real and honest response.

But then that edge of selfishness pushed in and he knew he

would rather defer her response and take the gift she had just given him. The one where she pretended that who he was and where he had come from didn't matter more than who she knew him to be.

Something shifted inside of him and he found himself walking over to meet her in front of the kitchen patio doors.

Sephy King was interested not in salacious detail, but in simply being his friend.

And wasn't that the real reason he hadn't told her about being a fostered child for more years than he'd actually lived with his birth mother?

Because he was interested in being her friend too and hadn't wanted to experience her possible rejection.

Luke shoved his hands in his pockets and stared out at the formal square patio laid out beyond the glass doors. 'My foster parents are good people. They're the kind of people who think that love is what makes the world go around.'

'Aren't you proof of that?'

He shot her a quick smile. He guessed he was. 'It's not like their expectations of love are unrealistic. But it's hard for them to understand I can be happy without being married. That favouring work over a relationship isn't compensating for a lack of a full life but that it can be equal.'

Sephy raised an eyebrow and he could feel himself getting defensive again. Ms Marriage-Phobic was hardly in a position to tell him he wasn't filling his life to its fullest.

'So,' she said, looking as if she was feeling her way around a maze, 'you told them you were getting married to…?'

'Look,' he said, 'obviously I didn't think it through. I didn't think beyond needing them to stop worrying about me. The lie slipped out and they started backing off.' He let out some of the breath that had been waiting in his chest for too long. 'I owe them a lot. I never imagined they would want to visit and "meet" the woman I finally gave my heart to.'

'Uh-huh.'

'You don't approve?' He shifted to look at her. 'Believe me, I already feel guilty enough.'

Sephy swallowed. 'Look, it's not like I've never told a white lie.'

'Yeah? When was the last time you did?'

She looked really uncomfortable for a moment and everything inside of him stilled as he wondered if it was to him.

'Okay, don't get mad, but,' Sephy squeezed her eyes shut and then opened one a tiny amount to look up at him. 'I might have implied to Ryan that you and I were seeing each other.'

'What?' Luke couldn't have been more shocked. Then, immediately, he was reaching out and sliding his hand down her arm to grasp loosely at the soft, soft skin of her wrist. Without his permission, his thumb feathered across her pulse point until he felt the jump of life there. 'Tell me he didn't do something way out of line to make you feel cornered into doing that?'

With a subtle twist of her wrist she jerked herself free. 'No. No, nothing like that, although while we're on the subject, don't think for one minute that I'm not going to grill you about a certain visit you paid him.'

Damn. 'He told you about that, huh?' He shoved his hand into his pocket and told himself he couldn't really feel a residual buzz in his fingertips from the slide over her skin.

'What on earth were you thinking?'

Thinking had had very little to do with it, Luke thought, remembering that mostly what he had *felt* was a compulsion to make it clear to Ryan that Sephy was coming out the other side of grieving for her father and wasn't in a place to be mucked around with.

'I was looking out for you and Daisy.'

Immediately her hands went to her hips. 'Do I look like I need looking out for, Luke?'

'Truth or white lie?'

'Wow.' She frowned. 'I thought I'd been doing a good job of –'

'You've been doing an excellent job of keeping it all together,' he asserted. 'I can't see what harm it does to have someone else on your side, though.'

She stared at him before whispering, 'Okay,' and the simple acceptance in her eyes made him feel hero-like.

'So why did you tell Ryan we are involved?' he asked.

'He – I just thought it would make the boundaries between us more set in stone.'

'You realise you've now locked yourself into this pretend-fiancée thing, then.'

'I wouldn't have come here today if I wasn't going to follow through.'

'Yes, but you weren't expecting to hear –'

This time it was Sephy who cut him off. 'I haven't heard anything to scare me off. I like that you want to protect your foster parents and make them happy. As long as we put in some ground rules to keep Daisy out of this, then like you've just told me, I can't see the harm in having someone on your side. You do the photo shoot with me and I pretend to be your fiancée for the length of your foster parents' visit. What could possibly go wrong?'

CHAPTER SIX

Sephy drew the sides of the turquoise silk wrap with its scarlet-embroidered edging together and retied the sash for the fourth time while pondering exactly how much longer she could stay locked inside Luke's en suite for.

She barely breathed as she listened out for any sign of movement in the bedroom beyond.

The bedroom.

Why was this all feeling suddenly so much more intimate than it needed to be?

She seemed to be having monumental difficulty believing she was about to step into Luke's bedroom, take off her robe, and show him how she wanted him to pose with her.

How had this all come about again?

Oh yeah.

It was on account of noticing Luke's gorgeous hands – which were about to get up close and personal with her.

This is what happened when you had an out-of-control imagination that ruled you, rather than the other way around.

Sephy leant both hands on the vanity unit and tried some deep breathing. All the time they had been talking about his foster parents, she had forgotten to be nervous about why she was here today. Listening to his bare-boned account of how he had obviously been fostered out for large chunks of his childhood had had her wanting to walk over to him, wrap her arms around him and hug him to her tight. She had wanted to assure him that he didn't have to tell her anything he didn't want to because she could remember only too well what it felt like to be on the receiving end of question after question about your personal family life. The questions floating about after Jared had gone to New York all those years ago had been invasive and endless.

For months it had felt as if all she would ever be was Jared King's baby sister – possible mine of information for gossiping purposes about why the heir to KPC had upped and left so abruptly. Nora had been nineteen and so much better than her at being the good child, at being the one who did what their father told them to do. Nora had made refusing to be drawn on the subject look super-easy, whereas Sephy, at fifteen, had really struggled.

With hindsight she could look back and see that as the youngest she had been too wrapped up in her own world to be aware of any but the most obvious undercurrents. By the time Jared left that summer, her existence was reduced to being stone-walled by her own family at every attempt to find out why the brother she hero-worshipped had upped and left.

Sephy had wanted answers and was used to getting her own way. She definitely wasn't someone who found it easy to fall into line like her sister had. There was too much of the rebel in her.

The less she had been able to toe the family party line when Jared had left, the more her father had dealt with her by cutting her out of the loop and pretending she didn't exist.

The partying and generally wasting her life had started before she had hit sixteen and it had continued for four years until she'd had Daisy.

Part escape, part antidote to all the questions, but mostly as a way of trying to make one thing in her family not be all about Jared, or KPC, but about her.

The shame of that sometimes still had the ability to overwhelm her, so, yes, while she might have shared with Luke some general family milestones and some of the heavier family issues, she had done so anecdotally and not with any particular emphasis on how those family tales had taken root deep inside of her, making her feel as if she sometimes didn't belong in her own family.

Every family had its secrets.

She supposed she could hardly blame Luke for not wanting to open up about his own childhood. But aside from his right to keep some things private, Sephy had to acknowledge that at every juncture where she and Luke might have grown closer, she had very deliberately set about re-establishing the boundaries of friendship she wanted to operate within.

Because…

Sephy looked away from her reflection.

She knew why she constantly boxed their friendship in.

But she sure as hell wasn't going to admit it out loud.

Especially not if the guy waiting for her in the adjoining room might hear.

Before she could out-think herself, Sephy dragged in a breath, and reaching for the bathroom door, tugged it open.

Luke, who had been sitting on the corner of the bed waiting for her, rose to his feet and automatically turned to face her.

As his gaze swept over her, Sephy felt the lick of flames a thousand times hotter than when Ryan had looked at her the day before. That was all it took for her to know one hundred per cent that the nerves in her belly weren't what had propelled her out of the bathroom and into Luke's bedroom.

It was the heady, fluttery mix of excitement swirling alongside the nerves. It was the long- forgotten need to chase that excitement that had spurred her on to open the door and step out.

Damn.

She really needed to be careful here because she had sworn off playing with fire the moment she had held Daisy in her arms and had realised she was wholly responsible for someone other than herself.

Yep. She definitely remembered promising herself no more

thrill-seeking. No more letting loose. No more not thinking things through.

But maybe she had reached the statute of limitations on behaving well.

Because now, as she stood in Luke's bedroom facing him, no matter how good her imagination was, no amount of creativity was able to shift this bedroom into an innocent beach scene where she was simply wearing the equivalent of a bikini and wrap.

'So this is the first,' Luke swallowed and gestured with his hand, 'outfit you want photographed?'

Sephy nodded, trying to pretend that she hadn't noticed that Luke's voice had got deeper, or that tiny goosebumps chased each other all over her body and fed the excitement she was supposed to be shutting down.

'Yes.'

'Nice,' he stated, his eyes sweeping from her shoulder line to bottom hem of the robe for the second time.

'Nice?' Sephy squeaked, her toes cramping against the polished wooden floorboards. Nice, as a word, wasn't going to cut it. The hours she had poured into making sure the design flowed and the fit looked expensive had her wanting more from him.

'More than,' he admitted, clearing his throat and flicking his gaze up to meet hers.

'Better,' Sephy heard herself say, enjoying the verbal reaction that went along with the darkening of his eyes.

'So where do you want me?' he asked.

The question sounded loaded with promise and damned if her betraying gaze didn't shift automatically to the bed, before colliding back with his.

Wow, was this kind of mortifying.

Sephy willed his dimples not to make an appearance. She hadn't even taken off her robe and the situation obviously had her transmitting completely subconscious thoughts to her *must-not-go-there-with* friend.

Figuring that the less she associated Luke Jackson with a bed, the safer they both were, she turned around to face the wall of mirrors. She was quite pleased with herself when her voice sounded semi-normal. 'I guess if we use the mirrors to, you know, figure out which poses work best, then we can provide Frazer with a list of specific shots. That will speed the whole process up, won't it?' She peered over her shoulder, waiting for him to approach her.

'Aren't you forgetting something?' Luke said, a smile tugging at the outer corners of his mouth.

'What?' she said with a frown as she whipped around to face him.

'Well, unless this photo is all about the robe, you probably need to lose it.'

Her hands went automatically to the silk knot at her waist.

The longer she stood there frozen, the surer Luke's smile became.

Oh God.

Other than his initial reaction to her coming out of the en suite, he didn't look one bit fazed by the fact that she was standing before him with hardly any clothes on.

That had to rank right up there with some of life's most unfair advantages.

Panic bubbled alongside the nerves and excitement as she started wondering what would happen if she accidentally on purpose forgot five years of good behaviour for one moment of insanity.

With her *friend*.

Ack.

This was so not about...Luke and...that.

Sure, with the air growing thick and the heat flaring in Luke's eyes and her breath coming shorter, it might seem like this was now all about the swirling attraction hanging in the atmosphere.

Or perhaps even that this was about pure lust.

Need.

Sex.

Between two supposed platonic friends.

But it wasn't.

Wasn't. Wasn't. Wasn't.

Screwing up her courage, she tossed her hair over her shoulder and lifting her chin a determined notch higher said, 'I drop the robe when you lose the shirt.'

If anything, as Luke studied her, the atmosphere heated and thickened further. Just when she thought she was going to be wearing this robe until she went home Luke shrugged, casual as anything, and then in a practised movie-smooth move, slowly reached behind him, grabbed a hold of his t-shirt and dragged it clear off over his head.

Electricity arced between them. With his t-shirt sexily bunched in his hand at his side, Sephy knew absolutely that her eyes were bulging.

Knew it and yet could do nothing to stop her reaction to the visual in front of her.

Saliva became a distant memory.

She knew he worked out. Had known the way his shirts stretched across smooth, taut muscle that the workouts were effective.

She just hadn't realised what an aesthete she was.

Stop staring, woman.

But how could she when he was so very prettily sculpted?

He had to know that, right?

What the hell was there to be shy about when you looked like this?

Sephy licked her lips and told herself for the gazillionth time that Luke was not for having and that she was not a person who went about life diving in without due care any more. For a start she depended on his friendship too much and absolutely did not want to jeopardise that.

'Your turn,' Luke said, staring intently at the knotted-silk belt.

She had to calm down. It wasn't like they were stripping all the way down to their skin, for each other.

All this was about was getting comfortable for the express reason of turning out the best ad campaign she could.

For her business.

The business that was going to support her and her daughter and therefore needed all of her attention.

'You know what would make this a little easier?' she asked, blushing when her voice sounded all croaky.

'Copious amounts of alcohol?'

Ha. Maybe he wasn't feeling as at ease as his body language suggested. 'What would help is if you weren't so,' she stopped before she said 'cocky', because as she looked closely she could see the slight lift of tension lifting his shoulders a fraction higher than normal. Under all that control, it was the glimpse of vulnerability in him that made it easy for her to finally draw one end of the silk through its knot and part the material.

Luke looked away and she frowned, unable to decide if she was grateful or not.

As he walked over to the leather armchair in the corner of his room and carefully folded up his t-shirt before placing it on the chair Sephy lowered her robe. Concentrating on the feel of the silk cooling her heated skin as it slid down her arms and off, she caught it before it landed on the floor and dropped it casually onto the bed.

Except now she didn't know what to do with her hands.

Turning to the wall of mirrors, she stopped in front of them and lifted her hand to fiddle with one of the bra straps. Seconds later and she couldn't help herself, her gaze flicked to the mirrors and she caught Luke staring at the robe as it lay seductively on his bed.

Not that he was necessarily thinking it looked seductive, she told herself.

When he continued to stare down at it, she whirled around

to face him. Maybe he had OCD and clothes needed to be neatly folded or hung up.

'I can pop it back in the bag, if you want?' she asked, her voice sounding like it had been mixed with sand.

Luke's gaze whipped up to hers and his hand went to the back of his head like she knew it did when he was thinking through one of his more complex problems. 'Huh?'

'The robe. If it's bothering you.'

'Why would it be bothering me?' Luke said, slowly removing his hand as if he had realised how it looked.

'I have no idea. But you looked as if you wanted it gone from your bed.'

'You're over-thinking.'

'Yes, well.' For once she was all in favour of over-thinking, analysing, rationalising and looking before she leapt. Anything that put the kibosh on feeling was definitely a good thing.

'Tell you what,' Luke said determinedly, 'let's just get this done, shall we? So,' he moved towards her and she turned back around to face the mirrors. 'Where exactly do you want me to stand?

'I was thinking directly behind me?'

Luke followed her instructions and as he stepped in right behind her Sephy tucked her lower lip between her teeth and lowered her head. She could feel heat radiating from that magnificent body of his.

'Okay,' he murmured, the word pouring into her ear and making her suck harder on her lip. 'Now, tell me where you want my hands.'

Sephy's head shot up, nearly bumping against the underside of his chin, because the way he said it…the husk in his voice made her feel as if he was asking her to order him to put his hands on her.

She searched out his expression in the full-length mirror in front of them, but he had been studiously looking at her shoulder when he'd uttered the words.

Sephy inhaled deep into the bottom of her lungs and Luke responded by matching her so that her back came into direct contact with his torso. Molten, hot mossy-green eyes shot to hers in the mirror and she watched, mesmerised by the metronomic beat of his jaw clenching and unclenching.

This was torture.

Blissful torture.

She should never have agreed to this.

'Seph?' His calling her name was so gruff there was no mistaking the edge of appeal in his voice. 'You want to tell me where you want me to put my hands, or do you want me to take charge?'

Mercy.

Yes.

She wanted him to take charge.

To end this.

To begin this.

To…no. None of this was supposed to be about sex and the two of them. All this was supposed to be about was creating a relevant user story that would have consumers craving to buy her lingerie.

Right there, right then, Sephy re-promised herself that when she went out to New York in a month's time for Jared and Amanda's wedding, she was going to get Nora to look after Daisy for a while and she was going to go off and find herself an outlet for all this churning, burning, all-consuming need that had to be about the fact she hadn't been with a man in a while and was absolutely nothing to do with Luke specifically.

Breathing through her mouth, she tried to clear her lungs of Luke-Jackson pheromone and concentrate. 'I think for the first shot,' she said, channelling her inner business-woman with all her might, 'you should place your hands on my ribs, under my, um, breasts.'

'Like I'm going to reach up and palm them?'

'Yes,' she managed to get out through gritted teeth, eternally grateful that this particular bra was padded and therefore Luke would hopefully not be able to tell that her breasts had swelled within the cups of material.

She watched in the mirror as Luke reached around with his arms to place his hands on her. She held her breath and at the first touch of skin on skin, Sephy's system burst into overdrive.

Luke's hands felt warm. Firm. Confident and capable and her imagination wept that she would never get the chance to experience full taking-charge Luke Jackson as a lover.

'This okay?' he asked quietly and straight away her imagination leapt ahead to thinking about all that generosity in him. Yes, she thought, breathlessly, he would be a generous lover.

Striving to claw back a sense of professionalism, she said, 'Move your fingers up so that they skim the underwire a little more.' She licked her lips as he did so and said, 'Yes. Just exactly like that.'

Behind her, Luke went completely still at her tone and after a few moments staring at his fingers – her willing them to stroke upwards and him – looking at her like he knew that was what she was doing, she husked out, 'We could crop the photos at your jaw-line. That way no one will necessarily have to know it's you in the photos.'

'I should take off my watch and –'

'No,' Sephy shot out. 'I like it. It looks good against my skin, I mean the lingerie.'

Again Luke's eyes met hers in the mirror.

Again she brazened out the fact that she was standing nearly naked, his body heat making her melt, the feel of his hands making her worry a whimper of need might escape her lips.

'Okay,' Luke said, dropping his hands from her and shaking them out a little. 'Next pose.'

'Right, so maybe if you moved one hand to slide a finger under my bra strap.'

In the next instant Sephy was trembling as Luke, oh so gently, swept her hair out of the way. Was it her heightened senses that imagined the way his thumb fleetingly caressed over her top vertebrae as he did so?

She swallowed and felt Luke turn his hand so that the backs of his knuckles brushed slowly across the skin of her neck and shoulder. When her knees buckled and she wobbled forward a step, his hand closed over her shoulder to hold her firm.

She should say something.

Maybe if they acknowledged this, it would be easier to put a stop to it.

But treacherously her better angels remained silent.

The look of intense concentration on Luke's face as he slid his thumb slowly under the bra strap meant he had to know the effect he was having on her, but was choosing to ignore it.

Why?

So that he could continue torturing her by enticing a response from her that neither would be able to ignore? Or because he couldn't stop himself, even if he wanted to?

'Like this?' he finally asked, sliding the strap a couple of inches down her shoulder.

'Uh-huh,' was all she could answer with.

Luke cleared his throat and said, 'And where do you want me to put my other hand?

'Um, maybe on my hip?'

He moved to do her bidding. 'Take your hand and place it over mine.'

She tried her hand at resisting that hot-butterscotch-sauce-over-ice-cream voice, but when she hesitated he urged, 'Go on, put your hand over mine and let's see what it looks like.'

'Yes, sir, mister expert-ad-content photographer,' she said, but did so, and was that her hand squeezing gently over his that caused his to clench against her hip seemingly in need, or had his hand clenched first, and hers had squeezed in agreement?

All at once it was too much.

As sensation after sensation rushed at her, Sephy pictured herself making the biggest fool of herself ever, and forced herself to step away and pick up the robe again, causing Luke to immediately drop his hands from her body so that she then felt ridiculously bereft.

Luke started pacing back and forth along the length of the bedroom wall. 'Out of interest,' he asked tightly, 'how many other sets of underwear did you bring with you?'

'Only two more. A corset like one of the models wore in the original ad campaign, and another set a bit like this, but in white.'

'A corset?' Luke asked, shooting her a look as he ruffled his hair again. 'I'm not sure that's a good idea.'

Wow. Okay. Sephy fiddled with the end of the robe's belt. He was as worried as she was that the game they were playing could spin out of control. 'I absolutely won't need your help to get me out of it,' she said trying to reassure him.

'I thought women wore corsets specifically to be undressed by the person seeing it on them?'

'A woman buys a corset to wear under a piece of clothing that calls for it, or sometimes as a top itself,' she said indignantly.

Luke laughed and the sound danced down her spine. 'I can guarantee you that isn't how a man sees it. What?' he asked when he caught the frown she knew was on her face.

'Nothing. I guess I'm not used to hearing you be so –' Sephy trailed off.

'Sexual?'

Heat flooded her. 'Yes.'

'Because that's not really how friends usually are with each other, is it?' he asked as if to double-check.

'Um, no. So...I'll be getting changed now.' She moved towards his en suite.

'Into the corset?'

'I guess we can skip that one.'

She thought she heard him mutter, 'Thank you, God,' but couldn't be certain. She definitely heard him when he said, 'I'll be right outside waiting.'

Sephy closed the door to Luke's en suite behind her and stared at the Seraphic bag on the vanity counter. Reaching forward she opened the bag and peered in at the black bustier with its miles of ribbon.

She was glad Luke had finally alluded to what was happening in front of those mirrors. Glad that he had effectively put a stop to the two of them pushing and pulling closer to meeting and then crossing the line between friendship into something way more complicated.

It wasn't a big deal that it was him who had the sense to put a stop to things. She wasn't going to get competitive about that. She was going to be mature about it.

As her hands went behind her to unhook the bra she was wearing she realised they were shaking and reminded herself that it would all be okay because she now had control over her natural propensity for stepping gleefully into trouble. The need to call attention to herself had left her years ago. She wouldn't slip up. Besides, it looked as if Luke had more than enough control for the both of them. She skipped being irked about that and decided to be impressed as hell.

Carefully she stepped into the final lingerie set – a pair of pure-white satin-and-silk bikini briefs with delicate lace trim and matching balconette bra that was the signature piece of her Seraphic collection. Hmm. She bit her lip. On her it didn't look quite as virginal or angelic as she had thought it would.

CHAPTER SEVEN

Sephy resisted the urge to pose in the doorway as Luke looked up. Especially when she heard him curse under his breath as his eyes once again swept over her.

Forcing her feet to move, she padded over to the mirrors and took up her previous position.

Luke wandered up behind her, running his hands down his jean-clad thighs as if to stop himself from reaching out to touch her before instructed to do so.

When you could fit perhaps a millimetre of air between his body and hers, he tilted his head towards her ear and murmured 'pretty', as his eyes, watching her reflection, lingered on her breasts.

Sephy swallowed. 'Yeah?'

'Come on.' His Adam's apple bobbed up and down in his throat. 'You have to know what you look like in that. Look in the mirror.'

Sephy had never in her life been shy, but it had been a while since she'd had the luxury of letting a man take his time looking at her the way Luke was looking at her.

'You don't need me to sex up your ad campaign, Seph. Look at you.'

But it was him making her look like this. Him that put the sparkle in her eyes, made her lips pout with anticipation and added the flush high on her cheekbones. Him that was making her nipples hard points jutting against the sheer fabric of her bra.

As if he couldn't help himself, Luke reached out and stroked down the length of her hair, before wrapping it all around his fist.

'Luke?' Wow that felt… 'I'm not sure this is a good –'

He tugged delicately, exposing the long length of neck to his gaze and delicious pin pricks of desire raced from her scalp to her belly, and lower.

With his other hand he reached down and splayed his fingers against her abdomen. 'What do you think? Should I hold you like this, or –'

Before he could slide his fingers down to the band of lace trim Sephy found her voice. 'Seriously, Luke, maybe we shouldn't be doing this.'

He stopped the descent of his hand and cleared his throat. 'It's fine,' he said through gritted teeth. 'Sorry. Just,' he tipped his head from side to side as if to un-kink corkscrewed muscle, 'be a friend and don't step back into me, okay?'

Immediately her body tried to take a step backwards and Luke breathed out harshly and his hand shifted at her waist to clamp over her hip and squeeze before holding her firmly an inch or two away from him.

'Damn it, Seph, unless you want to unleash a whole world of trouble between us, I really need you not to move, right now.'

'Sorry,' she whispered.

Only she wasn't. She wanted to unleash a *torrent* of trouble if it meant she got to feel the hard length of him pressed up against her.

'Quit wriggling too, okay?'

'Am I even allowed to breathe?'

'I'm thinking, no.'

'I'm sorry. I'm making this too difficult. I don't want this to turn into –' she was going to say a reason to lose his friendship, but he was way ahead of her.

'It won't. We're not going to let it.'

'Good. That's good. I mean we'd be stupid to…' her words

deserted her and her eyes drifted shut as she felt his thumb brush the indentation right at the small of her back. Pure heat rolled over her and a moan escaped.

His breath was heavy against her ear and she forgot any good intentions.

She turned her head deliberately to feel the brush of his lips against the shell of her ear.

'Luke?'

'Damn it. This is madness. I can't –' His thumb pressed into the nerve at the small of her back again and she moaned, arching her back in desperation to get closer to the heat of him. 'God, Seph, tell me you haven't once wondered what it would be like to feel my lips on yours.'

'I –'

'Tell me,' he repeated, only this time his voice was thick with demand and any resolve she had left melted right into nothing.

'All right. Maybe I have. Satisfied?'

Before she knew it, he had spun her around to face him. 'Satisfied? Not nearly.'

She stared up into eyes hooded with desire and one last attempt at doing the right thing made her say, 'We shouldn't. We *really* shouldn't,' she stopped because the words would no longer come. Instead she implored him with her eyes to be stronger than her.

Luke stared down at her, searching her gaze intently before finally raising his head to the sky, inhaling deeply and dropping his hands away from her.

'Yeah. Okay. You're right. I know you're right,' he said.

Sephy leant forward, laid her hand gently on his chest and felt granite muscle tremble under her fingertips.

Rising up on tiptoes she whispered, 'Thank you,' into his ear and then because it didn't seem enough after he had so kindly pulled them both back from the brink, she placed a light kiss of gratitude to his cheek.

She felt his groan to the bottom of her toes. She pulled back infinitesimally but Luke followed her movement.

'It's too late, Seph. I have to. Now that I know you've thought about this too,' and closing the distance he captured her lips with his.

Nothing compared.

Not that first taste of hot white chocolate sauce poured over blueberries that she awarded herself after hours and hours of sewing. Not the crisp tang of perfectly chilled pinot grigio after a really long day chasing Daisy around.

Not the mouth of *any* other man she had ever tasted.

As Luke's lips moved over hers, creating delicious friction, his hands tightened against her, dragging her up against the length of him and, holy mackerel. Kissing quiet, considerate, confident, supposedly shy, but undeniably uber hot, Luke Jackson-of-the-sexy-dimples was not supposed to be like this.

She wasn't supposed to get so lost in him she couldn't feel the ground beneath her feet.

Luke drove his tongue into her mouth and Sephy King ignited.

Emotion rose up inside of her, strong enough that it threatened to spill over. Leading with what she was feeling, because why would you think when you could feel all of this, she teased his tongue with hers, nipped at his bottom lip and felt the cold of the mirrors against her back as Luke reacted by pressing her back against the hard surface.

Her hands travelled up his beautifully sculpted chest, over his superb wide shoulders and as far down his back as she could reach. Revelling in the musculature that moved sinuously under her fingertips, her nails dug in as she dragged them back up and over.

Luke seemed to like that because he shuddered, tore his mouth from hers, dragged in air, and then set about creating a line of fire from her ear to her shoulder with his teasing hot mouth. Her nails dug in harder as his tongue dipped into her right clavicle and licked. Her eyes rolled shut and she rubbed against him, needing as much contact with his body as possible.

Smiling against her skin, he bent slightly and dropped a soft kiss to the top of her breast before edging further down and uncaring of the satin bra in his way, laid his mouth hotly over her breast and sucked her nipple into his mouth.

Sephy's head slammed back against the mirrors. She was going to expire from ecstasy. She was going to –

Her brows drew together. What on earth was that sound?

It didn't go with the galloping heart and ragged breathing that Luke was able to elicit from her with that wickedly clever mouth of his.

She frowned harder as music pounded into her consciousness. It kind of sounded like Disney music.

What the…?

Oh my God.

Sephy's nails dug into Luke's shoulders before pushing him away.

'Weird. I've never heard music before,' Luke muttered before reaching for her again.

As if he'd already imprinted on her, her body bowed in his arms before she got a hold of herself and pushed against him again. 'That isn't music. That's my phone. You have to stop. *We* have to stop. This is so wrong.'

'Wrong?' Luke took a step back, his chest heaving and with his voice dull and his jaw clenched, accused, 'You were into that as much as me. Wrong? What exactly are you saying?'

The music filled her head as all the heat that had been rushing through her collected in her brain, leaving her mad as hell with herself. 'I'm saying that is my phone alarm to remind me to pick up Daisy from school. You know,' she said pulling her bra strap back into place and moving past him to the en suite in search of her clothes, 'Daisy. My *daughter*.'

'I know who Daisy is,' Luke answered tightly, as he followed her. 'That wasn't what I was asking.'

Spying her bag, she snatched it up and rifled through it to pull out her phone. With shaking fingers she silenced the alarm.

'Want to tell me why,' Luke bit out, 'when you can bring yourself to meet my eyes, that is, you're giving me the idea you think I'm suddenly the devil incarnate?'

Oh, surely she stole that particular role. 'I can't talk about this now.' *Or quite possibly, ever.* She couldn't believe she had let herself get so carried away. Couldn't believe that one kiss and she'd been in – all in.

What the hell was wrong with her that she would throw away a year's worth of the best friendship she'd ever experienced for the sake of a couple of hours in his bed that would change everything afterwards? At root, had she not grown up at all, then?

With shaking hands she shoved her hair behind her ears. 'I have to get changed.' Wishing she hadn't chosen today to wear skinny jeans, she picked up the white trousers and with a flick of her wrists shook them out to step into them.

'Okay, I know things got a little out of hand,' Luke said from the doorway.

'Biggest understatement of the year,' she threw over her shoulder, thinking only that she had taken her eye monumentally off the ball and now her daughter was going to be kept waiting because of that. Sex was never, ever, supposed to shove her daughter lower down the scale of priorities. 'I can't believe we did that. I can't believe I let you – let myself…'

'What? Act like we're human?' Luke took a step into the room, making the walls shrink in and giving her an eyeful of half-naked aroused male as she turned nervously around. 'Give in to temptation?'

'Is that what this is all about?' she asked, stabbing her legs into her jeans and wriggling to pull them up. 'You lured me here on purpose, hoping this would happen? This was your way of getting me to step outside the very clear boundaries I set up?'

Luke folded his arms and looked at her derisively. 'Do you really think I would do that?'

Sephy blew hair out of her eyes as she looked down to snap close the button of her jeans. Reaching for her top she yanked it on. Guilt sat heavily in the pit of her stomach. Luke would absolutely never do that to her. Why was she making it worse? 'Thinking is clearly something neither of us were doing back there,' she said.

'That should tell you it wasn't premeditated.'

Sephy looked away because if she was being excruciatingly honest with herself, part of it was premeditated, wasn't it? From the first moment she had felt that flutter of excitement at finally finding out what it would feel like to have his hands on her, her subconscious had been playing dirty mind tricks with her. All that justification had been such waffle.

Shame poured on top of guilt.

'Why did you have to go and ruin everything?' she lashed out.

'Unbelievable! Are you always this melodramatic after being kissed?'

Embarrassment burned a laser hole through her middle. Luke was right. Where was her poise? Where was her grace? Where the hell was her, 'Oops. My bad,' and the ability to laugh it all off?

'I can't do this,' she whispered. 'I have to go. Will you please let me past?'

For a moment she thought he wasn't going to move and she was going to have to explain in words of one syllable that she wasn't in the business of letting her daughter's schedule suffer on account of her giving in to her more base urges. He took a step forward and, unprepared, she flinched and heard him swear succinctly.

'I thought you'd need these?' he said, reaching past her and then dangling her Seraphic bags in front of her. 'But thanks for making me feel like scum.'

'I –' Sephy broke off as her phone started playing Daisy's favourite Disney tune again.

Luke handed her the bags so that she could rescue her phone again and then, holding his hands up in a conciliatory manner, stepped aside to let her pass.

Concentrating on switching the alarm off properly she stashed it back in her bag and stepped past him to stumble through his bedroom, down the long corridor, jog down the steps and stop at the huge, imposing front doors.

When the front door didn't immediately open, she kicked it with her foot.

She had to get a grip. The last image Luke had of her exiting his house was *not* going to be one of her totally losing it.

Dragging in a breath, she said, 'Can you please show me how to open the door?'

Silently Luke reached past her and gently turned the doorknob. He had barely got the door open half a foot before she was squeezing herself through and running to her car. 'Can you open the gates for me?' she said as she unlocked her car door and practically threw her bags into the back. She turned before she got into the car to find Luke standing leaning against the door frame, his arms folded and an inscrutable expression on his face. She swallowed because she knew she had hurt him and right at this moment had absolutely no idea how she was ever going to make it up to him.

'I'll call you,' she promised ineffectually, before closing the car door and switching on the ignition.

Luke pushed against Sephy's doorbell for the second time and, this time, forced his finger to linger over the buzzer.

The guilt he felt about potentially waking up Daisy was outweighed by the need to get a few things off his chest before he set about getting his and Sephy's friendship back on track.

Finally the door opened and a justifiably angry-looking Sephy stood before him.

Christ.

She looked incredible and his body reacted instantly, which was so not helpful. He needed his blood pumping to his brain if he was to remain focused and get through to her.

'What are you doing here?' she asked in a hushed whisper.

'Hello, to you too,' he greeted.

'Never mind all the conventional mumbo-jumbo greetings. What are you doing here?' she repeated, drawing the sides of her baby-blue cardigan together as she folded her arms.

Luke fished his phone out of his pocket and made a show of clearing his throat while he searched and found the text she had sent him.

'Thanks for the help,' he read aloud, 'but I've decided I'm uncomfortable about the head of Seraphic being the model in her own ad campaign, so I'm cancelling the photo shoot. Will understandably be busy over the next few days sorting out the launch. Call you after.'

He finished and waited. Sephy merely raised an eyebrow in haughty enquiry.

'Not even an "xx" after,' he stated.

Even with most of her face in shadow from the light behind her, he could tell she was blushing. Well, tough, because he wasn't finished yet.

'Spend a long time getting the wording exactly right, did you? Try out a couple of drafts before finally deciding that was the one to go with?'

She swallowed as if, yes, it might have taken her more than a few minutes' consideration to trot out the biggest load of bollocks he had ever heard.

'I'm not ready to talk about what happened yet,' Sephy whispered.

'News flash. Not everyone in the world is willing to wait until you announce you're good to go.'

Something flickered in her eyes and her hands tightened their grip around her upper arms. 'I'm not sure what you want me to say.'

As angry as he was with her for shutting him out and now shutting him down like this, one look at her and what he really wanted her to say was screw it and then reach out, grab a hold of his shirt, pull him against the door and lay those sweet, sweet lips of hers against his.

But he was going to have to set all that want aside because, call him a glutton for punishment, he wasn't walking away. He didn't do that any more.

'I want you to say that you're better than that,' he said. 'Better than this,' and he held his phone, waving it in her face to show her the text she had sent him.

She looked at him like she really wasn't.

But she was going to have to be.

She didn't get to kiss him back like that – make him feel like he was "the one", and then look at him like she was absolutely devastated that she had.

She didn't get to reject him and run away.

'At least invite me in, since I've driven all this way,' he said.

Sephy snorted. 'It's maybe three miles.'

Luke dug his heels in. 'Why are you looking at me like you think I'm not the kind of guy to cause a scene until you let me in?'

'Because you love Daisy and you wouldn't deliberately wake her up.'

'Okay. I didn't want to have to do this but you leave me no choice,' he said as he held his phone up and started scrolling through information.

'What are you doing?'

Luke held up his hand to silence her until he found what he was looking for. Taking a deep breath, he pressed start, opened his mouth and as the opening bars to the *Frozen* theme tune started up, started singing.

Badly.

'Oh my God,' Sephy reached out to touch him and then, obviously thinking better of it, snatched her hand back. 'All right, come in, you don't have to break my ears first.'

The warm and mellow surroundings felt immediately welcoming as he followed her into her cluttered kitchen. The relaxed and pleasant ambiance wasn't simply because her place was small and cosy, because even the main house, with its huge rooms, felt homely to him.

Not empty, like his place.

He had almost given up wishing he could figure out what was missing in his home, but if he knew what it was maybe he could fix it. Buying a place he owned outright and that he could leave and know it would always be there to come back to had been a long-held dream.

Coming from his foster home, where it was always packed and so noisy you could barely hold a thought in your head, he had been so sure that space and silence was what he wanted. But even when he bought home acres of work from the space he rented in town and left it lying around on the weekend, the place never seemed cluttered and relaxed.

'I really was going to call you after the launch,' Sephy said as she picked up a bottle of red wine and indicated for him to get the glasses.

He crossed to the huge kitchen dresser, took two glasses from the uppermost shelf and carried them to the table for her to pour in the rich ruby-red liquid.

'And say what?' he asked when she pushed the cork back in the bottle and gestured for him to take a seat at the table.

'And say hi,' she mumbled, lifting the glass to her lips and then staring defiantly over the rim at him.

Luke took a gulp of his wine. No apology, then. Interesting. He took another sip and said calmly, 'I need you to call Nora and arrange for what's-his-face to do the photo shoot tomorrow.'

'No. Way.'

'Look. I get it. I really screwed up.'

A brief silence, and then Sephy admitted, 'We both really screwed up.'

Sort of an apology, then. That King pride was a killer, wasn't it?

'So we acknowledge that we made a mistake and move on,' he said.

'Just like that?' Sephy's eyebrow shot up with incredulity.

'Just like that,' he stated with a brief incline of his head, although his heart raced at the thought that she wasn't able to ignore what they had done or relegate it to simply being a mistake.

'I –' she trailed off to study him like she was worried that the first chance they got it might happen again.

Perhaps she had never realised how strong-willed he could be when it was needed. Admittedly it had been a long time since he'd had to channel his younger closed-off self. But, hey, once that was inside of you, it never totally left you, did it? A thought which sometimes kept him awake at night but which he was thankful for right now. 'We'd both been thinking about that kiss for a long time. We caved,' he added a shrug. 'It's out of our systems now. We can move on from it.'

Sephy fiddled with the stem of her wine glass.

'You're seriously going to throw away something you want,' he pushed, 'something you claimed you *needed* in order to give Seraphic a fighting chance, because of what happened between us?'

Studying the glass in front of her she said, 'You're only here because you want me to pretend to be your fiancée.'

Unbelievable. 'You want to bet?' he bit out.

Maybe she was so spooked by what had gone down between them that her saying that was a test. He couldn't really blame her. What they had indulged in had held all the elements of flying way too close to the sun.

When she finally looked at him, her eyes were cloudy with regret. 'Under the circumstances, I think we should forget about me pretending to be your fiancée.'

'For the record, I am more than capable of stepping up and telling my foster parents that I lied about you.'

'You mean about having a fiancée,' she whipped back, her gaze sharpening on him.

His heart kicked against his chest because when the lie had slipped out hadn't it been her that he'd been picturing? 'Like I said, I can be a big boy about it.'

'Well.' She frowned. 'That's good, then.'

'Friends don't force each other to do things they're not comfortable with, so consider yourself off the hook.' He paused for a fraction of a second and then added, 'But as your friend I am going to force you to realise you'll regret not doing the photo shoot.'

Sephy sighed and leant back in her chair. 'Luke, please don't.'

'Don't what?'

'Don't do the reasonable-friend thing followed by the tug-on-the-heartstrings thing. You know I can't resi –' her mouth snapped shut as she realised what she was about to say.

Luke grinned.

'I'm sorry I let that kiss get so beyond friendly curiosity,' he said, softly pressing his advantage.

'Stop it. Don't you dare fall on your sword, not for me.'

'I don't like the thought of you losing out because you're focused on the wrong thing. Phone Nora and organise the shoot.' He held her gaze steadily. 'I can behave myself. You have my word.'

Sephy rolled up the foil cover from the top of the wine bottle and flicked it across the table. 'You realise I can hardly look you in the face after what happened.'

'Yes. Why is that again?'

Sephy blushed. 'Because I completely over-reacted and acted like a crazy lady.'

Luke leant forward to make sure he filled her vision. 'Are you talking about the way you kissed me back, or the way you acted when you got reminded that Daisy comes first?'

'What do you think?' she asked searching his eyes.

What the hell did he know? He was still reeling from one minute feeling her writhe so spectacularly sexily against him and then the next minute seeing her flee the scene of the crime.

He was here to convince her the crime was too small to throw away a friendship over – it was the only way he was going to get to salvage something from the rejection.

'What do I think?' he asked, feeling the devil push in on him, 'Well, I could tell you that if that alarm hadn't gone off I'm pretty sure I would have ended up inside of you.'

Sephy gasped and went beetroot red, but Luke wasn't going to be put off.

'I'm not going to tell you that afterwards I would have regretted that happening because it didn't happen and now we'll never know. I can deal with you bolting when your phone alarm went off. But, Sephy, you don't get to act the coward and not even speak to me about it afterwards. That is not who you are.'

'I know. I really screwed everything up.'

'So unscrew it.' Luke reached across the table and picked up her phone and passed it to her. 'Phone Nora and set up the photo shoot.'

'But –'

'Seriously, do you see yourself jumping on me the moment I take off my shirt and put my hands on you? In the middle of a busy photographer's studio,' he added for good measure.

She shook her head.

'Didn't think so. Make the call. You need this for your business. I'm not having you launch your line and later making me a source of regret that you didn't get the pictures you really wanted for your publicity. And just so we're clear. I can guarantee you I won't be blurring any lines at the shoot or afterwards.'

'Because we're friends?'

'Because we're friends, yes, and because,' he added, unable to keep the steel from his voice, 'I'm not a man without ego. No way am I putting myself in the position of getting knocked back by you for a third time.'

CHAPTER EIGHT

'You might have mentioned Luke looked like a God without his clothes on,' Nora gushed as she pulled on the ribbon lace to cinch Sephy securely into the corset.

'Ssh,' Sephy whimpered, completely paranoid Luke would hear them. The tiny changing room in the photographer's studio had paper-thin walls. 'And will you please quit staring at him. He doesn't like it.'

Nora snorted.

'He doesn't. He's shy. Ouch,' she hissed as Nora tugged another pair of eyelets closed. 'I do have to be able to breathe, you know.'

Except, maybe she didn't deserve to. The guilt of realising just how shy Luke was as they had done the first set of pictures had nearly knocked her off her feet. It was in the way he held his breath when he knew the camera was focusing in on him and in the way he watched the photographer, Frazer, looking at each of the shots. As if he was waiting to be told they weren't good enough. It was even in the shrug of his shoulders when asked for input. As if he didn't – couldn't – get invested.

'If he's shy, why is he doing this for you?'Nora asked.

Because he's my friend.

Sephy closed her eyes to avoid seeing the betraying heat flash through her eyes in the mirror.

When she had fled his bedroom with all the moxie of a flighty fairytale character, the only thing that had saved her dying from embarrassment was the fact he had not come after her.

But then he had.

And telling her they weren't throwing their friendship away on his watch had stolen her breath, melted her heart, and reminded her of the months after her father's death, when romance had been the very last thing on her radar. She had barely been keeping her head above water emotionally as it was, but Luke's easy manner and the lack of drama he brought to her life had saved her.

Friend, she repeated as she chastised herself once again for dropping the ball on that friendship so that heat had started building between them again, until it had risen up, spilled over, and smacked her across the face with a dose of big fat scary need.

'Well,' Nora whispered loudly, 'I know you can't see what the two of you look like, but the photos are scorching.'

Ha. Sephy knew only too well what she and Luke looked like – *felt* like, together. The memories followed her around all day, making it impossible to move past without gargantuan effort on her part, and she was already feeling exhausted and stripped bare. Clearing her throat, she mumbled, 'Good. That's the idea.'

'I would think it's quite hard to fake heat like that,' said Nora carefully.

Oh, on the contrary, Sephy thought. Under the hot studio lights Luke hadn't reacted to her at all. Not in the way she had to him. Pride kept asking her how he could have escaped Flashback Land, when someone seemed to have downloaded a year's free membership to the place, taken her there and left her.

Ultra-sensitive to his every movement, every time he put his hands on her, she genuinely worried her heart was going to burst out of her chest and giggle uncontrollably as it skipped about at their feet.

Nora stared at her for a few minutes. 'Do you remember when you pushed me into your kitchen and forced me into spending time with Ethan?'

Sephy breathed in as much as the corset would allow. 'Luke

and I – we're not about that. *I'm* not about that. Okay?' She searched Nora's face for understanding. What her father had said to her in his letter was humiliating enough, without having to explain why a relationship with a man who had money – serious money, now felt out of the question for her.

'But –'

'No, Nora. I mean it.' She was already upset for succumbing to temptation as it was, she certainly didn't need to hear a lecture from her sister on how she couldn't be expected to live like a saint for the rest of her life. As it happened, she had no intention of doing so. She just wasn't going to relinquish that status with someone she cared about. 'What I need from you is support,' she added. 'I'm about to have a coronary thinking about this launch as it is. This business stuff doesn't come as easy to me, you know.'

Nora pouted. 'You are so not fun when you're in business mode.'

Sephy pasted on a grin and exited the changing room.

She had declined to wear stockings and stilettos for these pictures. She wanted to be bare-legged and bare-foot. If Luke was standing in jeans minus his shirt, she didn't want to be 'out-dressed' in full-on men's fantasy attire.

He said nothing as he slowly walked towards her. His acting was magnificent.

She stood on the white matting with the huge white backdrop behind her and waited for him to take up his position.

'Where do you want me?' he asked Frazer.

Frazer. Not her.

Not wanting to be seen caught off-guard, she chimed in with, 'It's important to show off the back of the corset as that's where the most detail is.'

She felt Luke studying the back of the corset and had a sudden burning need to do a quick burlesque shimmy before turning her head coquettishly to look over her shoulder at him.

Instead she stared straight ahead and thought about all the things she had left to do when they finished up here.

'If you want the detail picked up on camera, then you should be facing me,' Luke said, finally acknowledging her.

Sephy swallowed. *Now*, he wanted to get involved?

'What was that, Luke?' Frazer asked, stepping closer with his camera.

'Sephy should be facing me. That way you get the back of the corset in.'

'Sephy,' Nora suggested helpfully, 'turn and put your hands on Luke's chest.'

Sephy did as she was told, but not before she directed the sibling glare of death at her sister. Nora simply grinned back and continued with, 'Now Luke, can you think of some way to help show off the back of the corset without completely covering the detail up with your hands?'

Sephy's head tipped up to look at Luke. His gaze swept over her face, her shoulders, her cleavage and his nostrils flared and his eyes darkened to the colour of oak leaves.

She could feel his heartbeat beneath her palm. It was racing like a Formula 1 car with the finishing line in sight.

Not unaffected, then.

Thank God.

She wasn't alone in this, after all.

Pride had itself a little happy-dance as her heartbeat increased to match his.

'How about if I do this,' Luke said and reached out to gather up all of her hair and bunch it in his fist, reminding her instantly of what had happened the last time he had done that.

'Perfect,' sighed Frazer and Nora in unison.

'This might work, as well,' and with his free hand, Luke reached for one end of the bow and tugged.

Sephy's mouth dropped open in shock and Frazer started zapping away with his camera.

'Keep your hands on the ribbon end, Luke,' Frazer instructed. 'I want it to look like you're about to undress Sephy.'

Sephy thought she might have sort of mewed and damned if Luke's dimples didn't come out as if to say, 'You've got no one but yourself to blame for designing a piece of lingerie like this.

As his heated gaze seared her to her bones, she didn't register Frazer moving closer with his camera to snap shots from different angles. All she felt was the delicious tug on her scalp as Luke pulled her in even closer to him and then his gentle caress against her head as he seemed to realise.

Their lips were centimetres apart and Sephy wasn't aware of ever craving anything as much as she craved touching her lips to his.

'Luke?' His name left her lips like an entreaty and suddenly there was daylight between them.

'You get the shot?' he asked, releasing her and turning his head towards Frazer.

'And then some,' Frazer said.

'Great.'

Wait – what, the what?

Luke walked over to his chair, picked up his phone, and casually started checking for messages while she stood trembling as if she had just survived a hostage extraction and didn't know what to do or where to go.

What was real? The way his heart had raced under her palm, the look of 'mine' in his eyes, or this, cool, casual detachment?

Briefly she heard Frazer call it a wrap, but she wasn't really listening.

As she moved on auto-pilot to the dressing room, she was thinking about what it took for Luke to look at her like that one minute and shut it down the next. She never would have believed him capable of it.

Who had taught him it was necessary to protect his feelings like that?

She was still musing that as the four of them sat around Frazer's battered old desk looking at shot after shot so she could choose which ones she wanted gracing the banners in the ballroom. The rest of the chosen pictures would be put into glossy catalogues. The copy had been written. She simply needed to add the photos to the final layout.

'Frazer, these are really wonderful, I can't thank you enough,' she said as each shot paused on the screen.

'You could both model professionally. You in particular, Luke,' Frazer mentioned, running his gaze over him.

'I'll stick with the job I have, thanks. This was strictly a one-off favour.'

'She must be very persuasive,' Frazer joked, indicating Sephy.

'Very,' Luke replied, and Sephy felt heat zoom between them again.

Then, the first picture of her wearing the corset flashed onto the screen and Sephy forgot to breathe.

In the shocked silence, it was almost as if they had all forgotten how to breathe.

'Did you get any with Sephy's face in?' Luke asked tersely as each image filled the screen in slow succession.

'They'll be coming up,' Frazer placated.

'You're going to have to find one that doesn't have my face in it, or I don't give permission for you to use any of these,' Luke said in a brook-no-argument manner.

Sephy stopped watching the screen and started watching Luke. She saw his features pull tight as he stared at the laptop and she could understand some of what he was feeling because as she flicked back to the screen again she worried that what was captured on Luke's face was going to be reciprocated on hers.

Suddenly she would have given anything for this set of photographs not to exist. She could see now what she had missed when she was in the moment – when she was so wrapped up in what Luke might witness on her face that she wasn't seeing everything Luke was showing on his.

And what Luke was clearly showing was that in that moment

he was ensnared by her. Not that she was ever going to mention the fact to him. The problem was, without her face in the shot mirroring his expression, the photo looked completely one-sided. Sephy could see absolutely why he wouldn't like that being on show.

'Use that one,' Sephy said as the first one that didn't focus on either of their faces flashed up onto the screen.

'Are you sure? Frazer checked. 'From the brief you gave me, the others are better suited.'

There was sexing-up her ad campaign and then there were images that should remain private.

'I want the one I mentioned. Luke, are you okay with that one?'

Luke nodded and Sephy saw his broad shoulders relax a little, allowing her to turn her attention back to the screen and set about finalising all her choices for both banner and catalogue.

She nearly missed him leaving as they were packing up. He hadn't uttered a word since agreeing which corset shot to use.

Calling after him to stop him in the doorway she smiled tentatively and then mouthed the words 'thank you'. With a quick salute, he smiled, and was out the door. Sephy bit her lip. That smile hadn't reached his eyes. Moments later she heard his car engine firing up.

Hugging Nora tight she promised to call if she needed anything prior to the launch. Otherwise she'd see her on the big night.

Alone with Frazer she put on her best smile and asked him, as a personal favour to her, if he could please let her have all the proofs that contained headshots of her and Luke while she was dressed in the corset. When he loaded them onto a memory stick for her, she asked him for one more teeny-tiny favour and then watched as Frazer deleted from his camera and hard drive all the ones she knew Luke didn't feel comfortable with.

Luke squinted at the left-hand screen of three monitors. Not that that was going to make anything clearer. He had been looking at his code for the past three hours and still wasn't happy.

Was the world really ready for less zombie action? To compensate he brought one up onto the screen…and destroyed it.

'Wow, you have a slow-mo option for exploding zombies?' said a voice from his office doorway. 'This is the sort of thing that sets you apart, Action Jackson.'

'Never ever call me that again and expect to live,' Luke muttered as he put down the console and turned to Sephy. His heart provided him with a little somersault action. 'Shouldn't you be counting catalogues, checking invites have been responded to, and generally running around like a headless chicken?'

'I should. But I'm a King and so I laugh in the face of impending meltdown and choose to distract myself with a visit to a friend instead.'

Luke watched as she stepped further into the room, her gaze fixed with interest on the screens in front of her. 'You know, I've never actually played one of your games before.'

'Call yourself a friend?'

'Want to teach me to play?'

Luke clamped his mouth shut. She absolutely did not need to know the ride she had unwittingly taken his thoughts on. 'No time, today.'

'After the launch, then. I'll need something to do to de-stress.'

Again, his body prepped for an altogether different way of de-stressing and then he frowned as she set her huge leather tote down on the edge of his desk and started rummaging through it.

'Carry on with whatever it is you're doing,' she said, head in her bag, hand flapping about in the air. 'I'll be quiet as a mouse.'

'Doing what?' he asked suspiciously, his concentration on his code and his game totally shot to pieces.

Her head popped up. 'Wait right here,' she said, disappearing out into the corridor.

'Where would I go? This is *my* office,' he called out, but all he could hear was the sound of her heels clacking down the corridor.

What the hell was she doing here? He had been trying to give her some space because he knew she had a lot to do.

That was what he told himself, anyway.

It sure as hell shouldn't be anything to do with that photo shoot and the way the camera had picked up on what he felt when he had looked at her.

Instead of feeling as if his honour was intact by getting her the shots she wanted without making a fool of himself and reaching for her, he had been left feeling excruciatingly exposed.

The only good thing to come out of walking out that studio and putting physical distance between them was the concerted effort he had put back into his new game.

Gaming, to him, was an extension of losing yourself in a good book. When you were in a game you weren't worrying about what you were going to find when you got home that night or even where you were going to sleep.

A few hours spent saving the world made you feel like you could cope with your own reality.

As a teenager he had used gaming to escape and when he had started needing more and more escapism, he had started designing his own game. A talent and aptitude for programming and game design was the first thing he felt as if he could count on in life. Rejections and set-backs had been simply part of the industry. It hadn't felt like all the times he'd been personally rejected as a child. Pursuit of something he had wanted more than anything had enabled him to push past the debilitating shyness and distrust of people and allowed him to take a job as a programmer in a large company and work on that first game every spare hour he had.

Steve and Lily's belief in him – their work with local business to raise the money needed to get the game off the ground had meant failure was not an option.

Zombie Freedom Fighters had taken off and by the end of the second year, when the big names had shown interest, he had elected to stay indie rather than get lost in a large company and feel that creeping shyness re-emerge.

The success of his massively multiplayer online role-playing game meant he had repaid all his investors and built a company with a support staff to update the MMORPG and allow him the time to keep doing the work that had won him awards and made him an amount of money, which, frankly, he sometimes found a little embarrassing.

That reminded him. He needed to make some decisions about what to do with the latest chunk of money earmarked for investment, before his accountant got on his case again. The idea of opening up a facility specifically to offer support to foster and adoptive parents held real appeal. He wondered what Sephy would think now she knew a little of his background and felt a chill run down his spine. A 'little' of his background was all she still knew.

'Is it National Hug a Potted Plant Day?' he quipped when Sephy came back in loaded down.

'This is to make your office look less "techy" and more inviting,' she said, putting one of the large plants in the corner of his office and eyeing up where best to place the second. 'Your foster parents aren't investors or sponsors or, well, geeks, are they?'

'Why do I need to redo the office for them?'

'Luke, have they ever visited you, your home, or your office premises? Exactly,' she answered for him before he could open his mouth. 'Why not give them the full-ticket-price tour? Might help them to see how rounded and full your life really is.'

'You really think a couple of plants are going to achieve that?'

'Well, see, I have more.'

She smiled and his insides pulled in tight. 'More?'

Sephy delved into her bag and withdrew a photo frame. Luke needed only to glance at the photograph inside to feel as if all the oxygen had suddenly been sucked out of the room.

'I don't understand.' Luke grabbed the frame from her and stared down at the glossy image from the photo shoot. Tension coiled in his gut. Obviously he hadn't made it clear when he had stated categorically that he didn't want photographs with his face showing, to be printed.

'I thought that if your foster parents are going to be visiting your workplace, they would expect to see a photo of you and your fiancée on your desk.'

Luke's gazed bounced straight to Sephy. 'I thought we weren't doing the fiancée thing?'

A look of regret passed over her face. 'Don't tell me you've already broken the news to them that you're happily single?'

'Well, no. I thought it would be better doing it face to face.'

'Phew.' She shoved her hair back behind her shoulders and then tucked her hands into the top of her jeans pockets. 'I know I said that after we kissed –' She stopped, searched his face for a few seconds and there was a fine tremble to her lips that he found intoxicating, 'that I wasn't comfortable acting as your fiancée, but, I've changed my mind.'

'Just like that?' God, he really, really hoped all this wasn't about her feeling sorry for him. He dragged his gaze away from her face and those kissable lips to stare down at the plain gold frame in his hands. You couldn't see the corset in the composition. The image had been cropped so that mostly what you got was the two of them in profile, head to shoulders.

Without being able to see what she had been wearing, the picture should have felt much more innocent. But now it looked as if they were staring into each other's eyes, like – like they were each other's worlds.

Except Sephy had to be acting.

She was too brave to shy away from something she wanted and she had definitely shied away from wanting a deeper relationship with him.

Having learnt the harsh reality of human failings at a young age, Luke had never in his life begged for more than someone was obviously capable of giving.

'I bought something else for you too,' Sephy said, her hand pushing all the way into her pocket and withdrawing a memory stick.

Luke eyed it warily.

'It contains the photographs Frazer took while I was dressed in the corset. It's now the only file in existence.'

He tried to breathe evenly.

She came into his office with giant plants, photo frames and an announcement she was going to pretend to be his fiancée again and then handed him a file containing scorching-hot images of the two of them that were already burned onto his retinas?

Did she get off on thinking about him accessing this file and looking at the photos of her?

'What's wrong?' she asked, reaching out to touch him. 'I thought it might make you feel better to have the only version in existence. I know they made you uncomfortable.'

'Uncomfortable?' Understatement of the century.

'At the end of the shoot I asked Frazer to delete all the images on his camera and laptop. I only used the drive to access the least, um, provocative one and crop and print it out.'

Damn.

Her gesture was actually incredibly sweet. Even if he didn't like her in any way acknowledging what had been revealed in the photographs. He had really believed that he could school his thoughts, feelings, emotions, like he had done as a child, but something about Sephy in his arms made that impossible.

Luke's hand closed over hers as he went to take the pen-drive. Ignoring the spark, he gritted his teeth and murmured, 'Thank you,' and then taking it and using it as an excuse to gain that much-needed space, he walked around to the other side of his desk, opened a drawer and shoved it inside.

'Tell me again why you changed your mind and decided to act as my fiancée?'

'The photos look fabulous, Luke. Call it my way of saying thank you.'

He stared hard at her. She didn't look like she felt sorry for him. If they did this, he was only going to have to figure out a way of breaking the news later down the line to his foster parents, that he wasn't engaged any more. Sighing, he said, 'How am I going to explain plants and photos to my staff?'

Sephy shrugged. 'Bring them around on the Saturday or Sunday when there's not as many staff here. Put the frame in your desk drawer until then.'

'How are you going to explain to your family that you're suddenly spending a lot more time around me and my family? Don't you think it sends them false messages?'

'But that's the best part…Nora already knows it's not real.'

'You told her?' Why did he not like that she had found it easy to tell her sister that what was between them was fake?

'Of course. And with Mum in New York with Jared and Amanda, there's nothing to worry about.'

'What does Nora think?'

'That I'm mad, but as long as we both know I'm not…' she shrugged again.

'I'm not so sure. There's friends, and then there's calling in the sort of favours we've been asking of each other lately.'

Sephy stared down at her hands. 'To be honest, it feels really nice to be able to do something for you for a change. And we're only talking about a couple of meetings, aren't we? Maybe a few meals out? Nora's already said she'll babysit. If you still want to do this, I'm in.'

Maybe throwing them together would work and in some bizarre, twisted way reinforce to him that falling for Sephy King all the way was not an option. How could anything between them burn out of control in front of his foster parents? Sure, there'd be some hand-holding and maybe a couple of chaste kisses. He could manage that. Clearly Sephy thought she could, too. 'There's one more thing,' he added. 'When I thought this was a no-go, I phoned them and asked if they could bring their trip forward and arrive on the fifteenth.'

'But that's –' shock tracked across her features. 'You weren't going to come to the launch? Because of the photos?'

'Not only that. I didn't want you to feel awkward after my reaction at the studio.'

'I wouldn't have. I don't. You could bring them along to the launch.'

'I'm not introducing my foster parents to my fiancée at the opening of her lingerie collection!'

'They wouldn't approve?'

'That's not anything to do with it. The fifteenth is your night and you need to be able to concentrate and enjoy it to the full. We could meet the following day for brunch.'

Then, telling himself he was testing himself, he reached in to brush a kiss over her cheekbone. It had to be his imagination that she leaned in a little because when he whipped his head back to look in her eyes they were perfectly clear.

Yeah, if she could act like the other day was a complete aberration then he was going to make damn sure he did too.

CHAPTER NINE

Sephy stood in the double doorway of the ballroom and surveyed the result of weeks of hard work and stress.

She was going to be sick. Panic beat its unsteady drum deep inside her. Desperately she tried to contain the nerves. She absolutely positively didn't have time to be sick. She was already in her little-black-dress-and-high-heels ensemble. Her make-up was done, her hair was up in its elegant knot and she had spritzed her favourite scent on her pulse points.

This was it.

Everything she had been working towards for the past six difficult months.

Glancing at her watch she saw that there was less than an hour before curtain-up. She should be backstage making sure there weren't any hiccups with the models. It would look bad if guests started arriving to see her milling about as if she wasn't in complete control.

She pressed a shaking hand over her stomach. Who was she kidding thinking she was in complete control? What she wouldn't give right now to be sitting on Daisy's bed, reading her daughter her favourite bedtime story. She knew how to be Daisy's mum. She didn't know how to do this – was mad to think she could pull this off.

Her gaze flicked to the banners either side of the catwalk.

The nerves morphed into something more fluttery as she stared at the images of her and Luke.

Slick, sexy, sophisticated.

Yes.

Okay.

If she could get her lingerie to look smoking hot like she had, then maybe she could pull this off after all.

With a hand resting against her midriff as she counted her breath in, held it, and then counted slower as she released it, she wondered how Luke was fairing after the arrival of his foster parents.

'There you are.'

Sephy turned around to see Nora walking towards her with a huge smile on her face.

'I thought you'd be out the back by now, barking orders, hoisting up bra straps, checking make-up.'

'I'm supposed to be.'

'Well, that can wait a few more moments. I have a surprise for you in father's study.'

'Nora, no.' The very last place she wanted to be tonight was their father's study. 'I don't have time for surprises.' Unless…Her heart kicked up at the thought that maybe Luke had made it after all.

As soon as she'd had the thought she steeled her heart.

She didn't need Luke.

Luke was not for needing.

It was her and Daisy against the world.

Daisy was who she was doing this for.

'Hey,' Nora stopped in front of her, blocking her path. 'Everything is going to be all right, you know. What has you looking so haunted?'

'Nothing,' she replied not very convincingly as she thought about being in her father's study.

'We're all here for you. You're not doing this alone.'

'All?'

'Come and see,' and grabbing her by her hand, Nora dragged

Sephy across the hall, where a coat-check station had been set up and then she was standing outside the room that since her father's death she had always hesitated in front of before entering.

'I knew I should never have let you talk me into these shoes,' Sephy muttered as her footsteps slowed. 'And you know how I hate surprises.'

'You'll be fine, you do not hate surprises, and in about twenty seconds you're going to think I'm the best sister ever.'

Then, suddenly there was no time to worry if her father was watching over the proceedings tonight. Or worry even that she would catch a disapproving look out of the corner of her eye and turn her head, only to find no one there. Because all she could register as Nora threw open the doors was an overwhelming yell of 'Surprise!'

Jared, Amanda, her mother and Nora's fiancé, Ethan Love, were all standing there waiting for her with champagne.

Emotion rushed at her and tears gathered at the back of her eyes as she wished with all her heart that her father *was* there. Not a ghost but still alive and standing at her mother's side. With a fierceness that had her trembling she wanted to be able to see his eyes shining with pride for what she was doing. The way they had the first time she had placed his grand-daughter in his arms.

'Mummy,' Daisy popped out from behind the large, imposing desk. She was dressed in her PJ's and carrying her favourite cuddly rabbit. 'Why are you crying?'

Sephy sniffed and stepped forward to scoop Daisy up in her arms. 'I'm crying because I'm happy that you're all here to wish me luck, she said, making her smile extra bright so as not to worry her daughter.

'Granny said I could stay up to wish you luck. I made you a card too,' and out from behind rabbit came a beautiful hand-made card. 'Do you love it?' Daisy asked without waiting for Sephy to look inside.

'I love it,' Sephy laughed.

She gave Daisy a big kiss and put her back down on her feet so that she could move into the room and accept hugs from everyone.

'Mum. You look gorgeous,' she sniffed again, trying to dispel the lump in her throat. 'Have you been having a lovely time out in New York?'

Isobel King hugged her daughter and smiled. 'It's been the perfect tonic. I'm so proud of you.'

'I haven't done anything yet.'

'Oh, ssh. Don't think for one minute that I don't know what it takes to do something like this.' She held Sephy away from her so that she could look at her and her eyes narrowed perceptively. 'You look stressed and you've lost a couple of pounds, but you have a lovely light in your eyes.'

'I'm excited about tonight,' she soothed, ignoring the fact that a certain man with gorgeous green eyes instantly popped into her head. 'How long are you staying for?'

'Only until tomorrow night. If you need me I can stay longer.'

'No. Don't be silly. I'll be seeing you for the wedding soon enough.'

'I would like to have a talk with you at some point,' Isobel said and Sephy tried to decipher the unusual heavy tone in her mother's voice.

'Um, sure,' she replied, thinking that now that all the family was here it was going to be hard to extricate herself to make it over to Luke's for brunch.

Jared and Amanda moved in for a hug. 'So we've only just got here and already you're asking when we're leaving? Cramping your style, sis?'

'You could never cramp my style, Jared, for I have it in spades,' she teased.

Sephy hugged them both and, once again, refused to think about Luke and how the very next day she was going to be meeting his foster parents. As his fiancée.

His *fake* fiancée, she reminded herself as she looked at Jared and Amanda, Nora and Ethan and felt a pang of jealousy try to burrow in past what she thought were titanium-strong defences.

She watched Jared as he reached casually for Amanda's hand and brought it up to his lips to kiss. Sephy had only recently got to know her brother again, but she knew instinctively that he was happy. Amanda had softened those hard edges hewn into his personality and forced him to realise he wanted to be a part of his family before it was too late.

To her left, Nora was doing a little happy dance in her impossibly high heels and Sephy saw Ethan's soft smile as he glanced at his soon-to-be wife. Ethan had shown Nora that there was more to life than the family business and that she could choose her own destiny. Her sister had chosen Ethan first and foremost, but being a highly competitive King, she had also found a way to keep KPC too, and Sephy had never seen her sister more at peace with her world.

Before that pang of jealousy could make a stab at her again, she grabbed the glass of champagne Jared was holding out for her and took a healthy sip. She was only feeling out of sorts because she was nervous about tonight and feeling vulnerable thinking about her father.

'To Seraphic,' she declared, raising her glass, and then as everyone repeated her toast and raised their own glasses she felt her stomach pitch as her practical business head finally caught up with proceedings. 'Lord. I need to go and allocate some seating for you all.'

'Relax,' Nora said. 'I already took care of it.'

'How? You should all be seated up at the front, only that will throw the rows completely off balance.' Immediately she was back to thinking she shouldn't be in charge of something this big. She hadn't even organised rooms to be freshened for guests. Not that she had known her family was going to be flying back for tonight.

'Rather than change your seating order,' Nora said calmly, 'I simply added two chairs onto the end. Mum and Amanda are going to take them. Jared and Ethan are probably going to end up playing pool in the den.'

'Oh. Okay. Thanks.' She looked at her family and felt the emotion start to rise up again. 'I can't believe you all came. With the wedding so close, well, it means so much to me. Thank you.'

'Why wouldn't we?' Jared said with a hint of a smile. 'You go to all the KPC events, don't you?'

'You know very well that I do not.'

'Shocking. Disloyal. Flaky,' Jared intoned.

'Jared,' Amanda warned good-naturedly, 'No teasing until after the show.'

'Er, not even then,' Sephy tsked. 'School-boy error even thinking about teasing me until you've had your wedding present. I might have to go off-list, now.'

Jared shuddered and Amanda laughed.

'Mummy,' Daisy interrupted, 'Jared and 'Manda have brought me more furniture for my dolls' house. Can I play with it now?'

'Tomorrow. Right now you have to go to bed. Thank you for staying up to wish me good luck though. I really need it.'

'Don't worry, Mummy. I've told all my friends at school that soon all their mummies will be wearing your underwear.'

Well, that certainly explained some of the odd looks she had been getting from the other mums at the school gates.

'Why don't you let me put her to bed, while you show everyone the ballroom?' Isobel said, reaching down to pick Daisy up.

'Thanks, Mum.'

'Or I could put her to bed if you like?'

At the sound of the new voice, Sephy looked up to find Ryan standing uncertainly in the doorway.

'What are you doing here?' Sephy asked with a frown. When the one person she really wanted to be here couldn't be...well, she really hadn't envisaged her ex turning up instead.

Nora stepped forward looking flushed and worried as she

whispered, 'I'm so sorry. Is it not okay? Ethan and I thought it would be all right. Ryan wanted to be around for Daisy.'

Sephy stared at her sister because it wasn't as if Daisy hadn't slept in the main house on occasion, especially towards the end of Jeremy King's battle with cancer, when they had all taken turns to stay over and help. But then she watched as a huge grin broke out over her daughter's face as she raced over to Ryan to show him her rabbit. In that instant she was reminded clearly of whose genes had given her daughter that smile. While she wasn't ever going to allow herself to need Ryan again, the more time she allowed him to spend with Daisy, the stronger their relationship would become, and tonight, with Ethan and Jared around to help while her mother and Nora and Amanda were watching the show, Ryan would have backup if he couldn't get her to settle.

'It's okay,' she assured Nora before making eye contact with Ryan. 'And Ryan, I apologise. Next time I will make certain you're included in any family function.'

Ryan smiled his thanks and then accepted Daisy's hand and Sephy was reminded of the ease in which Luke picked Daisy up and how willingly she went into his arms. But now she understood Luke's natural ease around Daisy. He had been around children of all ages while being fostered at the Jacksons'. It was different for Ryan, but he would lose his nervousness soon and start doing the same. For one thing, Daisy was too charming not to pull him in and have him so besotted he forgot to be nervous.

'Well, I should probably go and check everything is under control,' Sephy said to the group. 'Can I leave you all to sort yourselves out?'

She was halfway to the door when she heard Nora say to Amanda, 'Wait until you see the photography. Oh, and you have to check out the catalogue.'

Sephy turned just in time to see Nora whip a catalogue off

the desk and open it up for Amanda – a professional photographer, to have a look.

Oh no.

In all the excitement about seeing her family she had completely forgotten the fact that now they were all here they were about to get an eyeful of her impromptu modelling assignment.

With Luke.

Not that the photographs were x-rated. They just felt x-rated.

'Wow,' Amanda exclaimed before snapping the catalogue shut as Ethan and Jared joined her to get a peek.

'What? We don't get to ogle models in their underwear,' Ethan asked trying a little smoke- and-mirrors move to get the catalogue out of Amanda's hands.

'Not this model, you don't,' Nora said, snatching it out of his hands, only to have Isobel whisk it out of her daughter's hands and open it up to look at.

'Oh my,' she said, staring down at the photographs.

Sephy wished heartily for more champagne as she looked at the shock on her mother's face. Was her mother thinking she had reverted back to her old attention-seeking ways?

'I would have warned you if I'd known you were going to be here,' Sephy defended, glaring at Nora as if to say 'now look what you've started'.

'That might have been helpful.' Isobel said quietly. 'I think it's fair to say I wasn't expecting to see my daughter standing in her underwear modelling.'

'What the hell?' Jared backed away from the catalogue like he was worried it was going to fall open in front of him.

'If I don't have the courage to wear them, what does that say about the confidence I have in my designs?' Sephy said, trying to downplay it all.

'The photography is really good,' Amanda remarked. 'And your lingerie looks incredible.'

'Let me see,' Ethan said, moving to stand so that he towered behind Isobel, Amanda and Nora.

'Don't make me come over there and punch you,' Jared muttered, draining his champagne.

'Hey,' Ethan laughed, 'she's not my sister.'

Nora punched him on her brother's behalf. 'She is practically your sister-in-law. One word: inappropriate.'

Ethan laughed, completely unfazed by Nora's fighting stance. 'But it's all right for you and Amanda to be drooling over the guy she's posing with?'

'Doesn't he seem familiar to you?' Isobel said.

Nora snorted.

Sephy's stomach just about dropped through the floor.

'Nora. Do. Not. Even,' Sephy warned through clenched teeth.

'Who is it?' Ethan, being so tall, had no trouble looking over their shoulders again as Amanda and Isobel turned their heads to a different angle and brought the catalogue closer to their eyes.

Sephy held her breath. It would be okay. As if any of them would be able to tell it was Luke she was modelling with. That was the whole purpose of only showing a partial view of his face.

'I can't understand why he seems so familiar,' Isobel said.

'It's his watch,' Ethan said suddenly. 'It's the same model as the one Luke Jackson wears.'

Oh for heavens' sake. Why did Ethan have to choose now to go all Hercule Poirot on the proceedings?

'A coincidence, then,' Sephy said, her voice unnaturally high, even to her ears.

'You're right,' her mother murmured, turning another page of the catalogue and bringing it up even closer for inspection. 'That's what it is. Funny how the model has the same leather cord around his wrist, too.'

Nora groaned and not so subtly elbowed Ethan in his midriff because he was to blame for mentioning the watch in the first place.

'Hey,' Ethan proclaimed, rubbing a hand lightly across his solar plexus before frowning and then putting two and two together and doing a double-take at the catalogue and exclaiming, 'Wait – *is* that your friend Luke Jackson?'

'The computer-game guy?' Jared asked, with a frown on his face.

Sephy glared at her brother. 'If it is him, and I'm not saying it is, what does it matter?'

'Of course it matters. What the hell are you doing posing nude with Luke Jackson?' Jared asked, his tone glacial.

'No one is nude and like now is the time to take a stab at acting like my big brother?' Sephy said, her tone matching her brother's.

'I don't have to act it, I *am* your big brother,' Jared said, refusing to give ground.

Sephy breathed in hot air as instantly she forgot about all the months Jared had worked to regain his place as the eldest King sibling, and, instead, remembered all the years of hurt and confusion after he had left.

'Now, now, children,' Nora warned, and, ever the peace-maker, automatically moved to stand between them. 'Let's not squabble.'

'Oh, stay out of it, sis,' Sephy and Jared shot back at exactly the same time.

Sephy stared at Jared and Nora as both of them stared back at her. It was the first time they had reverted to how they used to be with each other. Before Jared had left and everything had changed. A smile started to appear on each of their faces as it felt as if finally the last elephant had left the room.

Well, right up until Ryan helpfully chimed in with, 'It's okay – Sephy and Luke are together.'

'Together?' Isobel King turned to look at her daughter.

'I'm sorry, I thought you all knew,' Ryan added. 'She told me last week.'

Sephy swung around to stare at Ryan and damned if he wasn't

now frowning hard at her as if assessing the situation and finding the only reason she would not have told her family…was if she had lied to him and she wasn't really with Luke.

This was going from bad to worse.

'Nora? Did you know about this?' Isobel asked, as if she was accusing her middle child of deliberately withholding information.

Sephy swung straight back around to give her sister a pleading look not to divulge the whole fake-fiancée deal.

Nora squirmed like a fish on a hook.

Sephy couldn't believe it.

Tonight of all nights.

Well, she was going to go right ahead and pretend that her ex had not just outed Luke Jackson as her new lover to her entire family.

Pulling in a deep breath she announced, 'So I have a little launch party that needs my attention. If you'll excuse me,' and with her nose in the air, she turned on her heel and left the study.

'Seraphina?'

Darn! Sephy paused halfway to the ballroom, automatically turning at her mother's gentle tone.

'I really do have to see to the show, Mum.'

'I understand,' Isobel said, walking towards her daughter. 'I just wanted to say I think you and Luke make a lovely couple.'

Sephy's ability to remember the nuance between lie and white lie suddenly deserted her and had her blurting out, 'It's not what you think it is.'

'It's not?'

'No. I mean we're not –' she stopped, tried again, 'Luke and I are just –' this was ridiculous – why couldn't she make herself finish the damn sentence? With a deep breath in she went with, 'We're not serious.'

'You're not?' Isobel King asked, staring at her daughter as if she found the idea Sephy would let someone into her life and it not be serious, preposterous.

Sephy had no words. She took her friendship with Luke very seriously, but right now she couldn't do the double-speak required. Not with her stomach churning a countdown to the show. She was going to slip up and say the wrong thing. She could feel it.

'Will you be with Luke later tonight?' Isobel asked.

'No. Of course not,' Sephy said, blushing to the roots of her hair. 'And I don't want anyone thinking I'm going to be palming Daisy off on Ryan just so Luke and I can get some regular alone time.'

Isobel King's eyebrows rose in perfect unison. 'I swear I don't know how you get these ideas into your head. I was asking so I could work out if we could have that catch-up tonight, rather than tomorrow. Why would I think you would act like that?'

'Maybe because,' she looked down at the floor as she admitted, 'before I had Daisy, Ryan and I were hardly role-model material.'

'But it's hardly as if your father and I had to bail you out of trouble night after night, is it?'

'Do you think Dad would have bailed me out if I'd ended up in a police station, or do you think it would have been you bailing me out?' Sephy asked, unable to stop the question.

'I would have thought that knowing one of us would have turned up to collect you would be enough.'

Sephy fiddled with the pearls at her neck. She hated slipping back into the cycle of trying to get proof her father had loved her. But maybe it was easier to return to bad habits than deal with the guilt of all the years she had wasted partying.

Isobel reached out to grab hold of her daughter's arm. 'Don't you think it's time you forgave yourself? I admit you gave your father and I a scare or two and you might have had your reasons for rebelling like you did, but you hardly went off the rails and never came back to us. If Luke makes you happy, I applaud that.

I've never been comfortable with the thought of you deliberately being on your own.'

'I'm not on my own,' Sephy insisted, pride rearing its ugly head. 'I have Daisy.'

'Daisy is growing up. If Luke is there for you at the end of each day, to share your business milestones, to share what Daisy has been up to, I'm all for it.' Isobel squeezed her daughter's arm and lowered her voice, 'and if he can put the kind of smile you have on your face in your catalogue... Well, if I'd had the beautiful designs you've created when I was younger I could probably have persuaded your father to come back from the office earlier more often than I did.'

'Oh my God,' Sephy shuddered, 'we are so definitely not having a conversation about you and Dad and sex.'

Her mother laughed. 'You know, for someone always insisting they're one heartbeat away from behaving inappropriately, you really can be wonderfully conventional. Now, get up on that catwalk and do what you do – shine.'

Sephy gave her mother a quick hug and made her way into the ballroom.

The sound of excited voices, amplified in the semi-darkness of the room, had her butterflies quadrupling. On shaking legs she climbed the steps up to the catwalk and disappeared behind stage to check her models hadn't given up on her and got dressed again.

Looking critically at the line of models, she tried to focus past the nerves, past the lump in her throat over the subtext that her mother didn't want her daughter to be lonely, and past Luke and every confusing emotion he brought out in her.

Mentally she compared line-up with running order.

'It's going to be fine, Ms King,' said her head stylist, following her gaze.

'Actually,' Sephy replied, adopting what she hoped was a confident smile, 'it's going to be better than fine. Ladies, you all look fabulous – you have made my very first collection look fabulous… and I am in no doubt whatsoever, that in,' she glanced down at her watch, 'three minutes' time, every single one of you walking down that runway is going to one hundred percent *own it*.'

To the sound of cheers she made her way back to the stage area, willed the nausea to take a back seat, and stepped up to the podium.

As the lighting technician lowered the rest of the lights in the ballroom, Sephy felt the heat of the spotlight on her. Her heart raced as she checked her notes.

Thirty seconds to lights, camera, action.

She raised her head to look out over the audience of selected boutique, department-store owners and fashion press. Her mother and Amanda were seated at the back, Nora right in the front. There was absolutely no fear in their eyes. Were they crazy? Didn't they know it was entirely possible she was about to ruin the King name?

As the seconds ticked by and her throat tickled, her palms sweated and her insides jangled, the one thing she tried to stop was her thoughts from scrambling.

Oh, but she wished Luke was here, looking at her in that quietly confident way of his. As if right before he flashed her his dimples he was telling her he expected her to be able to do anything she put her mind to.

The intro music started and holding Luke central in her thoughts, her smile felt more natural and her confidence more real as she pulled in a breath and said, 'Ladies and gentlemen, welcome to the launch of Seraphic…'

She managed to keep her tone even as she described the jewelled tones of the first part of the collection. The fun part of the collection, where the bright colours of the super-soft Lycra bodysuits trimmed with lace were playful and flirty and meant to be worn under everyday clothes to make you feel the best you could be.

She was doing it, she realised, as the models strutted down the runway. As long as she didn't look to see if the audience were marking order forms or smirking while writing copy for tomorrow's magazines, she was actually doing it.

The last part of her collection came out – the more playful now mixed with a sense of seduction in the cut. Her floral and seraphim-embroidered lace combining with the romance of tulle to provide sheer and cut-away patterns on her bras, knickers, thongs, suspender-sets and bustiers.

This was lingerie that moved you from day to night with sensual ease.

This was the lingerie she had modelled with Luke.

Her stomach pulled in as the last model came out in the Seraphic showstopper.

Sephy's voice became breathy as she described the design. If she closed her eyes, if she so much as blinked, she knew she would be back in Luke's bedroom and feeling his mouth skate over her skin and his beautiful, confident, sexy hands soothe and excite as he taught her things about herself – about him – about what she was missing out on.

CHAPTER TEN

Sephy soaked up the silence of her father's study as she ran her fingers over the polished chesterfield desk he had loved so much.

'Well, Dad, I did it,' she whispered. 'Seraphic is officially up and running.'

The last guest had left half an hour beforehand, having placed an order for her chain of boutiques. Sephy had had to tense every muscle in her body to stop herself from reaching out to give the woman a thoroughly unprofessional hug.

That order had been one of several, and along with all the compliments, she was on such a high it would be hours before she'd be able to sleep.

Feeling restless, she had excused herself from the rowdy kitchen where toasted sandwiches and red wine were being passed around, and had gone to check on her daughter.

And then she had found herself in here.

No hesitating in front of the door this time.

She was so happy she'd done the launch here instead of London. Here was where she felt comfortable, but also where she had always felt inspired to do her best. There was something about the land and house, the structure of it all – the rightness, that came out in her designs.

Dropping her phone onto the desk she turned to stare up at the imposing portrait of Jeremy King that had once hung pride of place in KPC headquarters. Nora had recently removed it and chosen to hang a photograph of her father alongside all the previous family members who had once run KPC, instead.

Sephy marvelled at Nora having the presence of mind to do that. But then she had always had a much clearer-defined and better relationship with their father than Sephy had. The two had spoken the same language.

Sephy had never really spoken Jeremy King's language.

Where he had high expectations of her working at KPC, she had learnt to have low expectations of him ever truly accepting her for who she was – someone who was artistic rather than another home-grown candidate for his beloved business.

Not for the first time she wished she had got to show him what she could make of herself while he was alive. Was she stupid to think she'd receive an acknowledgment for tonight? Some sort of sign? Or, was she even more stupid for *needing* one?

She hated the ache that came with missing him. Hated that tonight, at twenty-five years of age, what she yearned for most was a hug, a kiss on the forehead and a 'well done' from her father.

A hot tear slid down her face.

Maybe she shouldn't have slipped back into this room and made herself sad when she had been feeling so elated. So positive for what she had achieved tonight. So proud of what this meant for Seraphic's future. For her and Daisy's future.

On occasions like this it was hard to remember she had forgiven her father for thinking Jared and Nora perfectly capable of providing for themselves, but not her. At the end of Jeremy King's life, Sephy would have given anything to have been treated equally with her brother and sister, but instead he had chosen to write three very different letters to his children. Nora and Jared's letters had been perfectly judged. Making it all the harder to realise her father saw her as someone who had no drive to achieve anything for herself.

Another tear slipped out.

His lack of faith in her was a wound that would not stop

seeping and unconsciously she brushed a hand over her heart as if to suture it shut again. How dared he think that choosing to accept his money while she got her degree would lead to her accepting someone else's money afterwards? How could he have really thought that living off others was the lesson she wanted her daughter to learn? But it was too late to impress upon him that what she was doing now was simply what she would have been doing two years down the line when she had finished her degree.

Sephy wasn't even aware that Jared had entered the room, and was standing beside her, until she saw the box of tissues being waved in front of her face.

That he had come to check on her made the tears come faster.

'I'm okay,' she sniffed, not really certain if she was telling herself or Jared. She took a tissue and wiped at her eyes.

'Of course you are,' Jared said, and then with a nod to the portrait added, 'It's hard to do the big things without him there to see.'

Sephy looked up at her brother as he smiled wryly and continued, 'What? You think out in New York I didn't ever once feel that? Try signing for the bank loan to start the company, finding business premises, the first property deal I shook hands on...the one that made me a millionaire. Every one of those times I wanted him there. Then I'd remember standing in here the night of Nora's nineteenth birthday. I'd remember the disappointment in his eyes. The stubborn tilt of his jaw.'

'The same jaw you have,' Sephy said, with a soft smile replacing her wobbling lip.

Jared turned his head to look at her. 'Ditto, little sis.'

Sephy swiped at another tear.

'I've been so busy the last few weeks preparing for tonight,' she told Jared, 'I thought I was handling it. I thought I'd accepted that he's gone, but when I walked in here earlier this evening and saw you all standing waiting for me, all I could think was that I wanted him back here too. Just for a while. Just to see this. To see me do this.'

'It'll get easier.'

Sephy nodded and reached for another tissue as the study door opened and Nora entered.

'Don't tell me the two of you are arguing again?'

Jared shook his head. 'We were talking about Dad and about all the firsts.'

Nora nodded and came to stand the other side of Sephy. 'A few days after I got the Moorfield account I drove over here and sat in this room and bawled my eyes out.'

Sephy turned to stare at her sister, hating that she had been so upset and hadn't stopped by for a cup of tea and sympathy.

Nora gave a toss of her hair and sat back against the desk. 'Oh, and the first big work function I went to after he had died? It was a good thing Ethan was with me, otherwise I'm not sure I'd have stayed more than five minutes.' She tipped her head to rest on Sephy's shoulder. 'It does get easier.'

'That's what I told her,' Jared said.

The three of them stood in silence for a while and then Jared added, 'I need you both keeping an eye on Mum at the wedding. It's going to be hard on her without Dad there.'

'Sort of bittersweet,' Sephy sighed in understanding. 'Of course we will.'

'Speaking of weddings,' Nora said softly, 'This might not be the best time and I know Ethan and I haven't set a date yet, but well I was wondering if at my wedding, Jared – you would give me away?'

'I'd be honoured,' Jared said, as his hand came around Sephy to squeeze Nora's shoulder, and then, as if aware of leaving his baby sister out of the proceedings, he bumped against Sephy to get her attention and added, 'I'd be equally honoured to be involved in your wedding, too.'

Panic invaded and Sephy didn't know whether it was the

mention of weddings full stop or the creeping sensation that she liked the sound of her brother giving her away at a wedding she had no intention of having.

'Well,' she cleared her throat, 'make sure you dot all the I's and cross all the T's for Nora's, because you both know I don't plan on getting married.

'Not even to Luke Jackson?' Jared managed to keep a straight face for about three seconds.

'Oh my God, you told him?' Sephy turned mutinous eyes to Nora.

'I'm sorry. He got Amanda to get it out of me. She's good – did not see her coming at all. First she was talking about your lingerie collection and then how she'd brought over our bridesmaid dresses to try on and then how tight your friendship with Luke must be and then she was wondering where he was tonight.'

'And suddenly you were telling her about him modelling and me posing as his fiancée? How does that just slip out?' she whipped her head around to Jared. 'You absolutely cannot tell Mum about this.'

'Definitely okay with me,' Jared replied. 'She's feeling vulnerable as it is. Let's not give her anything else to worry about.'

Sephy frowned. 'She asked to have a word with me before she goes back to New York with you tomorrow.'

'Oh.'

'What do you mean, "oh"?' Sephy's heart started beating faster. Why did it feel as if her world was constantly set on fast-spin these days?

'What if mum wanted to sell the estate?' Jared asked carefully. 'Do you have a plan for that, if she does?'

'What? No, I do not have a plan for that.' Sephy stared at him as if he was crazy and thought that was a statement guaranteed to produce a reaction from the grave.

But nothing happened except that Nora leaned forward into her sight-line to shoot Jared a worried look. 'Has she mentioned it to you while she's been staying with you, then?' she asked.

Jared looked rueful. 'A couple of times.'

'Why don't you seem surprised?' Sephy asked Nora.

Nora looked sheepish. 'She mentioned it to me a while back. Maybe she wanted to be sure of her feelings before she talked to you about it.'

'Why,' Sephy questioned, her voice rising, 'because I happen to live on the estate?' *Because this place is where I'm me and where I've made plans?*

'I don't know, Seph – perhaps she wants to give you some of the proceeds.'

'Oh for goodness' sake this can't be about the bloody will again,' she vented, uncaring if an outburst seemed disrespectful in her father's study. 'I don't need money. Why do you think I'm setting up Seraphic? Why does everyone assume I can't do this?'

'*None* of us assume any such thing,' Nora asserted, 'but if Mum comes to you tomorrow and brings the subject up, you can't jump down her throat. If it's about the money, she's coming from a good place, and if it's actually about her and how she feels about this place with him gone, you can't guilt her into staying.'

'How could you think I would do that?' Sephy felt the hurt sink in deep. More than being the baby of the family… it sucked being treated like she was.

'Mum won't sell up,' she said suddenly with conviction, 'Dad's tree is here.'

They had planted the tree for somewhere to visit and remember Jeremy King. It symbolised the best of each of their relationships with their father and Sephy knew that the first thing her mother would have done when she arrived back here today was visit him there.

Her phone suddenly rang, making all three of them jump.

Reaching across the desk for it, she glanced at the screen and when she saw who was calling, her anxiety about no longer having this place to call home vanished in a heartbeat.

'You do realise you've got this kind of gooey look on your face?' Nora observed.

Sephy's head shot up. 'I do not.'

'Must be the,' Jared lifted his hands in the air to finger-quote, 'fiancé?'

Sephy rolled her eyes at them and made her way across the study floor thinking only of getting some privacy.

Stepping out into the brightly lit hallway she smiled into her phone and greeted softly, 'Hey you.'

'Hey you, back,' came Luke's deep, reassuring voice. 'How did it go?'

'It went well, I think,' she said, and then all pretence faded as she quickly forgave earlier family tensions and started gushing. 'Actually it went really well. I have orders. Multiple orders. Come Monday maybe even more. Oh, and Nora arranged for Mum, Jared and Amanda to fly back from New York for it.'

'You sound like you have the biggest grin on your face, right now.'

Sephy's hand tightened against the phone. 'Seriously, Luke, I can't thank you enough for posing for the photographs.' When he didn't immediately respond she spoke again, 'How's the visit going?'

'Good. They love the house, so I guess I have to grudgingly thank you for adding all the stuff to make it look friendlier.'

'You can say cushions and candles without starting to foam at the mouth, you know.'

'Pretty sure I can't,' he said and then sighed happily. 'It's kind of great to see them. And they're really looking forward to meeting you.'

'Me too.'

'You are?'

'Definitely. I've made a two-page list of embarrassing questions to ask.' Sephy wandered over to the coat-check table that still held a huge display of flowers in Seraphic's signature colours of white, cream and antique gold.

'Yeah. About that,' Luke said his tone now cautious.

'Relax.' She reached out to stroke her finger over a rose petal. 'I won't ask anything too outrageous.'

'Why don't I feel better?'

'Baby.'

'Want to come over here and call me that to my face?'

Sephy went hot all over. It was so wrong that she suddenly did. So wrong that the best way she could think of celebrating tonight was to do what she had assured her mother she absolutely wasn't going to do, and pop over to his house…and encourage him to put those gorgeous hands of his on her.

Bad Sephy.

Very naughty Sephy.

'Sephy?'

Sephy whirled around to see Ryan descending the last few stairs.

Cripes. She'd been so wrapped up in Luke she hadn't even heard him coming down the wide curving staircase, although that was probably a good thing. At least it reinforced that she and Luke were together.

'Hang on, Luke,' she said and then addressed Ryan. 'Ryan. You off home now? Thank you for coming tonight.'

'Why is Ryan at your place this late?' Luke asked, his voice rough and loud in her ear.

'He isn't. I'm still up at the main house,' she said into her phone.

Ryan raised an eyebrow over what she suspected was an obvious flush on her face. He looked as if he was weighing up how far he could get away with teasing her and then, with a familiar wicked grin, said in a tone that was definitely designed for the person on the end of the phone to hear, 'Remember all the times, late at night, when I used to sneak you back in here and up to your room.'

Sephy's mouth dropped open in shock.

‘Tell him you have a man you don’t have to sneak around with any more,’ she heard Luke mutter.

Okay, she was ending this before it got any more out of hand. ‘I will not,’ she told Luke and then to Ryan said, ‘I’m glad you spent time with Daisy, tonight. How about I phone you in the week and we set something up for before Daisy and I go to New York for Jared’s wedding?’

Ryan’s gaze flicked to the phone and then back to her and obviously feeling appeased that she wasn’t going to put Luke before him when it came to him seeing Daisy, he relaxed.

‘I’d love that,’ he told her.

‘No problem. Want me to see you to the door?’

‘I can see that you’re busy. I know my way out.’

‘Okay.’

‘Thanks again. And well done for tonight.’

‘He gone yet?’ Luke asked and the jealousy he couldn’t quite disguise shouldn’t have pleased her, but did.

‘Yes, he’s gone and, just so you know, I did not invite him tonight. In fact, I didn’t even think about it. Nora and Ethan thought it would be a good idea and, to be fair, once I saw Daisy’s face when he arrived, I thought it was too.’

‘It’s okay. I get it.’

‘You do?’

‘Seph, I’m never going to begrudge a parent wanting to spend time with their child.’

The way he said it, well, now she knew a little more about his family background she could understand the tightness in his voice and wondered how little his birth parents might have wanted to do with him.

‘So, I know you’re probably tired, but do you feel up to taking a quick walk?’ Luke asked, cleverly bringing the subject back to her in that habit she realised he employed when he didn’t want to talk about himself.

‘A walk?’

'Mmmn. Down to the gazebo by the lake.'

'And why would I want to do that?' she asked, fluster mixing in with intrigue.

'Because I may be standing in it, with a little present I picked out for you.'

Warmth bloomed in her chest, along with an outrageous flutter of excitement.

'You bought me a present?'

'It's not a big deal.'

'You didn't want to come up to the house?'

'I can't stay long. It wouldn't be fair to Steve and Lily.'

'Okay. Keep talking to me while I walk down to meet you.'

'So Nora brought your brother and mother back specially to see your show, huh?'

'I know,' Sephy grinned ear to ear. 'I think I might have to buy her a pair of shoes as a thank you. It was so great to see them there, it nearly made up for…' she drifted off, catching herself.

'Yeah, I was thinking it was going to be tough not having your father there,' Luke inserted.

Sephy had been going to say for not having Luke there, so his intervention saved her opening the can of worms they were taking in turns to carry around, but did that mean he had deliberately picked the gazebo as a meeting place? The thought that he might have suggested it so that she could be close to her father's tree made something soften in the region of her heart.

Her heels dug into the soft grass of the landscaped gardens but she didn't care. The closer she got to the gazebo, the more excited she was to see him.

'I like talking to you in the moonlight,' she said, and then, mortified to have let romance and sentiment slip out, she immediately clapped a hand over her mouth.

There was a small pause and then Luke was saying, 'So I should only ring you late at night now, is that what you're saying?'

Her answer was a deep inhale of breath because she could now see him standing in the gazebo, under the millions of fairy lights he had strung up for Daisy.

Was it her imagination, or seeing him, but did the moon suddenly seem brighter? The stars more plentiful? The air more filled with the heady sense of possibility?

Her heart skipped several beats as she fought to keep romance firmly divorced from solid, dependable friendship.

As if he could sense she was close, he turned, and as his gaze locked onto hers, he grinned.

She mounted the three shallow steps of the gazebo and came to a stop in front of him.

'Hang up,' he said, his voice husky as he indicated her phone.

'No, you hang up,' she grinned.

His laugh sent a tingle up her spine as he put his phone away.

Being here with him, in this gazebo that he had so generously built for them all so that they had shelter when they visited the willow sapling planted at the foot of the lake, made everything suddenly incredibly real.

Emotion flooded her. 'God, Luke, do you think I've done the right thing? I mean, what if –'

'Seraphina King, do not even attempt to finish that sentence,' he interrupted. 'Besides, it's a bit late now. Your collection is out there.' His face shone with a quiet pride for her and she shivered because the sound of her full name on his lips sounded special. Intimate.

To stop herself being tempted into increasing the intimacy and stepping closer to him, she deliberately took a step back, turned, and leant her arms on the waist-high balustrade as she stared out at the calm surface of the lake beyond.

'I feel a bit sick,' she admitted as she thought about the evening and the fact that, yes, her collection was now out there. In the world. Being bought.

'Because it's real now?'

She nodded and when he arrived to lean against the railing,

she couldn't feel guilty at enjoying the way his body heat merged with hers.

'It's so peaceful out here,' Luke murmured and she sighed with contentment.

'When Daisy was a baby and she used to cry, and I was this close,' she held her thumb and forefinger a millimetre apart, 'to phoning mum and dad and asking for help, I would put her in her pram and walk down here. Something about the stillness would always lull her.'

'Why didn't you simply ask your parents for help?'

Unable to look at her father's tree just yet she looked at Luke like he had forgotten she was a King. 'Way too easy,' she said. 'I wasn't going to give anyone an excuse to tell me I couldn't cope. Instead I would come here and soak up the fresh air and secretly wait for the other shoe to drop because getting to walk around this land with my daughter felt way, way better than clubbing ever had.'

Luke looked back out at the water. 'Where was Ryan while you were nurturing your roots here?'

'Gone.' She shrugged philosophically. 'He had his own demons. I respect him for how he's working to be in Daisy's life now, but we were never meant to stay together.'

'You're very generous to forgive him for leaving you to deal with your pregnancy alone.'

Sephy swung her gaze to him and realised that Luke would never have left her to cope on her own. He was too gallant, she realised. Too heroic.

Too used to being the one left behind, to do it to someone else?

'It wasn't so hard to forgive him,' she said softly. 'Once I worked out you can't force someone to love you or your child, it wasn't worth holding onto the anger and I didn't want Daisy growing up with any negativity towards him. Besides,' she confessed, thinking of everything she had achieved tonight, 'I had this place to help me make plans for the two of us. Without even realising what I was doing,' she confessed, 'I think I was stitching plans together for Seraphic and this place.'

Under the twinkly canopy of soft light, those plans she had made, the ones she had never told anyone in case they sounded too grandiose, came tumbling out of her. 'It's a way off yet, but once Seraphic is sustaining a profit and I've proved myself, I'm going to see if I can convert one of the disused barns into production premises and turn the entire process in-house. Offshore factories are cheaper. But I don't want cheaper. At the moment I'm using a small factory in the UK, but eventually I'd like to give back to the community and have it all produced locally. I'll need to run it all past Jared because he'll be taking over the estate one day, but I think I can sell it to him. In the meantime I was thinking about turning all the outbuildings on the south side of the estate into artist's studios. You know – provide space for artists to make and then sell their work.' She ran out of breath around about the time a smiling Luke put a box into her hands.

'Sorry,' she stuttered, 'I probably sound mad going on about things that aren't even close to happening yet.'

'Open your present, Sephy,' Luke instructed her softly.

She looked down and then looked back up to him. 'Why am I holding an obscenely expensive jeweller's box in my hands?'

'Well, since you are why don't you go ahead and open it.'

His voice was a deep purr, making her hands tremble as she undid the bow and opened the box.

'Oh,' her hand reached in to gently remove the platinum charm bracelet and hold it up to the fairy lights.

'Is it okay?'

Punch-drunk with emotion, her heart released a sigh of happiness as it filled up with him.

'It's more than okay. It's too much,' she whispered, taking in the different charms – the tiny sparkling tape measure, thimble, sewing kit, sketch pad and Seraphic emblem. Her heart tripped over itself when she saw the little house with the crown stuck on top, presumably to resemble this place, the King estate, but it was when she saw the little daisy that her heart re-started and her bottom lip wobbled.

All the things most important to her in the world.

'Luke, it's absolutely beautiful. I love it. Thank you.' She stole a look at him and then quickly looked away to the bracelet again, afraid that he would see and recognise what she had been fighting the duration of their friendship – just how important a place he held in her world.

Luke cleared his throat. 'Congratulations on launching Seraphic, Seph. I knew you could do it.'

She thought she might be glowing as she clutched the bracelet and his faith in her, to her chest.

CHAPTER ELEVEN

Luke opened his front door and stared. 'You're wearing a dress.'

Sephy smiled up at him. 'As always, your powers of deduction never cease to amuse me.'

'You mean "amaze me",' he corrected, trying to stop himself from carrying out a second and way-too-obvious head-to-toe appraisal.

'Do I?' Sephy teased with an impish smile and then leant in as if to deliver a secret. 'It's called a tea dress,' she whispered helpfully.

What it was, was lilac and floaty and so not what he was used to seeing her in that he found himself leaning forward, matching her body language and closing the inches further. 'But we're having brunch, not tea,' he whispered back.

Sephy licked her lips. 'Should I go home and change?'

'No, of course not.' God, but she looked even more beautiful than usual. The dress made her look softer, somehow, overriding that unconscious sexiness with a new sweetness that was magnetic. 'You look perfect.'

Sephy smoothed the material over her hips. 'I don't look like I'm trying too hard?'

A female voice from behind him said, 'And why on earth wouldn't you want to try hard the first time you meet your future in-laws?'

Luke got a brief look at Sephy's eyes widening with alarm before she breathed in, smiled her warmest smile and then she was peering around him and saying, 'Hello, Mrs Jackson.'

'Call me Lily,' she was corrected. 'Luke, let the girl in so we can meet properly, or are we all to eat in the doorway?'

Sephy stepped past him, her floral scent filling his lungs and reminding him of how she had looked in his bedroom, how she had felt in his arms. At night she now owned his dreams. During the day wasn't much better. It had got so bad that he'd had to devote time to constructing a de-sensitisation room in his head to put those scorching-hot memories in.

'I knew by the fifth time Luke mentioned your name that you were going to be special to him,' Lily said, smiling at Sephy.

Luke watched his foster mother sweep Sephy up into a welcoming hug.

'You did?' Sephy turned huge questioning eyes to him.

'Absolutely,' Lily replied. 'He never mentioned any other woman he was seeing more than twice and then, what totally gave it away was that he then went conspicuously quiet about you.'

Luke tensed because he remembered thinking that he'd been talking about Sephy too much and that he absolutely needed to make sure he stopped before they got the wrong idea. He'd deliberately switched to talking about work and unwittingly created his own situation.

Sephy skewered him with an assessing look. 'He does have this way of not talking about things that are close to his heart.'

Luke tried to keep his smile in place as Lily looked at Sephy shrewdly as if she had passed some sort of test. So far so good, except he didn't know whether to be more concerned about any further little tests his foster parents intended peppering brunch with, or Sephy's public acknowledgment that he automatically shut down on a few subjects.

'Come on,' Lily said, grasping Sephy's hand and leading her into the kitchen. 'Come and meet Steve.'

Luke followed behind them, unprepared for Sephy turning back to check he was close by and catching him staring at the seductive sway of her hips. Her eyes darkened to the same shade of melted chocolate brown they'd gone when he had kissed her. Scrubbing a hand over his face he held up a warning yellow card to his imagination. She was only acting like any other self-respecting fiancée, but if she kept looking at him with those soft, sweet, doe-like eyes during brunch he was going to have a hell of a problem keeping control of this visit.

It had been hard enough to keep control last night in the gazebo when she had pulsed with energy as she'd told him about the launch and her plans. Then, when he'd given her the bracelet and she had looked so touched he had known he was sinking further under her spell.

He had been counting on some of her usual snark to put his feet back on solid ground, but none had been forthcoming and instead he'd forced himself to leave the gazebo with a casual farewell. With every step back to his car he'd wanted to turn back and check she was still there, pride and happy dreams swimming in her eyes, and on her lips that incredible soft smile. Produced especially for him because she'd realised he'd spent more than five minutes thinking about a gift for her.

In the kitchen his foster dad gave Sephy her second hug in as many minutes, leaving him the only person not to have hugged her. Maybe he should remedy that. A little test of his own control.

Walking over to join them, Luke went for something more personal than a hug, and reaching out, did what he always found himself wanting to do when he was with her. He allowed his hand to stroke down that glorious mane of silky black hair as he smiled down at her. She lifted her head to rub her lips against his shoulder in a quick kiss. Her movement was so natural, Luke couldn't help himself, his hand lowered to settle proprietorially at her hip, his thumb stroking casually along her hip bone as he held her to his side.

Sephy looked up at him and stuttered, 'C-coffee?'

It was wrong that he liked the stutter.

Acting and control.

That's what this morning was all about.

Not laying his lips over that stutter and seeing if he could get her to moan like she'd moaned for him the other day.

Easing out a breath, he dropped a quick kiss on the top of her head and agreed, 'Coffee,' before reluctantly releasing her to pour them both an extra-strength cup.

'So,' Steve Jackson said, pulling out a chair and indicating that Sephy should take a seat at the table loaded with food. 'Luke has been telling us all about your special event last night.'

Luke added sugar to their coffees without looking at what he was doing. He was too focused on Sephy.

She smiled, reached for the plate of bacon, put some on her plate, and said, 'Yes. Last night I launched my new lingerie collection to buyers.'

'From what Luke told us, it sounded pretty big,' Steve said.

'I'm hoping it will be. I've been mostly doing couture pieces while finishing my degree, but it feels like the right time to go for it and expand properly into stores.'

'That's a huge commitment to undertake with a young daughter,' Lily remarked.

'Hey,' Luke warned Lily as he put a coffee in front of Sephy and sat down beside her.

'I guess there's never a perfect time to start a business with a young child, but I'm very blessed,' Sephy answered. 'Daisy is at school and I have a large support network. My mother is nearby and helps out. Daisy's father lives locally now and, of course, Luke is brilliant with her.'

'Luke had to do a lot of helping out when he was younger and I guess that has stuck. He has a very generous quality about him,' Lily said, shooting him a look that Sephy caught.

'That's not why I'm with him,' Sephy replied, lifting the plate of mushrooms and tomatoes and passing it to Lily. She leant forward conspiratorially, 'Obviously I'm only with him for his technical and programming skills…I mean,' she winked, 'it's not as if he's a charming, caring, charismatic, creative self-starter, is it?'

A second's pause and then Lily and Steve laughed and Luke relaxed a little.

'You're right about his generous nature, though,' Sephy continued, 'I'm forever having to stop him from buying Daisy the world.'

Steve laughed. 'Oh, you don't have to tell us about Luke and spending money.'

Luke winced as he felt Sephy turn to look at him while Steve continued with, 'Admittedly, it took us a while to fully appreciate just how much money he was making. The first time he tried to pay off our mortgage we thought he was joking. When we wouldn't accept the money, he went out and bought us a bigger car to help ferry some of the younger children around.'

'And did you accept the car?' Sephy asked, not taking her eyes off of Luke.

'Didn't have much choice after he got the old one towed away. The following year he bought us a second car so that we could both save time ferrying the brood around.'

Luke felt the blush stain his cheeks. What the hell was wrong with spending money on the people you cared about? Couldn't take it with you, could you. 'I'm sure Sephy doesn't want to know every single gift I've treated my family to over the years,' he said quietly.

'Oh, I don't know,' Lily said, looking at Sephy with a warm smile, 'perhaps you can convince him we really don't need money for an extension to the back of the house this year.'

Luke felt Sephy's hand reach under the table to squeeze his thigh, and with a look that said, 'Relax, I've got this,' she turned to his foster parents and said softly, 'He's just showing you how much he loves you.'

Steve and Lily blinked and then smiled warmly at Sephy.

Luke picked up his knife and fork and cleared his throat. 'So now that the Luke Jackson appreciation society is in full session, shall we eat?'

Lily made it nearly twenty minutes of chatting about general things before, not so subtly, steering conversation back to her favourite subject. 'So tell us about the wedding? What plans have you made so far?'

For the first time since arriving, Luke sensed Sephy's hesitation. He watched as her fingers slid over one of the charms on the bracelet he'd had made for her. Almost as if she was stroking it for comfort or to ground herself.

'Well, we haven't made too much headway,' she told them. 'I guess we're just enjoying being engaged, you know?'

'But you must know the big things,' Lily demurred. 'Are you thinking you want a traditional church service or are you going for a civil ceremony?'

'Um, not church. Right?' she looked to Luke for panicked confirmation.

'Actually, I think Sephy would love it if we got married on the King family estate,' he said on her behalf.

Sephy stared at him, her strained expression taking on a wistful quality that had him swallowing because suddenly he pictured himself standing in that ballroom waiting nervously for the double doors at the end to open…

Damn. His insides lurching in reaction and before his imagination could go completely kamikaze on him, he reached for his coffee and chugged it down. To combat the images, he deliberately added zombies to the fading scene in his head and focused on dispatching every single one of them.

'That sounds lovely,' said Lily. 'And are you thinking big "do" or small, intimate family gathering?'

Again he felt Sephy turn to stare at him for help.

Luke looked at his foster mother. 'Are you hankering for us to have a wedding big enough to invite the whole brood?' he teased, thinking the higher he built this all up the further they were all going to fall, if the guilt didn't kill him first, that was.

'You've attended some of your brothers' and sisters' weddings. It's important to maintain links with them all. You know we've always wanted each of you to feel that family support network behind you.'

'If Luke wants all his brothers and sisters there, then I want that too,' Sephy interrupted, looking like she'd recovered her composure a little. 'Family is important to both of us.'

'I'm glad,' Lily approved, then looked at Luke and in a quiet voice said, 'It's such a shame Claire won't be there to see you get married.'

'Who's Claire?' Sephy asked innocently.

In the echoing silence, Luke's mood instantly downshifted. He swung a quick look to Steve and Lily, who looked shocked that the woman he purported to want to spend the rest of his life with didn't know.

Luke's gaze shot to Sephy and the look of distress on her face hit him hard. She might not know who Claire was, but she realised that in not knowing she'd committed some terrible faux pas.

He cleared what felt like steel shavings from his throat. 'Claire was my birth mother. Claire Jackson.'

He tried to fill his head with zombies, but all he could think was: don't ask. Don't ask why she won't be there.

'Of course. I'm sorry. I wasn't thinking. I don't think you've mentioned her name before.'

He could kiss her not asking – for trying to cover asking who Claire was in the first place. He didn't want her upset when his reaction was his problem to deal with. His hand dropped down to cover hers and squeeze reassuringly.

'Why don't the two of you go out into the garden while we clear the table,' Steve suggested wisely.

'Great idea.' Luke shot to his feet, his hand still clasping Sephy's as escape beckoned. Pushing against one of the patio doors,

Sephy's hand feeling small in his, he pulled her out into the fresh air.

'I'm so, so sorry,' she whispered and his hand tightened on hers.

'Not yet,' he answered, striding further down the garden, until he could be certain they could talk without being overheard.

'I've ruined everything,' she said when he started to slow his steps. 'I should have kept silent.'

'It's fine.'

'Luke, obviously it isn't fine. The look on their faces when I asked who she was.'

'Don't worry about it. You covered really well.'

'The look on your face…'

Luke stopped and turned to face her. He still had hold of one of her hands. Couldn't seem to let go. 'They pulled a sneaky one – they know I don't usually talk about her.'

'I feel really bad.'

'Why? For not knowing my birth mother's name? How could you when I didn't tell you?' He stared down at their intertwined fingers and pushed the next sentence out. 'For not knowing she died when I was fifteen? How could you when I didn't tell you?'

Right along with the shock and compassion on Sephy's face, Luke could see the questions lining up one by one in her eyes. He braced, but she didn't lend voice to any one of them. She simply waited.

And the waiting killed him. Why was it so much harder to tell the story when patience was her weapon of inquiry? It gave him too much space to breathe. To feel. If the words were dragged from him inch by patient inch, he was going to lose that practised detachment he'd fought so hard to gain.

'My foster parents were coming from a good place,' he defended, 'but they were testing me, not you.'

He felt the back-and-forth stroke of her thumb against his hand.

'Luke, you shouldn't feel pushed into telling me about your mother. I know what it's like to be on the receiving end of questions you don't always know the answers to.'

Luke tipped his head back and let out a sigh. 'I know some of the answers. The ones that matter, anyway. I just –'

'Choose who you share it all with,' she finished for him. 'I understand that too.'

He looked down into her face. Seems like they'd both had their share of people wanting to know them for the family curiosity value they offered. By the time Luke had ended up with the Jacksons, he'd had a gutful of living with strangers, changing schools, and all the endless playground inquisitiveness that came with it. He'd lost all ability to trust anyone's motives for liking him and spent most of his time waiting to be sent back or sent on. Steve and Lily had had their work cut out for them.

Luke didn't want to let them down now by reverting to not being able to simply say what his childhood had been like. Worrying about Sephy's reaction was ridiculous. He couldn't change his past and he wasn't defined by it. He was bigger than any judgement she might make. Wasn't he?

With a half smile he admitted, 'I can't tell you how easy it made it for a fourteen-year-old kid who was tired of explaining why he had a different surname to the people he lived with, to turn up at a house where the foster carers happened to have the same name.'

Sephy nodded with understanding. 'You could pretend you weren't fostered.'

'For a while.' Until Claire Jackson had died, and once again the curious had gathered and he'd retreated back into his shell, silently waiting and wondering when the Jacksons were going to tell him they didn't want him.

Sephy glanced back towards the kitchen and as Luke followed her gaze he could see his foster dad standing at the patio doors.

Sephy turned back to Luke with a worried frown on her face.

'I don't like feeling they're thinking I'm out here haranguing you for keeping secrets or that I'm demanding a lot of answers from you.'

Christ, did she even know how sweet it felt to have her go in to bat for him?

'Okay, don't bolt,' he found himself saying, 'but I have to kiss you right now.'

Those gorgeous dancing eyes of hers widened and the endearing stutter returned. 'W-what? Why?'

'Because,' he tugged on the hand still captured in his. *Because you lift the weight of my past from my shoulders. Because you have my back. Because you're prepared to talk about weddings even though it makes you uncomfortable. Because you're prepared to not talk about my birth mother.* 'Because we have an audience,' he said aloud instead, nodding over her head towards the kitchen patio doors.

'Oh,' she said, her expression clearing, 'you're thinking we could save this?'

What he was thinking was that he didn't stand a chance any more against the craving that was impossible to keep locked down.

Taking a tiny step towards him, Sephy sighed dramatically. 'Well, go on, then. Lay one on me. It's all about taking one for the team, right?'

His chuckle came from out of nowhere, lightening his mood but not lessening the want. Bringing his free hand up to slide along her jaw-line he let his fingers splay into her hair. All he could think was, no way was he about to rush this. He was going to have to savour the stubbornness, the sexiness and the just plain sweetness of her.

Sephy felt Luke's hand tenderly tilt her head to the perfect angle for their mouths to meet. She was expecting a quick, hard kiss, so when his head descended with enough time for the look in his eyes to confound her, she wanted to say, 'Wait. I need to prepare,' but then there was contact and he was sliding his lips slowly, reverently, cherishingly against hers and she didn't stand a chance.

She forgot about audiences. There was no acting. No pretending.

Reality was reduced to the fact that Luke Jackson's second kiss was different and yet the same as his first. Different because it felt like *more* when it absolutely shouldn't. The same, because right away it was hot and sexy and tender and so, so good that she opened her mouth for him. Felt her heart fill with him.

Don't make this mean anything.

Yet she kissed him back with the same consideration, the same concentration, the same commitment she felt from him.

When he groaned and changed the angle of his head to claim her mouth again, his possession was so assured that she couldn't help but surrender more to the world he created. She had known he was skilled at world-building, but this? This was sublime. This was…

Don't make this mean everything.

Her inner strength had her pulling back to heave in a breath.

Not wanting him to see how much he'd affected her, she buried her face in his chest and mumbled, 'Have we still got an audience?'

Luke was silent for what felt like an eternity and then he dropped a quick kiss to the top of her head and said, 'Yep. Come on, we've been out here long enough for you to have raked me over the coals, me to have told you my entire life history and both of us agree that there won't be any more secrets between us. Let's go in and get this visit finished up.'

'Okay,' she offered him up a quick smile, her gaze snagging on his lips, making her want to repeat that kiss. Repeatedly. In private.

Wow, she was so in over her head it wasn't funny. She had to remember why a relationship with Luke wasn't a good idea. She was no longer a fan of messy endings. They took too much out of her when it came to new beginnings.

She needed to prioritise Seraphic and income.

Maybe she'd avoid being alone with him for a while. She had learnt certain sensible life skills. It was probably time to reapply them. After all, she was already busy proving to the world she could provide for Daisy. Why not take the opportunity to prove to herself something else – that she wasn't stupid enough to fall for a friend.

Steve and Lily were waiting from them in the kitchen.

'I hope I haven't caused trouble between you both,' Lily was quick to say, looking worriedly at Luke.

'We're fine,' Sephy assured. 'Luke and I don't expect to know every single detail of each others' lives before we marry. But we do know the important things about each other. I knew before today that he was fostered from a young age. You don't have to worry that he can't talk about it. He knows there isn't anything he could ever tell me that would change the way I feel about him.'

Beside her she felt Luke's sharp intake of breath. She had thought that in *not* asking she was showing him she wasn't one of those pushy, carelessly nosey people he'd had to deal with when he was younger. But maybe she should ask him some questions sometime. Maybe he did need to be pushed to talk. Immediately she forgot all about limiting time with him and only wanted to help.

'Well you've certainly made me feel better,' Lily said, reaching out to grasp Sephy's hands, only to pause and stare down at them.

Sephy wondered what on earth she was looking at and then she saw the faint frown and with slamming realisation knew Lily Jackson was wondering why Luke hadn't put an engagement ring on her finger.

'It's being resized,' she lied, feeling awful for yet another deception.

'Oh. For a moment there,' Lily laughed lightly, 'I suddenly thought "don't tell me Luke's learned his lesson about lavishing money on loved ones at the worst possible time".'

'No. Big diamond. Huge. Obscenely expensive. Bit large, though. It won't be ready for a few weeks, will it Luke?'

'Um, no,' Luke answered, staring at her hands still held in Lily's and probably feeling awful for deceiving his foster mother too.

'This is the bracelet he bought me for the launch last night,' Sephy said lifting her wrist to show it off. 'It's worth a fortune,' Sephy licked her lips. Oh, fabulous. Now she'd made herself sound like a gold-digger able to tell a bauble's worth in the blink of an eye. She felt an urgent need to allay this woman's fears with talk of her own money. Except, technically, she didn't have any, did she?

Beginning to panic, she felt the gushing begin, 'It's also, aside from the ring he picked out for me, just about the most gorgeous, personal present I've ever been given. See how he chose charms that mean something special to me?'

'It's beautiful,' Lily remarked.

'For a beautiful woman,' Luke said, coming to the rescue, picking up her wrist and turning it so that he could place a soft kiss on her pulse-point.

Every nerve ending in Sephy's body pinged with delicious awareness, but as she stared into Luke's eyes she could see him silently telling her to stop rambling before she stepped on another family landmine.

'Let me make up for earlier,' Lily suddenly said. 'I'd love to take you and your mother out to lunch tomorrow.'

'Oh. I'm so sorry but my mother is actually flying back to New York tonight with my brother and his fiancée. They're getting married at the end of next week and Mum is helping out with the details.'

'How lovely. But Luke, you might have mentioned we'd need to vacate the house a little earlier than planned?'

Luke looked confused. 'Why do you need to leave early?'

'Well, with the two of you in New York, you won't want us staying here.'

Luke coughed on a leftover croissant he'd picked up from the plate Lily had left out.

Rushing to the sink to grab a drink of water for him, Lily watched him drink some down to clear his throat. 'I'm sorry, have I said something wrong again? I assumed as Sephy's fiancé that you would be attending the wedding with her.'

'I'm not –'

'What he means,' Sephy interjected quickly, 'is he's not happy about you having to leave because he's off to New York with me. He was going to ask you if you wanted to stay on here and use the place as a base while you visit some of your other children. Weren't you, honey?'

'I was? I mean, I was. That's right. I'm Sephy's plus one at the wedding. We'll be in New York for –'

'Two nights,' Sephy said and when Luke shot her a look she couldn't decipher, she realised she'd said it with heavy portent. 'And days,' she added. 'Obviously we'll be there for the days too.'

Sephy stared down at the floor, not trusting herself to look at Luke or the Jacksons. Exactly how in hell had she managed, in one short visit, to make it so that the Jacksons were now staying longer in Luke's house while Luke was joining her in New York?

New York.

The place where she'd promised herself some letting loose… some distraction from the man standing beside her.

CHAPTER TWELVE

Sephy painstakingly pored over the columns in her spreadsheet, and then, feeling like something had changed within the private plane bound for New York, she looked up and realised Nora had stopped tapping away on her laptop.

Now that Nora had her attention, her sister nodded her head towards the scene in front of them before shifting her gaze back to Sephy with an expression that said, 'Tell me that is not the cutest thing you've ever seen?'

Sephy glanced at what her sister had been looking at and swallowed at the heart-melting sight before her. Luke's impressive frame took up most of the cream leather seat opposite. His head was thrown back and he was sleeping soundly, and sitting curled up and cosily fast asleep in his arms was Daisy. It was Daisy's first trip in the private plane and for the first few hours it had taken Nora, Ethan, Luke, herself and her bag piled full of toys and treats to keep that excitement focused in play before Daisy had calmed down enough to demand Luke read to her. Sephy's gaze drifted down over him to the book grasped loosely in his hands.

He'd very generously read to her daughter while Sephy sent emails confirming new appointments with buyers for when she returned from New York. He was so good to her – to her daughter, and as she watched her daughter's chest rise and fall, and noticed Daisy's small hand curved trustingly over Luke's forearm, Sephy realised it was too late to monitor Daisy's attachment to Luke. It had been there right from the beginning. She had been too focused on monitoring her own attachment to Luke, which had also backfired on her because every time they were together now she was finding it harder to keep those barriers up.

She looked across at Nora and, unable to hide her emotion, was surprised when her sister took pity on her and didn't comment. Instead, with a soft smile, she jerked her thumb towards Ethan sitting beside her. Sephy leaned forward and saw that he too was asleep.

'Men,' Nora declared with a roll of her eyes. 'Here we are, two hot, intelligent women working in our downtime, and what do they do? Fall asleep. They should at least be trying to distract us. It's a disgrace.'

Sephy sighed, thinking that even in sleep Luke had the ability to distract her, for her head hadn't totally focused on the figures in her spreadsheet.

'I guess Ethan is used to sleeping as and when,' she whispered to Nora, acknowledging the fact that Ethan had flown all over the world and worked in places where sleeping was done in a makeshift tent with only the basics for comfort in his job as a disaster-relief worker.

'True,' Nora whispered back and then paused and said, 'He's going back out to do some field work for the charity when we get back from New York.'

Sephy wasn't totally shocked. Although Ethan had stopped being part of a disaster-relief rapid-response team and seemed happy running his chain of deluxe gyms, Sephy supposed it was hard to completely let go of something you felt that passionate about.

'I'm going to finish my training so that next time I can go with him,' Nora said.

'What?' Sephy forgot to keep her voice down and winced as Daisy stirred and then burrowed further into Luke, whose arms automatically came protectively around her despite him still being asleep.

Sephy's heart melted just that little bit more.

Nora glanced to Sephy and then back to Luke and Daisy. 'I want to go out on deployment with Ethan a couple of times before we get married and start a family. I'm nervous about him travelling and living in difficult areas if we have children, so I want to experience it for myself first. Make certain I'm not going to put my foot down over nothing.'

Sephy took in Nora's softer expression as she watched her niece sleeping. So she and Ethan wanted children right away. Sephy wondered if Jared and Amanda were thinking the same.

More change. In fact, it felt like her world hadn't stopped changing since the week of her father's diagnosis. Was it any wonder she constantly felt one step behind? If she couldn't keep up was she always going to feel lost and left behind? But then she pictured Daisy bossing her cousins around as they raced all over the King estate and smiled.

'What?' Nora prodded.

'Oh, I was thinking it will be nice for Daisy to have some cousins around.'

'You ever think about having more children?'

A sudden and clear image of her having Luke's child had her sitting up straight and reaching for her seat buckle to pull it reassuringly tight as her world bent all out of kilter. 'Absolutely not,' she said determinedly, glancing back down to the safety of her spreadsheet.

'Why not?'

She flashed her sister a dark look. 'Looking after Daisy and now Seraphic is more than enough challenge for me.'

'If you had someone at your side you could do both,' Nora said.

Nora wouldn't get it, but what did she have to offer Luke? Daisy came first and foremost. Seraphic came second. No man wanted to come third in a woman's life. She looked at the way Luke's arms protected her daughter and wondered if Claire

Jackson had placed her son first in life. Wondered if every time she had given him away it was so that he could have better. Or was it because she didn't want him?

Whichever the answer, Luke deserved to be at the top of someone's list. She wasn't confident she had learnt how to put any man at the top of her list. If she had, Ryan wouldn't have walked away.

As if Nora knew the direction of her thoughts, she said, 'Ethan mentioned that Ryan was seeing Michelle again. How do you feel about that?'

'What do you mean, how do I feel about it,' Sephy shot back defensively. 'He told me when he dropped Daisy off the other day and I think it's great that they're trying again. He wanted me to know that they're taking it slow and that he wouldn't bring Michelle back into Daisy's life until they were sure they were going to work this time. I hope they do work out. I like Michelle. I think she's good for Ryan.'

Like Luke was good for her?

Needing to push the thought right out of her head, she used all her powers of concentration to focus on Nora and what she was saying.

'Well, I'm glad you're glad. I mean, I know you said you and Ryan weren't ever going to be –' Nora broke off when she witnessed Sephy's bored expression. 'Okay, okay,' she placated, 'Sorry – old habits. I know he has an important place in your life because of Daisy, but I also know that's where it ends.'

'Well, finally, she gets it,' Sephy whispered to the heavens.

'So you're not into thinking about something serious at the moment…what about some good old-fashioned,' Nora waggled her eyebrows and then aimed a slow wink towards Luke before looking back at Sephy with more waggling of her eyebrows.

'I don't have time for that, either,' Sephy said, thinking about the way Luke had kissed her in his garden and how it hadn't even started out as playful. It had started out as serious and ended up as complicated.

'Are you quite sure about not having time for fun?'

'Never been more sure.'

'How many hours have you worked this week? You need to find some way to let loose a little or you're going to lose perspective. It was always you lecturing me on working too hard and not taking time for myself, remember? Take some of your own advice, please.'

Sephy sighed because the irony wasn't lost on her and it wasn't as if she hadn't been looking forward to this trip to indulge in a little 'letting loose', as Nora referred to it. She'd been banking on Nora or her mother looking after Daisy so she could take all her pent-up energy and emotion over Luke and divert it onto someone else for a few hours.

As if she could purge him from her system.

No way was she going to get to do that now, when he was right here with her for the entire trip.

Not to mention the fact that she was going to have to keep up the pretence that they were together for her mother. Which probably meant more touching. More kissing.

More...

Sephy squirmed in her seat.

What if she forgot herself and reached over to kiss him in front of Nora or Jared – the only two people who knew they weren't really together.

And what if Luke responded?

And kept on responding?

And one thing led to another and she found herself succumbing to all this need raging inside.

'I'd have loved to have seen the look on your faces when the Jacksons pushed you into coming to New York together,' Nora giggled. 'Priceless.'

'They did not push us into coming together,' Sephy asserted indignantly. 'They naturally assumed he would be my guest at my brother's wedding.' Sephy stopped. No way had they tricked her and Luke.

No way.

That would have to mean they knew she and Luke weren't really engaged.

She shook her head at the paranoia and deliberately looked back down at her work, effectively stopping all talk of Luke.

Taking the hint, Nora indicated the spreadsheet opened on Sephy's laptop screen and offered, 'I can look that over, if you want.'

'Thanks, but I'm pretty certain I have it.' At least she hoped she did. She didn't have time for errors now.

If she'd thought she'd worked hard before the launch, forget it. Being able to carve out the three days to attend her brother's wedding had meant that she'd worked flat out during the time Daisy was at school and then at night when Daisy was in bed she'd spent a few more hours working up until the early hours.

On the plus side, falling into bed exhausted meant she was too tired to dream about Luke and his eyes, and those dimples… and his mouth and those hands.

'Did you and Mum manage to get that chance to talk before she flew back?' Nora asked.

Sephy felt the flash of guilt and shook her head at her sister. She'd arrived home from Luke's so off-kilter, so tired after the launch the night before, that she'd really felt that if her mum did want to talk to her about selling up, she'd lose it. So she'd chickened out.

'No doubt she'll corner me over the next couple of days. It'll be fine.'

The declaration didn't unravel the knots in her stomach, but rather made her feel antsy and breathless. No matter how many times she told herself she'd listen to whatever her mother wanted to tell her, with grace and an open heart, she had a feeling hearing the words was going to make her control snap.

Giving up on work she packed it all away with the sound of Nora's resumed typing and Ethan's soft snoring in the background. Then, rising to her feet, she gently pulled Daisy off Luke's lap and sat back down with her sleeping daughter cradled in her arms.

Pressing a kiss to the top of her daughter's head, she stroked the hair away from her face and thought about how she was going to work her fingers to the bone to ensure she had an income coming in for her.

It was a solid plan and it had to be her sole focus.

When her eyes, of their own accord, drifted to the man sitting opposite her, her breath hitched. Add one more thing needing her attention or her consideration, and she would muck everything up. She knew she would. Yet, disappointment crashed through her because it felt like she was limiting herself – and what if one day she had to watch Luke kissing another woman the way he'd kissed her? Would she be strong enough to see that and remain his friend?

Suddenly Luke's eyes opened and he stared straight at her. His eyes shifted from sexily slumberous to alpha-hot shrewd in a nanosecond, so that she felt as if he was stealing into her soul to see what she was thinking.

She felt hot and exposed and vowed she wouldn't forget she had plans and choices.

She didn't have to give up her focus on Seraphic. And she didn't have to allow herself to be seduced by Luke. She told herself she wasn't developing a weakness for him. She was strong.

In the muted light of the hotel's restaurant, with wedding chatter as the conversational backdrop, Luke watched Sephy try to stifle a yawn.

The last few days were bound to be catching up with her, but there was something more going on. She'd been tense when they'd landed, but the tension had been wound even tighter since they'd all emerged from their rooms to meet up with Isobel, Jared and Amanda for an evening meal. Energy and emotion fizzed under Sephy's skin. She was definitely het up about something.

Could it be her and him?

The look in her eyes when he'd woken up on the plane and caught her staring…like she wanted him but had told herself she couldn't have him.

Luke looked down into his drink, swirled the amber liquid against the ice and refused to allow the thought to take hold that it was because he wasn't good enough. He'd left that nonsense behind years ago.

Glancing back up, he found her gaze locked on him.

He knew she knew that kiss in his garden was about as far removed from acting as possible. Was the mixing in of emotion why she had reminded herself they couldn't have each other, because he was damned if he could remember why they couldn't any more.

Tipping his drink in salute to her, he lifted the glass to his lips and took a sip. Sephy frowned a little and looked away and he noted her twisting one of the charms on the bracelet he'd given her.

Maybe she was worried about leaving the business for even a few days. He knew she had something against weddings, but there was no way she would miss her brother's wedding – not even for her business. She wasn't that selfish.

Amanda had to call Sephy's name twice to draw her back into the conversation and when Sephy did turn her head to listen it was like she was more observer than participant. Luke realised he recognised the emotion hiding out at the back of her eyes. It was the look that said she was waiting. Waiting for the inevitable to happen. The question was: what was the inevitable for her? Definitely something to do with her mother, he thought. Sephy's gaze kept going to her before flitting onto anyone else.

'So, I have you all booked into the spa tomorrow at noon for manis and pedis,' Amanda was saying.

'No way.' Jared gave an exaggerated shudder. 'I absolutely draw the line.'

'You know I'm talking about the girls.' Amanda gave her fiancé a little elbow-to-ribs action. 'Sephy, I was asking if it's okay for Daisy to get one too?'

'Yes, Mummy, can I?'

Sephy smiled weakly at her daughter. 'Well, I guess it is for a special occasion.'

'Great,' Amanda said, laughing at Daisy's clapping. 'It's all organised, then. You'll have your spa sessions and then you need to make your way to the bridal suite that I've booked so that we can all get ready. I don't care what you guys do,' Amanda said, turning to Jared.

'Really?' Jared returned with a huge grin.

'Okay – within reason. But seriously, how much trouble can you get into when you haven't even organised anything?'

'Prepare to be amazed…this is how real men organise.' Jared looked at Ethan and Luke. 'Gentlemen. Tomorrow. Sports bar. With my friend Mikey and a few other friends and business associates. You both in?'

'In,' answered Ethan, lifting his glass in toast.

'Doubly in,' answered Luke, lifting his own glass.

Jared smiled at his bride-to-be.

Amanda sighed. 'Well as long as you are ready to stand in front of the celebrant at the appointed time. With all your limbs in working order,' she tacked on.

'Yours too,' Nora told Ethan.

The table waited for Sephy to warn Luke he'd better arrive in one piece as well, but she missed her cue.

Luke didn't miss the look that passed between Jared and Nora.

Nor did he miss the interested look Isobel gave her daughter. 'Sephy,' Isobel said softly, 'perhaps we could have that talk tomorrow during our spa session?'

Luke saw Sephy's shoulders tighten. What the hell was going on?

'I think it should wait until after the wedding, when we're back at home,' Sephy said slowly.

'I don't. I really wanted to have spoken to you by now.'

'I told you. What with the launch and,' she flicked a flushed look to Luke, 'what not, I didn't have time. I'm sorry.'

'It really can't wait any longer, Sephy,' Isobel King insisted.

'Fine,' Sephy said. 'Why don't we have it now?'

'Now? But –' Isobel scanned the rest of the table.

'Fine,' Sephy repeated in a less-controlled, spikier tone. 'If we need privacy, then I should be putting Daisy to bed anyway, so why don't you come with me and we'll talk in my room.'

'All right.'

Mindful of Daisy, everyone sitting at the table said their goodnights, but when Isobel obviously waited for Sephy to tell Luke her plans, he stepped in to cover the awkwardness.

'I can put Daisy to bed and stay with her if you and Isobel want to talk in the bar, or something?'

'No. It's better in private. Thank you,' and then with a quick look at her mother, Sephy reached back to Luke and brushed a quick kiss over his cheek. He caught the fine tremor in the hand that rested on his shoulder.

'Come back down to the bar for a drink afterwards,' he said.

'I can't. I won't leave Daisy.'

Isobel stepped forward. 'I think that would be a good idea. I can stay with Daisy. In fact, let's talk in my suite. She can sleep in the spare bed tonight and that way you don't have to worry about her.'

Luke watched as Sephy bent down to look at her daughter. 'Daisy, do you want to camp in Grandma's suite tonight?'

'Can Rabbit come too?'

'Absolutely.'

'Yay,' Daisy bounced up and down and hitched Rabbit to her side.

Sephy stood back up, picked up the cup of coffee that had been sitting untouched in front of her and drank the whole lot down in one go. 'Right, then, say goodnight to everyone, Daisy.'

Amidst kisses and hugs for Daisy, Luke watched Isobel and Sephy. Both women looked as if they were quietly preparing for battle. Standing up, he reached out and took hold of Sephy's hand. Leaning in, he said quietly, 'I'll be right here or in the bar if you need me, okay?'

Sephy stared at him for a few seconds and then squared her shoulders, pasted on a smile and nodded her head. None of her actions convinced him she didn't feel incredibly vulnerable, but before he could drag her close for a life-affirming kiss, or something, she was breaking contact and walking away with her daughter and her mother.

Luke took his seat back at the table, aware of the uneasy silence. Whatever was about to go down, they all knew about it.

Except him – he didn't know.

Luke hated being the last to find out about things. It wasn't how he liked to organise his life now.

'Maybe I should go up with them,' Jared said.

'And what?' Nora asked, pushing at the handle of her coffee cup.

'Mum shouldn't be laying this on her right before my wedding.'

'It might turn out fine,' Amanda soothed.

'What if Sephy can't handle it?'

'She'll handle it,' Nora said determinedly. 'She handles everything life throws at her.'

'Damn it.' Jared pushed his coffee away in a show of frustration. 'You want to know how crap I feel that I don't know her well enough to be able to say that? To trust that?'

'Then trust me when I tell you she'll handle it,' Nora said. 'I know the timing's bad but the sooner she knows, the better.'

'What do you think?' Jared asked Ethan.

Ethan ran his hand over the back of his head. 'I think I've been in a few disaster zones in my time and this has all the markings of another.'

'I knew it,' Jared said. 'Right. I'm going up there.'

'I really wouldn't if I were you,' Ethan said quietly. 'You can't stop it from happening and you'll only inflame the situation if you wade in there and try to tell either of them what to do or say.'

'Ethan's right. If you go up there now you'll only remind her of Dad.'

'Let it play out and be around to help any casualties after,' Ethan offered.

Luke felt as if he was one head-turn away from a serious case of whiplash as the Kings et al talked about Sephy like she was about to hear something absolutely devastating.

'Okay, enough,' he interrupted, making sure he eye-balled everyone sitting at the table. 'Someone want to clue me in on what the hell's going on?'

Shocked silence as they all looked at him as if they'd genuinely forgotten he was there.

'Well?' he bit out, waiting.

'Look, no offense,' Jared said, meeting Luke's stare head-on, 'but, no. If Sephy hasn't already told you, then no one sitting at this table is going to say anything.'

He got it.

He wasn't family.

Another time he was sure he'd have found their loyalty to their sister commendable. But right now he wanted answers so he could figure out how best to help Sephy.

'Nora,' he looked over at her, knowing she had always liked the fact that he and Sephy were friends.

'I'm sorry, Luke. If she wants you to know –'

'She'll tell me?' Luke finished. He wasn't so sure. He was beginning to suspect there were a lot of things Sephy didn't share with him. Not that he could blame her. When it came to opening family wounds he wasn't exactly Mr Tear and Share himself, was he?

'Maybe what I'm saying is if anyone can drag it out of her, you can,' Nora told him.

Luke's laugh was laced with sarcasm. 'Yes, because out of all you Kings she's the only one who responds to interrogation, isn't she?'

'You obviously have something to say about how we conduct ourselves as a family,' Jared confronted him, 'no need to be shy. Spit it out.'

'Jared,' Amanda reached out to squeeze her fiancé's arm. 'Luke's just trying to look out for Sephy. You would do the same for me if the situation was reversed.'

Luke was submitted to a long appraisal, which he had no problem absolutely not backing down from. Finally, as if satisfied, Jared inclined his head and said, 'I apologise. The last thing we need is to start a war zone down here.'

Luke took his time with his own appraisal. Sephy wasn't going to be too enamoured with him if he made things worse for her and her big brother, especially at the family gathering for his wedding. 'Fine. I really don't have a right to comment on your family dynamics. I got a little carried away.'

'Only natural,' Jared appeased. 'You and Sephy are obviously much closer than I realised.'

'We are. Now, how about we all move to the bar for drinks and Sephy can find us when she's ready.'

By the time Luke spied Sephy entering the crowded bar an hour later, the conversation had shifted to embarrassing stag dos and Ethan was recounting waking up with an unfinished dragon tattoo on his back.

Luke drowned out the laughter and focused on Sephy. Her usual innate sexiness had been replaced with a brittle, haughty demeanour that still held the power to draw more than one man's gaze, but she looked to be completely oblivious to that.

As he watched, she headed straight for the bar, her heels clacking a sharp staccato, her back ramrod straight, her fingers clenched against her clutch.

'Excuse me,' he murmured, getting up from the table to head straight over to her.

He told the barman to put whatever she was having on his tab. Sephy didn't even react. It wasn't until he reached out and stroked a finger down her forearm that she turned her head to look at him.

'Hey you,' he greeted, gently.

Her eyes were red from crying.

Luke's heart hammered in his chest. Sephy never cried.

When the double vodka was put down before her, she picked it up and drank the whole lot down in one go.

'Better?' he asked.

'I will be. After another.'

Luke signalled to the bartender for another.

'We have a table over in the corner, or you and I can stand at the bar for a while and talk.'

Sephy looked over her shoulder, 'Jared and Nora at the table with you?'

'Yes.'

Sephy took a slower sip of her drink.

'You've been crying,' he said, hoping to get her to open up and tell him what had upset her so that maybe he could fix it.

'It's fine.' Sephy turned her head as if to search for the table and then turned back to the bar, picked up her drink and drank half the second vodka down. She stared down into the glass for a moment. 'Screw it,' she muttered, making a move towards the table where her family was sitting.

Luke shot out his hand and caught her by the upper arm, forestalling any further movement. 'Are you sure you want to head over there right now? You seem a little,' he hesitated as her eyes turned fiery, which was maybe better than the crushed look she had been wearing when she had come down. Maybe. 'Het up.'

Sephy paused for a second and then, seemingly having made her mind up about something, shook free from his hold and said, 'I am. And this isn't going to wait.'

CHAPTER THIRTEEN

Sephy sat down on the seat Luke pulled out for her, hugging her vodka close like a security blanket.

'Well, it's official,' she delivered into the expectant silence. 'Mum's definitely selling the estate.' Damn, but her words were coming out too bright and too brittle, but hiding how she felt was impossible. For days, ever since her siblings had mentioned what her mother might be thinking of doing, she'd been feeling like she was tied to train tracks, waiting endlessly for the impact of her mother's intentions to hit her. Now that she'd been run over with the news, instead of feeling flattened, she felt adrenalised. Like an accident victim who doesn't accept they've been hurt until their body or mind gives up on them.

'We might leave you to it,' Ethan said, with a nod towards Amanda.

'I'll see you afterwards in our room,' Nora told him quietly.

Amanda got up from the table and leant down to give Jared a quick kiss. 'Text me later and we'll have a drink before you head over to Mikey's for the night.'

As she watched Ethan and Amanda depart from the table, Sephy realised Luke hadn't moved as much as a muscle. She cast him a quick look and got a full dose of, 'Seriously, if you want me to leave you, you're going to have to make me.' She considered it for a moment because this was a family thing and she didn't want to drag him into it, but then she thought she should save her energy for what she was about to have to ask her brother and sister. With a shrug for him she took another sip of her vodka and waited for its numbing affect.

But she didn't experience the numbness she craved. Instead the shot of alcohol fuelled the maelstrom of emotion already churning, twisting and turning inside of her, making her feel sick. What she probably needed was another double, but as if Luke could tell that was what she was thinking, he slid the jug of water closer towards her.

Ignoring the pitcher of iced water she raised her glass of vodka in a toast. 'To homelessness.'

'Seph,' Nora said quietly and Sephy really wished her sister could have withheld the note of chiding because it only made lashing out easier.

'What? Too dramatic?'

'You know it won't come to that,' her sister asserted.

'Do I? Hey, maybe Daisy and I could house-sit for you and Ethan when you're in the field?'

Nora said nothing, but she did reach over for the water and poured herself a large glass to place next to her glass of red wine.

'Jared? What do you say?' Sephy looked to her brother. 'Should Daisy and I relocate to New York? That penthouse of yours is so big. You and Amanda are bound to rattle around in it.'

Jared was obviously under the impression she needed to get this all out of her system because he too chose wisely to remain silent. Even if that muscle in his jaw was ticking double-time.

'Why will you be homeless if your mother sells the estate? Luke asked, turning in his seat to study her.

Sephy flipped her hair over her shoulder in a delaying tactic, although she might as well get it out there and tell him the sorry details. He was going to find out soon enough anyway because there was no way the King estate would take long to sell. It was prime real estate.

The breath she dragged in made her feel light-headed.

Briefly she wondered where her pride had slunk off to and

figured it had probably headed for the bar the moment she'd begged her mother to wait a year so she had a chance at getting together enough income to go to the bank and ask for a loan. 'Why will I be homeless? Well, because I have zero money to my name. Dad put it all into a trust fund for Daisy – which,' she said adamantly, 'I was absolutely fine with, being that I'm determined Seraphic will make enough money to support us both. You two,' she said, looking back at her brother and sister, 'were the ones who kept offering me money.' She paused and gathered the courage to ask the questions she was afraid of hearing the answers to. 'Did you know that Mum had wanted to sell all along? Is that why you kept offering me money? Because you should have just said. At least I'd have had time to –' *get past it. Get okay with it. Get over all those stupid pipe dreams I kept building in my head.*

'We offered you money,' Jared replied, his voice tight, 'because how the hell do you think we felt when Dad gave us each an inheritance and tied up all of yours? Do you have any idea how hard it has been to stand by and do nothing out of respect for your wishes? Do you know what it has done to Mum to see you struggle?'

'I am *not* struggling for money,' she said, barely keeping a lid on her voice rising high enough to deafen the whole bar. 'You're seeing what you want to see because you don't have any faith in me. None of you do.'

'How can you think that?' Nora interjected, dismay and concern etched across her face.

'I don't just think it,' Sephy flung back. 'I *know* it. I *feel* it.' The fissure she thought she'd sutured up inside her chest burst open all over again and in the silent fallout she felt the shame of uttering the words aloud.

'This is complete bullshit, Sephy,' Jared said and when Nora went to lay a warning hand on his arm he shook his head and told her, 'No. She needs to hear this. If none of us had any faith in you,' he said, skewering Sephy with a look that reminded her so much of their father it was hard to hear over the drumming of her heart, 'why the hell would we have supported you through getting Seraphic up and running? Mum is selling because the estate is too much for her now Dad has gone. There are too many memories. Watching you pull yourself together after what Dad wrote to you, watching you tell us all to forgive and to heal filled her with pride. She knew that you understood he would never have meant those words to come across the way they did – but if she can see a way of easing the financial pressure on you by giving you some of the proceeds from the sale of the estate… You can't tell us you wouldn't do the same for your daughter.'

That was beside the point.

Sephy drained the glass of vodka.

They didn't get it. How could they not get it?

'He wrote Mum a letter too,' she whispered.

'What?' Nora's hand crept up to her mouth.

She forced herself to look at her brother and sister and the shock on their faces told her that at least they hadn't known about that – at least her mum and brother and sister hadn't all been worrying about what to do about poor little Sephy.

'He wrote her a letter and told her that it was okay to sell whenever she was ready to and that after taking out a specified amount of money for her to find a house, the rest should be ploughed back into KPC.'

'There must be some mix-up,' Nora insisted. 'He told me I could sell KPC if I wanted. He would never have wanted millions ploughed into the company if he thought I would sell it.'

'Maybe he knew you would never sell,' Sephy replied. 'Maybe he knew you would choose to keep KPC even if you didn't actively run the company.' It hurt more than she could put into words that her father knew Nora would keep KPC and that KPC would get investment for years, but that the house and estate would be lost to them all.

Frustration and sadness blended with the anger and hurt.

Because from the lack of instant reaction from Jared and Nora – they still didn't get it.

'The estate has been in our family for generations,' she said, trying to prompt them into feeling as lost and aggrieved as she was. She had always known that the heart of Jeremy King beat mostly for KPC, but she had always believed he had at least had his roots deep in the land she called her home. Never, ever would she have believed that having her connection to the estate severed would make her feel like this. But the estate was her shelter. It had provided a haven for her and Daisy when they'd needed it most. She took strength from the family links there.

She couldn't imagine not even being able to visit.

'How could he do that? How could she?' she asked, her voice barely a whisper.

'Mum will have only wanted to see you financially secure,' Nora soothed.

'I don't care what she wants. I don't care what he wanted. Not if they thought selling would be the answer.' She leant forward, her hands pressing against the white linen tablecloth as if she could pull them closer to her side of the argument. 'Don't you care that it's not being left to either of you?'

Nora and Jared exchanged a look and her heart started to race.

It was inconceivable to her that neither of them loved it like – it turned out – she did. Inconceivable that they wouldn't want the King homestead for themselves. For the family they were each going to have. For their connection to their father.

For roots.

For family.

For all that the estate could be.

'Jared, please,' she implored. 'I know you didn't want KPC, but you must at least want the estate?'

'I'm sorry, honey. My home is New York. Here is where I put down roots.'

Sephy swallowed hard. 'Nora?'

'I know it's the only place you've ever lived, but my roots aren't there either, any more. My home is with Ethan and that's London, or wherever we end up.'

Sephy shook her head and refused to give up. With all her pride left out on the table in front of them she did what she had resisted doing every time they had offered her help. She asked them for money. 'You could both buy the estate and I'll manage it for you.'

'I know this is hard,' Jared said. 'But I seriously doubt Nora and I could raise the millions needed. Most of our money is tied up in the businesses and investments.'

That was it? When it came down to it they weren't even fussed about raising the funds?

'You could raise the money if you tried. We could all do it together. You can't let it go. You can't.'

'Seph.'

She wouldn't let herself hear the gentle compassion in Luke's voice.

'No.' Sephy felt the sob rise up in her throat, but she'd gone too far to stop. Looking at Jared and Nora she implored, 'I can't be the only one out of the three of us who wants it. Don't make it be me. You know he would hate that.' Not when it turned out she was the only one who had ever dreamt up plans for it.

'Of course he wouldn't hate that,' Nora said, reaching out to try and hold her hand, but Sephy couldn't bear the pity in her sister's voice and so she snatched her hand away.

'You have to help me change Mum's mind.'

'I won't put that on her,' Nora said.

'You can count me out, too,' Jared said firmly. 'No way am I guilting her into anything. We might not be willing to raise the millions needed to keep the estate in our name, but you know we'll give you the money to buy a decent place for yourself and Daisy, and enough for you to get Seraphic through its first business year in profit. Don't allow self-interest to stop Mum from being happy.'

Self-interest? Sephy stared at them as if they were crazy. She had wanted to build a legacy for her daughter. How could that be construed as selfish?

Her heart was breaking because although she could understand them protecting their mother, she simply couldn't believe they didn't want the estate enough.

She thought about how she had felt reading her father's letter to her. How his lack of faith in her had cut right through to the deepest corner of her soul.

Was this some sort of test? Was she supposed to give up on fighting for something she hadn't even realised she wanted and just let it be taken from her? *Was* she supposed to let it go? And in doing so let her father go all over again?

'So that's it?' There really was no point hiding the bitterness from her voice, 'One lousy discussion and the baby of the family is firmly put back in her place?'

'Perhaps if you stopped acting like the baby of the family…' Nora came right back at her with.

'Are you serious?' Sephy stared at Nora open-mouthed. 'What? Dad says it's okay to sell and straight away you're "Whatever he wants"? I thought you'd stopped following and started l –'

'Do not even think about finishing that sentence, Sephy,' Jared said, standing up.

'And you,' she said, rising to her feet to stare Jared straight in the eye, 'you're going to up and run away again because the going gets –'

'Whoa, time-out.' Luke rose to his feet too. 'Let's end this before somebody says something they can never take back.'

'Stay out of it, Luke, this is a family thing. You wouldn't understand.'

'Seph, trust me. I do understand.' He reached out to clasp hold of her hand, leant in and said into her ear, 'Say goodnight and then you and I are going for a little walk to cool down.'

'What the hell,' Sephy felt the warmth of his breath in her ear, the stroke of his fingers over her hand and cursed that his quiet strength started to have an automatic calming effect on her. 'You can't order me about,' she said, not wanting to calm down because she needed to fight for the place she hadn't even known she couldn't bear to leave.

'This conversation is ending now,' Luke insisted. 'The three of you, along with your mother, are going to celebrate Jared's wedding tomorrow and a happy time is going to be had by all. If you can't do it for each other, do it for Amanda. Jared, I'll see you tomorrow in the foyer of the sports bar. Nora, Sephy will see you tomorrow for her spa session.'

Sephy broke free with the intention of heading straight for the bar to drown her sorrows.

'It's okay,' she heard Luke mutter to Jared and Nora. 'I'll look after her.'

She'd nearly made it to the bar before Luke caught up with her to steer her firmly in the opposite direction. 'You drink another couple of doubles and in the morning not only will you hate yourself for what you said to Jared and Nora, you'll be able to add a stinking hangover to the mess and your brother's wedding will go down in your family history as a day that sucked for you.'

'You don't understand. I need –'

'To cut a little loose, I know. Wait here,' he said, plonking her down in one of reception's large armchairs.

By rights, as soon as he wandered over to the concierge, she should have turned around and headed wherever the hell she wanted to. But, where would she go? Back up to her mother's suite for another go at dissuading her from selling? Left alone for a moment, all she really wanted to do was howl at the world and all the change it imposed on her. Sob that she was going to lose the home she loved and that last physical connection to her father.

Shame suddenly hit her right between the eyes, making her frown a little. Had she really accused Nora of kowtowing to their father, and Jared of running away whenever the going got tough? She shivered. What an almighty spectacular show of immaturity. Thank God Luke had been there to do what she'd been incapable of – make them all pull their punches.

She watched him as he conversed with the concierge. The concierge turned to look at her and humiliation washed over her afresh. Luke was probably asking for advice on where you took someone who needed to get a temper tantrum out of their system. A few more minutes of discussions and then Luke passed the concierge a bundle of notes in exchange for what looked like a key card. Her frown deepened as he turned to walk confidently back over to her.

When he reached her he held out his hand and without thinking twice she rose to her feet and placed her hand in his.

'Where are we going?' she asked as he pulled her over to the main bank of lifts.

'You'll see.'

In the lift, he entered the key card and punched the button for the top floor. Seconds later, the lift doors pinged opened and Sephy stepped out, her eyes going wide.

'This is the rooftop pool,' she claimed.

'As always your powers of deduction never fail to amuse me,' Luke said with a smile as he quoted her own quip back to her from the other day.

'But what are we doing here?'

Sephy took a couple of steps further into the room, admiring the beautiful inset backlit pool at its centre. Arrested by the way the water reflected against the walls of the pool and shone out to bounce off the glass walls and ceiling, peace and serenity started to coat all the adrenalin that had been coursing through her from the moment her mother had told her she wanted to sell the estate. Curiosity had her taking a couple more steps and before she knew it she was walking the perimeter of the pool. Palm trees in gigantic mosaic pots created private alcoves where loungers had been placed. Outside, the glow from competing sky-scrapers cast a mellowing hue on the night sky.

'We're here so that you can swim off some of that hurt that's bouncing around inside of you,' Luke said.

'What?' Of all the things she had expected him to say, that hadn't even been on the list. 'But I don't have a costume with me.'

Luke merely folded his arms and grinned at her.

The imp started letting loose in her before she had given it permission. 'You brought me up here to go skinny-dipping?'

'Sephy, you do know it's Heathstead's worst-kept secret that you have a wild streak running through you?'

Immediately she went hot all over. 'I am not that person any more. I haven't done anything wild since...' since Daisy was born, she finished silently.

'Yeah, yeah, you're the original responsible adult now. But do you see me running at the thought of seeing a flash of that wild streak?'

'I told you. That's not who I am any more.'

'To be fair, this hardly constitutes wild. For a start I'm the only person with the key, so no one else can get up here and I got the key from the concierge, so someone knows we're here. If that's not responsible, I don't know what is.'

'You had to give him money to get him to give you access. Clearly we're not supposed to be up here.'

Luke threw back his head and laughed. 'Wild we are, then. So, you going to strip or am I going to dump you in this pool as you are?'

'You wouldn't.'

'Want to bet?'

'I really don't see what you think swimming a few lengths of this pool is going to achieve?'

'You. In a state of bliss – or at least a state that will see you through Jared and Amanda's wedding tomorrow. You've been on the go for weeks. Swim some of that fear, exhaustion and hurt out of your system.'

He made it sound so easy. So therapeutic.

So tempting.

'All right. Let me go and get my costume and I'll meet you back here.'

Luke shook his head at her. 'This is a one-time offer. You walk back into that lift and you'll talk yourself out of coming back before you've even reached your room. And then you'll decide you need to check on Daisy and end up upsetting your mother again.'

'You think you know me that well?'

'Yeah.'

Sephy stared down at the water.

Luke clucked like a chicken and the sound echoed in the huge room.

Sephy felt her chin tilt up. Felt her hands plant themselves on her hips.

'Come on,' he teased, 'it's not like I haven't seen you in your underwear.'

She would absolutely *not* return his teasing smile.

'Strip and swim, Seph.'

'And while I'm swimming you will be...?'

'Keeping pace with you.'

The conversation with her mother and then downstairs with Jared and Nora suddenly all seemed further away.

She looked across the pool at him. 'I've never seen you in your underwear.'

His dimples flashed. 'I can go commando if you prefer.'

She watched as his hands went to his trouser fastening and her mouth dried up. 'I thought you were shy?'

'Like I said – never with you,' he reminded her.

Slowly Sephy reached for the tuxedo jacket she'd teamed with camisole, skinny jeans and high-heeled ankle boots and shrugged it off her shoulders. Was it really only going to take a proposition to swim in her underwear for her wild streak to bloom back to life? Or was it because it was Luke playing with the rebel in her?

Luke grinned but didn't move.

'How come you're not stripping?' she asked.

'For all I know you're hot and simply removing your jacket.'

'You think I'll chicken out?'

Luke folded his arms and waited.

Okay then.

Bending she slipped off her boots, but it was only when she reached for the hem of her silk camisole and pulled it loose from her jeans that Luke smiled and started to unbutton his shirt.

In seconds she had stripped to her underwear and with a shriek of delight she dived into the deep end, surfacing in the middle with a huge grin on her face. The water felt incredible.

Luke hit the water moments later and in unison they struck out for the far end of the pool.

Up and down.

Matching each other for pace.

Smoothly cutting through the water.

And with each length Sephy felt the knots in the pit of her stomach loosening until finally her lungs tired and her pace slowed and when she next reached the side she stopped and put her elbows up on the ledge of the pool to rest.

Luke swam silently up beside her and mimicked her pose. He wasn't even breathing hard. Sephy let her feet tread water and her mind float. If anyone had told her a few hours ago that she'd be swimming in a closed pool on top of this five-star hotel at close to midnight she wouldn't have believed them. But somehow Luke had known that up here all the hurt would begin to feel manageable.

The water took away all the energy she had for fighting, which was good because fighting with her family always reminded her of being young and feeling every slight too keenly.

'You know,' Luke said casually, 'if you're really worried about being homeless, you and Daisy could always move in with me.'

CHAPTER FOURTEEN

Sephy's heart scudded to a stop. If ever she was presented with an opportunity to take a miss-step, Luke's absurdly generous offer was surely it.

Live with him?

As house mates?

Because they were best mates?

Even though lately it felt like they were only one step away from becoming *bed mates…*

No. It was a completely, utterly, ridiculously ill-thought-out idea that she would be insane to even contemplate.

Turning from the pool's edge to swish her hands back and forth through the water, she said slowly, quietly, firmly, 'Thank you, but no.'

'Seriously, you know the house is too big for me,' Luke said, oblivious to the panic edging under her skin as he warmed to his theme. 'You've already made it more homely. Don't you think Daisy would like a bigger room? It's closer to her school, so more time for you to spend on Seraphic.'

'It's very generous of you,' she said, deliberately making her voice dull and, she hoped, final.

Luke regarded her thoughtfully. 'Is generosity the only reason you think I'm offering?'

'I guess I don't know if you're asking or offering,' she countered.

'What's the difference?'

What was the difference? Sephy bit down on her tongue. One meant he wanted them to live together. The other one meant he felt bad about her and Daisy needing to find somewhere to live.

One made her skittish, the other like she was a charity case.

She studied the water moving through her fingers.

Luke watched her for a while and then said, 'Well, the offer's there.'

To stop herself from responding, she ducked down further into the water, feeling the level bob against her lips. The sensation only made her think of his mouth against hers. If she moved in with him, she could definitely see herself wanting more of his mouth, more of him…more of them.

She lifted her head from the water and went back to moving her fingers back and forth around her.

'So now that there's at least twenty-five floors between you and your brother and sister,' Luke said, 'tell me instead why you haven't told them about your plans for the estate?'

Emotion swam immediately back up to the surface.

'I thought I had time to prove myself first. Stupid, huh?'

'No. Just surprising you would feel you needed that behind you.' As if Luke knew what was coursing through her, he jerked his finger towards the other end of the pool. 'You need to take in another couple of laps?'

She shot him a quick smile and turning, she stroked through the water, forcing herself to swim the knots out while Luke watched from the side.

Her very own private lifeguard.

In *and* out of the water, she realised, as she made the smooth turn and closed the distance back to him.

'Bit better?' he asked.

She nodded and then rolled her eyes. 'I hate feeling angry. It reminds me of hating KPC when I was younger.'

'Better to hate KPC than your father.'

'Oh, there were times when I hated him too.' Then, feeling bad, she added, 'but even hating him, I still loved him.'

Luke nodded. 'I know what it's like to have a parent obsessed with something to the point you realise they don't see you.' He turned his head to stare out of the windows in front of him. 'The difference was my mother wasn't obsessed with a business. She was obsessed with men,' there was a fraction of a pause, 'and later, drugs.'

Sephy needed a moment to absorb his words. She couldn't even begin to imagine what that meant he might have been through, but it definitely sounded like it had included emotional abandonment.

Above the sound of the pool's pump and the water lapping against the edge of the tiles, she asked, 'Do you know who your father is?'

'Nope.' Luke turned his head to meet her eyes, challenging her silently, and her heart filled up for everything she realised he hadn't had as a child.

'That must have been hard.'

Luke shrugged. 'I never knew any different and after I worked out the type of men my mother was drawn to and that they weren't exactly the type of men you'd want for a father, it got even easier.'

'Do you want to be a father one day?'

Green eyes stared unflinchingly back at her. 'Yes.'

There was no hesitation. No shadows in the green depths and she was pleased for him.

'Because of Steve Jackson?' she wondered aloud.

'He was the first male role model who acted like how I thought a father should act. He made the time. He imposed the boundaries. He didn't give up on me.'

Sephy thought about her own father. In hardly reacting to every boundary she'd overstepped, it had certainly felt as if he had given up on her. But now she had Daisy, she understood how difficult it was to choose those boundaries and impose them religiously. So what exactly would she have had her father do – lock her up?

'Did your father really not leave you any money?' Luke asked.

Her defence was automatic. 'He left me a huge amount. He just put it into Daisy's pot.'

'Maybe I can see why he did that,' Luke murmured thoughtfully. 'If Jared or Nora had had children, do you think he would have done the same?'

'That,' Sephy whispered, 'is the million-dollar question, isn't it?' The one she used to ask herself over and over until she decided the only way out of feeling like she'd deliberately been treated differently was simply to forgive. For Daisy, she had to be okay.

'How much do you figure the estate will go for?'

She tried for a casual shrug. 'I would think in excess of five million.'

Luke blew out a long whistle.

'Mmmn. Not exactly an amount within my reach. But, then, it's not really about the money.' Feeling her eyes fill with moisture she stared down at the surface of the water. 'It's about feeling like my chest was going to cave in when Mum told me,' she whispered.

'Yeah. Discovering you want something that badly will do that to you.'

Sephy whipped her head up to look straight into eyes that sharpened, darkened.

Butterflies beat their wings wildly inside of her and she turned back to face the edge of the pool so that she could cling to the tile. She concentrated on the ebb and flow of the water against her shoulders because she absolutely could not ask if he was still talking about the estate.

As if sensing he'd strayed into dangerous waters, Luke pushed a little away from the side and dipped fully under the water. When he came back up for air he shook his head and water droplets haloed around him as he grounded the subject again. 'Try not to feel too bad about tonight. I would have fought not to have to leave Lily and Steve's. I did fight.'

'How many places did you live before you got to the Jacksons'?'

'Too many.' He looked at her out of the corner of his eye. 'You know what sofa-surfing is?'

She shook her head and he grimaced. 'It's where you sleep on friends' sofas. In my case I slept on my mum's friends' sofas whenever we got evicted from our flat for not paying the bills.'

Sephy would never let herself do that to Daisy, no matter what she'd churlishly said downstairs to her brother and sister about living with them.

But then she didn't have an addiction.

'Did she spend all her money on drugs?' she asked softly.

Luke shook his head. 'Not in the early years. In the early years she spent it on whichever man paid her attention.' After a few moments he cleared his throat and added, 'Sometimes she'd go and live with them and if they didn't want me around I got dumped on her friends.'

'Where you slept on the sofa?'

'Or on the floor.'

Sephy asked herself what the hell she ever had to complain about from her childhood.

'You learn to be pretty quiet and as little trouble as possible,' Luke added matter-of-factly. No, she thought. It was worse than that. He had learned to be invisible.

'And I guess you learn to travel light,' she surmised, now understanding why his house had seemed so devoid of knick-knacks. It was a testament to who he was, she thought now, that he hadn't thrown her sentiment for the King estate back in her face.

'Self-preservation,' he admitted, his voice low. 'Bed down for the night. Get up. Leave no trace. I'd been at the Jacksons' three months before I felt comfortable not packing my bag before I went to sleep at night.'

His name slipped from her lips on a whisper of pain for him.

'I might not have lived in one place long enough to put down the kind of roots you have,' Luke continued, 'but I understand why you wouldn't willingly give that up. By the time I got to Lily and Steve's I'd been placed, or been forced to bunk down, in fifteen different homes.'

Sephy bit back a gasp. 'But that's more than one a year.'

'A few times she placed me in temporary foster care, always working hard with the authorities to get me back when it didn't work out with the guy. Then, she started seeing someone new and within weeks he'd introduced her to drugs. It got really bad and I,' he paused and heaved out a breath. 'I couldn't stay there. So I volunteered for temporary foster care and ended up with the Jacksons.'

She wanted to touch him. Ease some of the conflict in his voice, but she didn't want to stop him from talking either.

'Part of the agreement I signed, and because Steve and Lily wouldn't have had it any other way, was that I had to maintain some contact with her. I'd been seeing her once a fortnight for six months, the most regular contact I'd had, and then,' he frowned, then seemed to gather himself, 'that was it. One night she fatally overdosed and I got to stay with Steve and Lily permanently.'

'I'm so sorry.' Sephy whispered, knowing it couldn't have been as cut and dried as he made the words sound.

Luke acknowledged her and then his gaze slid away to stare hard at the water. 'I was relieved.'

'No one could blame you for feeling that,' she insisted. 'It can't have been easy – having to re-establish a relationship with her. Working out where your boundaries were – you must have wished it was her setting high standards for you, not the other way around.'

Luke sighed and said quietly, 'Mostly I wish she'd had higher standards for herself.'

'But maybe she had no one to show her that when she was younger?'

'Yeah. You just figured out what it took me years to learn.'

She wanted to take away the cloudiness from the green of his eyes. Help him feel better, the way he always made her feel better. 'Hey, want to race me a couple of lengths?'

Luke frowned, as if confused by the lack of judgement and follow-up questions. He studied her for a moment and then said slowly, 'I've never noticed any swimming trophies at your place.'

'I didn't notice any at yours, either,' she countered.

'So we're pretty evenly matched.'

Sephy threw back her head and laughed. She pushed off from the side and looked over her shoulder. 'I'm a King. You think I'm not going to give it everything to win?'

He laughed and then somehow, without looking like he was even exerting himself, he was in front of her, his magnificent six-pack and broad shoulders made for racing. She made every effort to keep up, but for once, instead of her competitive nature overriding what she was doing, she was content to let him swim off some of his own hurt.

He beat her by half a length, his chest pushing in and out as he leaned his elbows back on the ledge and waited for her to swim up to him.

'So what are you going to do about the estate?' he asked.

Sephy stared up through the glass roof and tried to feel okay about it all. 'I guess I'm going to let it go,' she said, aiming to keep her voice light.

'Just like that?'

'I'll get over it,' she said, thinking that after what Luke had gone through it was time for her to face this latest news and thank her lucky stars that she had at least got to put down roots.

Roots, she knew, grew again as long as you tended them. Wherever she ended up, Daisy would be with her and she'd have Seraphic too. She wasn't going to be left out in the cold like Luke had been for so much of his life.

'You really think it's that easy to let go of something that's inveigled its way into your heart?' he asked, studying her again.

'No.'

'So how are you going to do it?'

'Like I get over everything else, I guess.'

'Ah,' Luke nodded sagely, 'mustn't forget the key King trait. You're going for stubbornly, then?'

She flicked water playfully at his chest. 'I prefer determinedly.'

He flicked water back.

Sephy laughed and pushed away from the edge to spin around and around in the water. When she became aware that Luke was quietly watching her from his position at the side of the pool she stopped.

Awareness whispered across the water between them and, as quickly as that, those butterflies came back.

'Thank you for tonight,' she said, her words carrying huskily across the body of water between them. His friendship had helped her expel the suffocating shock from her system so that she could breathe easier, rally from the hurt and box up some of the negativity so that she would enjoy her brother's wedding tomorrow.

'For what?' Luke responded with a smile. 'For forcing you to strip down to your underwear and making you undertake physical exercise?'

'For stopping me before I went too far downstairs. For having my back. For sharing about Claire.'

Luke pushed away from the side of the pool and swam over to her to tread water in front of her. 'Kiss me and we're even.'

At his outrageous flash of dimples she laughed again. 'How about we don't, but you can say we did?'

Luke's grin grew bigger. 'What happened to letting loose? You know that wickedly wild part of you wants to.'

Sephy watched the water droplets clinging to his shoulders and before she knew what she was doing she was leaning forward a little.

Because yes, now that he mentioned it, that wickedly wild part of her did want to.

Because he was gorgeous and strong and patient and kind and had a mouth that, when it was on her, had the power to make the butterflies always burst free from her.

Luke reached both his hands forwards, hooked his thumbs under her bra straps and pulled her forward until they were nose to nose.

Her hands automatically clamped onto his shoulders and her legs encircled his hips. She felt his strong arms come around her and his hands rest at either side of her waist. Water lapped seductively all around them.

'How is it that lately we always manage to end up back here?' she said breathily.

'Tell me where "here" is.'

'Oh, one small step away from indulgence.'

'And there was me thinking it was just a kiss.'

She stared into gorgeous green eyes. 'Okay, then,' and closing the distance, she dropped a quick chaste kiss on his lips.

Leaning back in his arms she raised her gaze to his and saw raw, undiluted heat.

'Luke,' she whispered in protest, but the protest was weak and when Luke didn't let go she didn't pull away either. 'No fair. I'm just needy enough right now to say, okay, let's indulge ourselves and to hell with afterwards and consequences.'

Luke's hand reached up between them to gently tilt her face up to his so that she couldn't hide from him. 'Needy? Or needing me, and this,' he questioned before covering her mouth with his.

He tasted like he was starved, drank like he was dehydrated, took like he was possessed.

She matched him kiss for kiss. Nip for nip. Lick for lick. Slipping speedily under his spell.

Her fingers went into his hair as she stretched her head back to allow him access to the line of her throat, her breasts… anywhere he wanted. When she felt him release the catch on her bra and then felt his hands move up to hers to free her hold on him, she didn't protest. She wanted to feel him skin on skin. So much so that when he peeled the wet material from her she took it from him and flung it up onto the concrete floor.

Luke's gaze raked boldly over her. 'Jesus, Sephy, you take my breath away.'

Fierce longing exploded in her chest because he took her breath away too. She aligned her body with his and loved that he breathed in sharply, that his body went rock-hard with awareness, his hands automatically sliding to her waist as if to steady himself – steady both of them.

She wound her arms around his shoulders and lay her mouth on the tight cords of his neck. She felt him shudder as she opened her mouth to lightly bite, grinning against his skin as he groaned and moved against her in the water.

He pulled her head back so that she was staring into his hooded, intense gaze. 'You've always taken my breath away, Seph.'

She closed her eyes because tonight with her family she had surely shown him past her defences to the structure underneath and the shaky foundations.

'Don't,' he commanded, pulling her in close again. 'All you need to think about is that this is mutual between us. *Mutual*,' he repeated, and as if to seal the truth between them, he took possession of her mouth again, his tongue stroking hers as he dragged her under the water, where there was no noise, no distractions. Only she and Luke entwined in a crystal body of warm blue enchantment.

When they touched the bottom of the pool, Luke pushed them back up to the surface so that they came out of the water breathing hard before then kissing again. Deep, drugging, can't-believe-we-haven't-been-doing-this-from-the-beginning kisses that fed the fevered want between them so that she tightened her legs around his waist and moved against the long, hard length of him, desperate for escalation, and seeking fulfilment.

Luke groaned and moved his hands to either side of her hips

to hold her still against him as he tore his mouth from hers and, breathing hard, brought his forehead to rest against hers.

'Better not start something I can't finish,' he panted.

She wasn't even aware she was pouting or that her hand had travelled the length of his impressive torso, needing to keep touching him, until she felt his hand clamp around her wrist. 'Sephy, you'd tempt a saint but I'm no saint and I don't have any protection.'

'Oh.'

'Yes. Oh.'

She couldn't believe she hadn't thought about that and she was the one with a daughter. Her only excuse was that Luke made it so incredibly hard to think through the veil of yearning.

Hesitantly she turned to swim back to the side of the pool, but when she made to lift herself out of the water, Luke was there behind her, his hands staying her.

'Wait. I won't leave you as tied up in knots as when I brought you here,' and one of his hands went into the wet rope of her hair to move it aside so that his lips could string soft, barely there kisses across her shoulder blades.

Sephy's breath grew shallow as she chased the sensation, trying to anticipate where his lips would travel next.

'Hold onto the ledge,' he instructed as he unwound his hand and lowered it into the water to slip beneath the material of her bikini briefs and slide deftly into her folds.

'Luke,' his name released from her mouth on a moan and her head slammed back against his chest as his fingers found her clitoris and circled, stroked and lightly pinched.

'Let me take care of you,' he groaned.

Her hands clutched against the hard edge of the pool as his fingers moved to stroke up into her. Her inner muscles contracted. 'I –' she shook her head, unable to form words. Unable to do anything but arch against his back and move against his hand as his fingers stroked in and out and the need for release built and built.

'Look up at the stars, Seph. Look up at them and let loose.'

Sephy looked up through the glass ceiling to the inky sky above, with all its stars twinkling and sparkling. She moaned as Luke increased the pressure and speed and the pleasure was so intense and made her fly so high that surely she could reach up to pluck one of those stars clean from the sky.

As if he knew exactly what would push her over the edge, he raked his lips down the side of her neck to bite where neck met shoulder. It was the extra she needed to have her body tightening and contracting as it bowed in climax against him.

Her breath heaved in and out and her heart felt like it could hardly be contained in her body and all the while Luke nuzzled her neck and soothed her beautifully through to the end of the ride.

'Feel good?' he whispered into her ear.

Sephy nodded, her hand releasing from the ledge to reach behind her, around the back of his neck and gently squeeze because she wasn't sure she could find voice to express just how good.

Luke pressed a light kiss at the base of her neck and gently removed his hand from between her legs. 'You should probably get out of this pool before I forget again that I don't have any protection with me.'

Again she nodded and prayed her heavy, sated limbs would actually lend her the strength to haul herself over the side of the pool. With a sigh she placed her palms on the cold hard tiles and was grateful when Luke put his hands on her hips and boosted her out of the water. Out of his arms and with her feet on solid ground reality had room to return.

She didn't welcome its intrusion. Greedily, she only wanted to be with Luke.

'Let me get a couple of lengths in and then I'll come out,' Luke said, powering up and down the pool with quick, decisive strokes and she realised he was working some of his arousal off before coming out of the pool.

With shaking hands she bent to pick up her bra and put it back on. Getting into her skinny jeans was going to be impossible. As Luke swam, she picked up her cami, balled it up and stuck it into the pocket of her tuxedo jacket. She really hoped the jacket would be long enough to cover her modesty. With any luck no one would be on their floor when they returned to their rooms.

Separate rooms?

She heard Luke climb out of the water, heard him slip his trousers and shirt on, and as she squeezed the excess moisture from her hair, her head tipped up and she captured a last glance of the stars.

She would never be able to look at the night sky without thinking of this. Without thinking of Luke taking care of her needs with a generosity that was as natural to him as breathing.

In the confines of the lift they stood silently side by side as the air pulsated around them. Sephy sucked on her bottom lip. She had got wickedly wild with Luke Jackson. She should be feeling mellow and sated and she was.

She was also feeling like she wanted to do it again.

And again and again.

That was what the air was crackling with now.

She shifted slightly to look at him, but he was staring resolutely ahead.

The lift doors opened and Luke pocketed the key card. Putting a hand out to stop her exiting he stepped out first to make sure they wouldn't bump into anyone. The gesture was so sweet she considered dropping the folded jeans and heels she was carrying and hauling him back into the lift for more wicked wildness.

Luke lifted his hand away and gestured for her to come out of the lift. They would get to his room first. How did she casually say goodnight after what they had just done.

At his door, Luke withdrew his wallet from his trousers and took out the key card for his room. 'Think you'll be able to sleep now?' he asked with a slow smile for her.

Was he kidding? She'd be up all night remembering, reliving, wondering…

Staring up at him she shook her head.

He reached out and stroked down the length of her wet hair. 'I can always take you through the first few levels of ZFF.'

Sephy took the key card from his hand and inserted it for him. It was his fault, she thought, as her heart dipped deep in her chest before righting itself and picking up steady pace. He'd been the one to bring out the wildness in her. He'd been the one to initiate her into how good it could be in his arms. Earlier tonight, she'd lost out on something she hadn't even known she wanted. She didn't want to lose out on this too. She pushed open his room door.

'I don't want to play ZFF. I don't want to play any games. Not any more,' and stepping over the threshold she turned, took his hand in hers and then pulled him into his room.

CHAPTER FIFTEEN

Inside his room, Sephy pushed Luke back against the door, her fingers going to his shirt to release buttons, and at each fresh inch of skin she exposed, she placed her lips and worshipped. Forget the chlorine from the pool – he tasted good. Better than good. He tasted like he was made for her consumption.

She came to the last button and yanked his shirt out of his trousers. His skin was still damp from the pool and she had to tug and push to get the material down his arms. When the shirt refused to float to the floor she forgot about releasing his cuffs and set about releasing him from his trousers instead. She wanted him naked. She wanted him inside her. She wanted him to make her soar again.

Luke's shirt-cuffed arms came up to still her movements. 'Sephy, wait.'

Wait? Was he kidding?

'Tell me you have condoms somewhere in this room,' she groaned out, moving in to skate her lips down the length of his throat and delighting in his sharp inhale of breath as she repaid his earlier kindness and used her teeth a little.

'I do have condoms in this room.'

She smiled against his skin. 'Then, strip,' she commanded. 'Please,' she added, looking up at him when he didn't move.

'You're absolutely sure about this?'

'You said this was mutual,' she accused, letting vulnerability creep in for the first time.

'Oh, it is. But you can want something for the wrong reasons.'

Sephy's gaze flicked up to Luke's, and then quickly away again. She wanted to seize the moment. She absolutely did not want to think about whether she was sublimating her wanting to keep her home with wanting to have Luke for a while.

'I just need to make sure this isn't pity sex,' Luke said quietly.

Sephy's head swung up to stare at him. 'What the hell?'

Luke grimaced and searched her eyes. 'It's a lot to take in – all the stuff I told you about my mother, about how I lived when I was younger.'

Shock had her not thinking before she spoke. 'Have women taken you to bed after you've told them before?'

He looked uncomfortable and God – that some complete idiot of a woman would treat him like that – or that he could even think she would do that to him. 'You know what,' she stepped forward to place her fingertips softly against his lips. 'Don't answer that. I'll answer for you.'

She could practically hear him grinding down on his molars as he braced to receive her answer.

'No, Luke,' she shook her head and smiled, 'this most definitely isn't going to be pity sex.' Her hands drifted up over his sculpted chest, across his shoulders, up his neck and into his hairline. She never, ever wanted Luke to think she pitied him. She was in awe of him. She'd wanted him way before sharing secrets in the pool. This past year had seen an escalation in their chemistry with all those looks… All those innuendoes… She really didn't know how she'd resisted him for so long because the heat had been building from the beginning and although at various points they'd both denied it, both of them had continued to stoke that fire. 'I'm pretty sure that the correct phrase to categorise what we're about to have is "hot, hard, fast, and intense" sex.'

Luke's breath hissed out.

'You okay with that?' she asked, chewing on the inside of her lip when he seemed to consider the question.

A grin that was wolf-wide and she had her answer. 'I believe you asked me to strip?'

'I'll help.'

Their stripping of each other on the way to the shower was done amid laughs and kisses and sighs and moans. When the hot steaming water rained down to cocoon them in a cloud of steam, they didn't even notice. They were too busy savouring the sensation of standing skin to skin, slippery, wet, and on fire for each other.

It was only as Luke snapped the water off and opened the shower door to reach for a huge fluffy white towel to envelop her in that the pace slowed enough for thinking to intrude.

As he hitched a towel around his hips and ran another over his head and chest, Sephy watched. She could hardly believe it had only been days ago that she'd been given to wonder how he could be shy with a body like his. But she knew now that his shyness was nothing to do with what he thought he looked like. His shyness was to do with being passed from place to place and waiting to be told this was where he fit in.

She wanted to show him he fit in with her.

She wanted to show him she saw him and she wanted to tell him he mattered.

So much.

Maybe too much.

The panic came. It flared in her abdomen and stretched up to encompass her heart. Being with Luke was a step she never thought she'd let herself take. It was going to change everything. And yes, she knew that they'd been dancing around each other and silently negotiating *the when* for an entire year. But it was one thing to finally admit what you'd been wanting and reaching towards, and it was quite another to selfishly take it.

'Hey you,' Luke paused in his rubbing down. As if he knew she was starting to overthink, he reached out and put two fingertips under her chin to tip up her face. His lips pressed feather-light to her closed eyelids, to the tip of her nose, to each cheekbone and she marvelled that although she could feel the fine tremor in the hands that moved to softly slide into her hair, he was completely in charge of the need coursing through the both of them.

Her lips parted in preparation for his kiss and she emitted a tiny moue of disappointment when his mouth instead grazed her jaw-line. He chuckled lightly but didn't break his concentrated exploration of the underside of her jaw and down her neck, where he worshipped at the pulse-point that beat so fast, so excitedly, so desperately for him.

Sephy's hand slipped from around Luke's neck to his chest. She had thought they would come together in a fevered, explosive rush that would assuage the ache, but Luke was showing her his own slower and expertly controlled seduction. By the time he'd made his way back up to her mouth, she was the one trembling as butterflies danced, her vision clouded and she opened her mouth to invite the bliss.

'Hey you,' she whispered back right before his mouth sipped from hers.

He dragged the towel down across her sensitised skin and her breathing hitched. His hand moved between them to flick his own towel off and then his hands were on her again, splaying possessively against her back to hold her against him as his kiss turned deep, creating the burning pace that she was certain was what she needed to ease the trembling and set her on the fast track to gratification.

Heat and fire.

She moved against him.

Friction and spark.

She wanted him inside her.

'Condoms?' she muttered, reaching for his hand and tugging him out of the bathroom.

His chuckle trickled over her skin as he followed her into the bedroom and walked her backwards towards the dressing table. Reaching over her, he pulled open a drawer.

'This what you're looking for?' he asked, taking out a few foil packets.

With a grin, she hooked her foot around the dressing-table chair, spun it around and twisted to push Luke down onto it.

'Wow,' Luke laughed as he landed with a thud and then pulled her down so that she was sitting astride him. 'Impressive moves you have there.'

'Want to see some more?'

Her eyes didn't leave his as she reached for a condom.

Luke's face tightened as she slid it over his hard length. Gone was the laughter, replaced with a serious intensity as he demanded, 'Show me everything you've got.'

The first rise of her hips as she moved on him had his head tipping back to watch her, his eyes obsidian and glazed.

She moved again, rejoicing in the sensation of how well he filled her, her feet resting on the chair struts for purchase as she watched desire chase over the strong features of his face.

Luke grunted with pleasure and her hands clutched against his shoulders in agreement.

His hands swept up her sides, palmed her breasts, trailed up her neck, pushed her hair back from her face and everywhere he touched became hyper-sensitive. It was like he knew exactly where to touch to elicit a sigh, exactly how feather-soft he should stroke to induce a moan, and exactly where to kiss to have her writhing for more, so that the want grew more desperate inside of her and the need drove deeper.

Her head tipped back as her hips rolled forward.

Luke's eyes squeezed shut and his hands moved back to her hips. She moved on him, looking down at him through heavy-lidded eyes. The hands that were clenched against shoulders slipped and trembled as she quickened her pace.

The building pleasure made all these feelings rush to the surface and afraid she was going to voice them she leant down to cover his mouth in a blistering white-hot kiss. One of Luke's hands moved to the small of her back, pressing her down harder onto him as he drove up into her.

'How is it you make me lose myself so?' Sephy sighed, the words coming out on a moan as he thrust up into her, harder, deeper. 'It's crazy.' She bit down hard on her lip as something so much more than simple pleasure danced in the air around them, linking them.

'You do something to me, Seraphina. Something that pulls me inside out and makes me need to sink myself to the hilt and never stop.'

His words wrapped themselves around her as her world narrowed to him and her. 'This. Us,' she voiced, her soul laid bare that he could wring so much from her, 'it's too much.'

'You can handle it,' Luke muttered with conviction.

Could she? She hadn't counted on the fact that they knew each other so well. Knew what drove each other. Knew what inspired each other. And in this, she realised, they were learning what could destroy each other, also. Emotion rushed through her as the gates of pleasure opened, leaving her chasing for more. More pleasure. More speed. More intensity.

Her arms came around him to hold him inside her as the rhythm increased, so that any minute she was surely going to fly out of her skin. 'How do you know I can handle it?' she whispered desperately.

'Because I have faith in you,' Luke assured her, gripping her hips as he thrust up into her, his words and movement causing the totality of emotion to burst free of her as she crashed into a mind-bending, soul-ripping, heart-surrendering orgasm.

Sephy took one last look at Luke lying gloriously naked and asleep in the rumpled super-king bed and opened the door of his room as quietly as she could. Screwing up her eyes to combat the bright light of the corridor, she stumbled out, fishing in her clutch for the key card to her room.

It has to be in here somewhere. Has to be.

She didn't know what she'd do if it wasn't. She had one goal and that was getting into her room to shower and change before she went up to her mother's suite to see her daughter. Luckily, that goal had enough in it to make thinking about Luke and what they'd done impossible.

Mostly.

The memory of her shuddering to orgasm after orgasm in Luke's arms had her hands trembling as she searched for her room key.

Come on, how can you get lost in such a small amount of space, for f-

The next thing Sephy knew she was bouncing off someone. Damn it, she'd been so focused on getting into her room she hadn't been looking where she was going.

'So sorry,' she mumbled, looking up to discover that of all the people to be walking this particular corridor, at this very particular time in the morning, she'd walked right into her sister.

Nora took one look at what Sephy was wearing and one look at the room her sister had exited and her eyes went bug-round and her mouth dropped open.

Perfect! As if she didn't feel on the verge of a meltdown already.

'All right, all right, all right,' Sephy said, holding her hands up, as if she was being interrogated to within an inch of her life. 'Yes. Me. Walk of shame. Happy now?' It wasn't like Nora hadn't seen her do the walk of shame before, she thought, feeling even worse. Of course, that had been years ago when she'd been a complete mess of a person. Obviously some things didn't change, she thought woefully.

'You slept with Luke,' Nora realised in a shocked whisper.

Sephy winced as if Nora had shouted the news down the corridor. Flapping her hands in a shushing motion she glared at her sister.

'*You slept with Luke*,' Nora said more loudly.

'Oh my God,' she rolled her eyes, 'please, can't you announce it a little louder? I don't think the guests on the other floors quite heard you.'

'Seph,' Nora said, stunned.

'What?' She made a show of searching her clutch again.

'Seph.' This time Nora said her name so gently Sephy found stupid tears forming at the back of her eyes.

'I can't find my room key,' she whispered miserably.

'Give it here,' Nora said, calmly taking the clutch from her. 'Look,' she said, pulling out the key card. 'You have a rip in the lining and it fell down the side of it.'

Sephy gratefully took the card, inserted it and turned to her sister. 'I can't talk about this. I need to shower and change before I see Daisy. She will have woken up by now and –'

'Well, isn't it lucky for me, then,' Nora interrupted, shoving her through the door and following, 'that you don't suffer from my inability to multi-task when overwrought? So spill. What happened?'

Sephy crossed to the wardrobe and yanked it open.

'What do you think happened?' Sephy replied over her shoulder with a side of sarcasm as she took in her sister's yoga bottoms and loose t-shirt and pulled out something similar for the spa session later on that day. Striding into the bathroom she shut the door firmly behind her and sat down heavily on the edge of the tub.

She'd woken up in Luke's arms, her head cradled against his chest. Her eyes had opened, but she hadn't had that 'what the... where am I?' moment. She'd known exactly where she was and exactly what she'd done.

All night.

Sephy closed her eyes as a moan escaped.

That had been when the attack had occurred. Lying there in his arms, arrow after arrow of poisonous guilt had pierced through the veil of their one night out of time, where the only responsibility they'd had was to share each other and give each other pleasure.

In daylight, weighed by the anchor of the real world, caught on the spear of faith he had said he had in her, she was left feeling utterly overwhelmed and so she'd done something completely cowardly. She'd risen from the bed, pulled on her clothes, picked up her clutch…and headed for the door.

Dully, she reached into the shower cubicle to turn on the water. Luke was everything you could want in a lover and – no. She couldn't, *wouldn't*, let herself think about all the ways in which he was generous and all the ways in which she now felt selfish.

'What are you doing up here anyway?' she asked Nora above the sound of the water.

Nora pushed the bathroom door open. 'I've been up all night – I wanted to catch you before you went in to see Mum and Daisy. I wanted to check you were okay.'

Sephy stepped into the shower cubicle. She'd been up all night too. But unless Ethan had been keeping her sister's mind off of what had happened earlier in the evening, it wasn't the same at all.

'I'm fine,' she answered.

'Not better than fine?'

'Stop fishing,' she said, reaching for the liquid soap.

'I'm happy for you.'

Wow. Direct hit. Sephy felt rotten all over again as a new arrow of guilt found its mark.

'This isn't what you think it is,' she said shakily as she rinsed off.

'It isn't? Did you, or did you not, have sex with Luke Jackson?'

Sephy opened the cubicle door and Nora passed her a towel, waiting for confirmation.

'I did.'

'Hot sex?' Nora checked.

'Incendiary,' she answered truthfully.

'Still happy for you, then.'

Drying herself vigorously she felt all the nerve endings that Luke had stroked over the night before, reawaken.

'So is this going to be a regular thing?' Nora asked.

Absolutely not, she whispered to herself. She never repeated mistakes. And it had to have been a mistake, didn't it? She wouldn't be feeling so spectacularly guilty if it was truly meant to be the start of something.

A swarm of butterflies swept in.

Like she could sustain the start of something with Luke. It was ridiculous. She didn't know what she'd been thinking. Except, she hadn't been thinking, had she? Not above getting something she wanted.

'Want me to ask Ethan to ask Luke for you?' Nora teased when she didn't answer.

'No, I bloody-well do not. In fact, don't even tell Ethan about this.'

Nora regarded her thoughtfully. 'It was hard enough keeping schtum about the modelling thing and this is way, way bigger.'

It was monumentally big, Sephy thought, swaying a little. 'Norsies?' she looked up at her sister, using the special name she gave her for when they were talking about the big stuff. 'I think I've screwed up. Really, royally screwed up.'

Last night there was absolutely no part of her that had pitied Luke, of that she was sure. What she wasn't sure about – what horrified her because it would be far worse if it turned out to be true, was that she might have used him.

Used her friend.

That was why she was feeling so guilty, wasn't it?

'Why do you think you've screwed up?'

'Because it's what I do.'

'What on earth are you talking about?'

Sephy bit her lip. 'Well, Ryan and I –'

'Ryan and you were kids,' Nora said brushing her worry aside.

'Not really. We weren't. I was twenty when I had Daisy.'

'Emotionally you were teenagers. Don't tell me you weren't. The way the two of you lived. No responsibilities. No desire for anything except putting the future off as long as possible.'

That was true. Hadn't she practically told Ryan that herself when he was hinting that they could maybe pick up where they'd left off?

'Look, I can hardly believe I'm going to advise this,' Nora said, 'but I think you should let things develop naturally with Luke.'

'Nora, I just left his bed while he was sleeping. I didn't even leave a note.'

'Ouch. Okay, that's a bit one-night-stand-ish. But understandable. You've been friends for a long time. This is a big thing. You can explain that to him. He'll give you that time, Sephy. You know he will. Give him that time back. See what happens.'

'What if what happens is that it all goes wrong and I hurt him? He hurts me? We hurt Daisy?'

'You know, someone used to tell me not to jump straight to worst-case scenario.'

'Well, who the hell did that?' Sephy shot back, knowing it had been her. 'That's the dumbest advice I ever heard.' How did you protect yourself – protect those around you, if you didn't go to worst-case scenario and check you could survive the fallout.

Of course what she should have done was do that *before* she slept with Luke. But no, in this instance, for something that was incredibly important to her, she'd instead reverted to type. How many times had she told herself Luke was not for having...Luke was not for needing?

All that guff about having no control over what was happening between them – she'd been managing the situation for the whole year beforehand, hadn't she?

'You owe it to yourself,' Nora urged, 'not to ignore the significance of, you know, having incendiary sex with your friend.'

The friendship short-hand she had with him was a given. But relationship short-hand was different. It took more than one night learning each other's bodies inside and out. Didn't it?

She stepped into fresh clothes and ran a brush through her hair. It was six-thirty a.m.; Daisy was definitely going to be up by now, her mum too if Daisy's usual happy morning chatter was anything to go by.

'I know I can't ignore it forever, but right now,' she told Nora, 'I have to. Because honestly if I can't apologise to mum because I'm hot-flushing on memories…'

'All right, permission granted. Damn,' Nora said as she held the room door open.

'What,' Sephy asked, collecting up the key card to exit the room.

'I should have said on condition you tell me some of the details,' answered Nora, as she walked with her to their mother's suite. 'Incendiary is good, but it doesn't cover visuals.'

'Hey, you have your own hot man. Leave mine alone.'

Mine.

God, she thought, as she tapped lightly on her mother's hotel-room door, this was where it all got so confusing. She shouldn't be thinking of Luke as being hers.

Not after one night in his arms. Not if she was feeling like she might have used him simply because she'd been feeling vulnerable.

The door to her mother's suite suddenly opened and Sephy started.

'Mum – I,' she looked at her mother and could tell she hadn't slept well after their altercation the day before. A new battalion of archers took up position just past her defences, pausing to dip their arrows in the bucket marked 'guilt'.

Sephy stepped inside the suite, wanting desperately to feel her daughter in her arms. Her brightness and chattiness would help soothe, help distract. 'Where's Daisy?' she asked, expecting a whirl of movement and a 'Mummy' of excitement followed by a hug.

'She's in the other room, still sleeping,' Isobel said with a smile. 'I think the excitement of yesterday must have thrown her system out.'

Sephy poked her head into the bedroom and saw her Daisy sleeping like an angel. Her hand came up to her chest. Sometimes the pride she took simply from looking at her nearly made her heart too big to fit inside her. With a sniff and a blink she pulled herself together to face her mother.

Nora had sat down on one of the sofas and picked up a glossy magazine to read, effectively making herself invisible.

Sephy looked at her mother. 'Mum?'

Isobel smiled gently at her youngest daughter and opened her arms.

Sephy crossed the room and went in for a hug. 'I'm so sorry about the way I spoke to you yesterday.'

'It's really all right.'

'It's not. It's just that I –'

'Didn't realise quite how much the place meant to you?'

Sephy nodded. 'It'll be okay. I'll work through it. I promise.'

'I should have told you earlier. But you've had so much going on, what with Ryan coming back into Daisy's life and then getting Seraphic up and running.'

Not to mention lying to Luke's lovely foster parents and her own mother by pretending to be with Luke.

Oh, and then having confusing, incredible, world-changing sex with her friend/fake fiancé/fake boyfriend. Sephy squeezed her eyes shut and tried to get Luke out of her head for five minutes, at least.

'I didn't want to add to your stress,' Isobel stated.

It wasn't really any surprise she was feeling so overwhelmed. Everything had been so full-on since before her father had died.

Sephy sighed. She had a feeling she'd be sacked as a friend when Luke discovered he'd been some kind of physical outlet for her. Even if he had helped her cut loose in the pool beforehand.

Thank goodness today would give them both some breathing space.

She wouldn't be able to talk about Luke during the spa session. Not with Daisy present. Then, later, well everything should be about Amanda. It was her special day. Sephy wasn't going to let her own inability to navigate relationships spoil that for Amanda.

'Would you like to read the letter your father wrote me?' Isobel asked.

Sephy felt the breath back up in her throat. 'You have it here with you?'

'I carry it everywhere.'

Sephy blanched. Her father had said everything he had wanted to say to her in her own letter. Unless… oh God, more tears threatened. What if it was more advice to her mum on how Sephy should live her life? Coming straight after sleeping with Luke, she didn't think she would be able to bear it. Sephy backed up a step. 'No thank you. You should keep it private for you,' she said with an attempt at swallowing the lump in her throat.

CHAPTER SIXTEEN

Luke fiddled with the cuff of his snowy-white shirt and had a sudden, vivid flashback to the night before, when Sephy had him pushed up against the door while she traced his flesh with that sinfully sweet mouth of hers.

Feeling like what he was remembering was written all over his face, he stared down at his feet. He probably shouldn't be thinking about what he and Sephy had got up to hour after hour last night. Didn't seem quite appropriate at her brother's wedding, with all the guests politely making small talk while they were waiting for the main event.

He fought a grin and concentrated on straightening his tuxedo jacket, before looking back up and catching Ethan's knowing expression.

'Try thinking about how many grains of rice are in a kilogram bag,' Ethan intoned. 'That's what I do.'

Luke gave him a little side-eye. 'That definitely comes under the heading of "bizarre", but thanks, I might try it,' he answered under his breath, checking to make sure Jared wasn't listening.

It had been a really long day. Good, but long. He'd enjoyed getting to know Jared better over a few games of pool. But he'd rather have been in bed.

With Sephy.

They burned up the sheets like he'd never experienced before. But it was more than simply the best sex of his life, though. What they shared cut deep and straight and true to the heart of each other.

At the onset of another grin filling his face, he tried thinking about rice and when that didn't work, he tried to distract himself by focusing on Jared again. The space next to him was empty because his best man, Mikey, was also Amanda's brother, and he was going to walk her down the aisle. Luke had been roped in as honorary usher and given the responsibility of checking the staff had made the aisle wider to accommodate Mikey's wheelchair and whatever size dress Amanda might be wearing. No doubt about it. Jared was a dot-all-the-'I's-and-cross-all-the-'T's kind of a guy. Nora wasn't that different.

He liked that Sephy's artistic nature left her more open as a person, less risk-averse.

Not that he thought of *himself* as a risk.

Okay, he had. But last night Sephy hadn't made him feel like she was playing at risk-taking with him. After he'd told her about Claire, he'd expected the familiar shyness to kick in and entangle his emotions, yet somehow Sephy's stillness in the water – her waiting for him to fill the gaps – hadn't felt pressurised and he'd realised that she would never look at him and see only that troubled, lost teenager he had once been. She would always be able to separate the before and the after. Her showing him how much he had moved away from who he had once been had made it easier to re-visit his younger self for a while and talk about his mother with her.

And by the time he and Sephy had made it back to his room, nothing from the past could have intruded. They had been far too wrapped up in each other to let anyone or anything else in.

This morning, after one night together, he'd woken up and automatically reached for her. Finding her gone had brought an immediate stab of hurt until he'd realised she would have wanted to check on Daisy and then would have a thousand and one things to do to get organised for the wedding ceremony and reception. He'd sent her a quick text from the sports bar, but he hadn't really been surprised when she hadn't responded.

Turning slightly, he cast his gaze over to the doors to make sure there were no more guests waiting to be seated and found his gaze colliding with Isobel King. Hoping to hell she wasn't looking at him and seeing what he and her daughter had got up to last night, he felt a sudden and intense need to run his finger around the collar of his shirt. As she continued to look shrewdly at him, he clenched his hands to stop the betraying gesture and wondered instead if she realised that in selling the estate, none of her children would ever get married there. But maybe she couldn't afford to care about that because maybe she didn't see that any new memories made there could outweigh the pain of Jeremy King's last days on the estate.

He didn't like to think of her still mourning so keenly, but he also didn't like the thought of watching Sephy have to lose the place she loved either. Not when he was fairly sure she thought of it as the last connection to her father.

What would Isobel say if she knew of what Sephy had hoped to build on the estate? Would it make a difference?

As the wedding music started up and everyone rose to their feet, he thought about that next tranche of money his accountant was expecting him to invest and his plan to start looking for suitable land to build that adoption and fostering resource centre. He thought about how Sephy took solace from the King estate and how she'd wanted it to help provide her and Daisy with a future she had some control over.

He thought about how she was like the willow tree they had planted for her father –whatever life threw at her she tried to bend with it – not break.

And he thought about how he wanted to show her that he cared.

Then the banquet-room doors were opening and there, standing on her own, cute as a button, was Daisy. Luke saw her eyes widen as she took in the standing crowd, saw the fear flash in her eyes and he actually took a step forward before he could help himself. He wanted to sweep her up in his arms and tell her it was all right.

In the next instant, Sephy appeared and bent down to whisper reassuringly into her daughter's ear. Whatever she said worked because a huge smile appeared on Daisy's face and, with her chin tipping up stubbornly unafraid, she took slow, measured steps up the aisle, scattering flower petals from her basket as she did so.

Luke's heart clenched with pride when Daisy drew up alongside him and beamed as if to say, 'Look, Luke, I did it.' He bent and held his hand up so that she could high-five him and then finally he allowed himself to look fully at Sephy.

He felt himself do the slow-blink thing he always did. Yeah. No doubt about it. He could get lost in Seraphina King and he didn't think that would be a bad thing at all. In fact, wasn't he more than halfway there anyway? Would it really be so bad to fall all the rest of the way?

She looked incredible in a column of midnight-blue satin, her hair up in a soft knot and a delicate strand of pearls at her throat. He might have even groaned because as Sephy and Nora walked past them to stop at the front of the aisle and wait for Amanda and Mikey to make their entrance, Ethan leaned forward and said sotto voce, 'Yeah, start counting those grains of rice, mate.'

Luke turned to look at Ethan, but the man only had eyes for Nora.

He turned back to look at his own woman. The one who'd captured his heart. And then had himself a mini heart attack because, wait just a minute…captured his heart? As in…

Straight away the imagination he usually applauded flashed back to the ballroom at the King estate, and Luke started sweating. To combat visualising Sephy standing at the ballroom doors of the King estate in a wedding dress, he started imagining zombies instead. For extra measure he imagined getting all the zombies into one small room and started logically working out how many kilogram bags of rice you would need to block the doors.

When that didn't entirely work he tried to remember how marriage-phobic Sephy was.

He willed her to look at him because surely he'd see that sexy, playful smile of hers and that would make him think of one thing and one thing only. Not hearts and flowers and declarations. After one night, she'd bolt if she knew that was what he was thinking.

Finally Amanda and Jared stood opposite each other and as the rest of the wedding party lined up he knew Sephy would finally get a chance to look at him.

When her eyes did land on him, he smiled, expecting a smile back, maybe a blush. She did blush, but instead of an intimate memory-swapping intense look over the bride and groom, Luke got beautiful brown eyes darkening, a worried frown and then she looked away.

What the hell?

He stood there, staring at her, willing her again to look at him.

As if she couldn't help herself, her brown eyes flashed on him, this time for maybe a nanosecond longer and then she looked away again.

Guiltily.

Shock hammered through him as the first kernel of doubt exploded inside him like a bomb.

Damn it, he'd asked her if she was sure last night and he'd counted on her courage to tell him the truth. Ice-cold anger formed a protective shell over his heart. If he'd been standing here thinking about hearts and flowers and declarations all while she'd been busy working out a way to pretend last night never happened...well, she was going to find he had something to say about that.

Him and her?

They weren't just a night out of time.

They were more than that and she damn well knew it. So whatever the hell was going on with her, he'd get to the bottom of it. He'd spent half his life not asking questions. Not causing ripples. But that wasn't this half of life. Now, if there was something that affected his future he never shied away from confrontation.

'So, I really like your Luke,' Amanda said, sinking down into the chair beside Sephy and smiling as she fluffed out the skirt of her wedding gown.

'Oh. Well.' With a glass of champagne clutched in her hands, Sephy sank slowly further back into her chair. Now that the reception dinner speeches were over, staff were busy moving a few of the tables off the edge of the dance floor and Sephy had suggested they all move to a table further back so that the music wouldn't be so loud and they could all talk.

Shooting a panicked look to the others sitting around their table, Sephy saw that they were all thankfully either watching the dancing or chatting amongst themselves. Her gaze moved across the room, automatically searching for Luke, who she located chatting to her mother. She wondered what they were talking about. Clearing her throat, she steeled herself and whispered to Amanda, 'He's not really mine.'

'Are you sure about that? He certainly acted like he was yours last night.'

'What?' Mortifying! Did everyone know she'd spent the night with Luke? That he had acted like he was hers and she had acted… true to form and taken what she wanted?

'Mmmn,' Amanda continued. 'While Isobel was telling you about selling the estate, Luke was busy demanding Jared and Nora tell him what was going on so that he could make sure you were all right.'

Oh. Sephy swallowed. Wasn't it just like Luke that while she was in full-on panic mode, he was in full-on protection mode?

As if he knew he was being talked about, he turned slightly and immediately locked gazes with her. She tried to send a silent, pleading apology for earlier. He was so generous, surely he'd accept it? But the slight she'd dealt him, when he'd reached down to kiss her cheek in front of her family earlier, was patently too much.

She really hadn't meant to shy away from his touch. She'd simply been thoroughly unprepared for it. Seeing how his skin had pulled tight as he'd looked at her, then at her family and then back at her, had made her feel awful. She'd tried to make it better, but when she'd put her hand on his arm to draw him into the conversation, his gorgeous green eyes had chilled to ice as he'd subtly brushed it off and removed himself to go and chat with other guests.

He'd shut down on her and she couldn't blame him. She'd tried to gather her words and find an appropriate time to drag him to one side and talk about the night before, but this wedding seemed to have something formal going down every blessed second and she'd either been needed for photographs, or to help Daisy hand out chocolate truffles, or help Nora decorate the honeymoon suite, or sit with her mother and make sure she wasn't feeling too sad.

'Jared can be quite intimidating when he wants to be,' Amanda continued, 'but Luke definitely gave as good as he got. And, well,' Amanda lowered her voice, 'aside from Isobel selling the estate, you look really happy and so that's why I like your Luke.'

Sephy watched Luke frown and turn back to concentrate on his conversation. She fiddled with the stem of her glass and added in a careful voice, 'It's not because of Luke, it's because Seraphic is doing better than I even dreamed it could.'

Amanda laughed delightedly, 'Yeah, it's not a business that puts that kind of light in a woman's eyes.'

Sephy felt herself blush. She should be pleased she was looking happy on her brother's wedding day. That all the turmoil she was feeling on the inside wasn't showing on the outside and that none of the undercurrents between her and Luke were on display for others to see.

'Speaking of business, though,' Amanda said, 'I feel awful for not realising how famous Luke actually is. He definitely downplays his accomplishments, doesn't he?'

'He's shy,' Sephy automatically defended and then frowned. 'What do you mean, famous?'

'When I mentioned to Mikey last night that Luke would be joining him and Jared at the sports bar, Mikey went into some weird-geek-crush trance and kept asking if it would be inappropriate to ask him for a selfie.'

Sephy's gaze drifted over to where Michael was chatting with his wife, Janey – Jared's personal assistant. 'Ah. I take it Mikey plays ZFF?' she asked, determined to concentrate on the conversation.

'Apparently he didn't just play ZFF, he lived it! Said it helped him battle through physio after the accident. I guess he had a lot of demons to slay and zombies made a good substitute.'

Pride for Luke's achievements filled her because knowing more about his background now Sephy could understand that slaying demons was exactly why he had created ZFF.

Zombie Freedom Fighter was all about rising up and fighting back against injustice, alienation, isolation and destruction. It was about joining forces with others and then leading others to reverse their virtual world's shortfall of hope. She could imagine Mikey would have needed that after the construction-site accident he'd been involved in had ultimately set him on a very different course.

Sephy wondered if the zombie slayings had started out as a way of Luke slaying his shyness and the need to be invisible. She could certainly see how others playing the games could conquer their own inner demons. Once you started playing you discovered that you couldn't give up or you'd let the dark shadows in the world win.

'Did you know Luke was interviewed in *Fortune* magazine earlier this year?' Amanda asked.

Sephy stared at Amanda in shock.

No. She hadn't known that.

'Mikey says the article was really impressive. All about how he's self-made and wants to use his wealth to create a legacy to help kids who feel they have restricted choices in life, to push through those barriers and succeed in spite of their backgrounds.'

Sephy couldn't believe Luke had potentially risked his reputation and his future plans by helping her out with her photo shoot. If she'd known all this beforehand, she never would have asked him to help her model.

Urgently laying her hand on Amanda's arm, she said, 'Can you not tell Mikey about the photo-shoot – about Luke being the model. I didn't realise his business plans were public and I don't want anyone to use the photo shoot to damage his progress.'

'Okay, I won't say anything. I guess I just wanted to say that I like seeing you look this happy, and I like that it's Luke who's putting that smile on your face.'

Sephy opened her mouth to deny that during the past few weeks, with every inhale and exhale of breath, it felt like she had been creating space inside her just for Luke and the warmth, safety and laughter he offered so generously, but Amanda was already getting to her feet.

'Time for more bride business,' she said, waving her bouquet as she walked towards the stage area.

Sephy took an urgent gulp of champagne and hoped that no one would notice her blending into the damask wallpaper behind her as all the women ventured onto the large dance floor to try and catch the bridal bouquet.

With Amanda instructing the women to get ready, Sephy allowed herself a small smile. The bride was already turning around to face away from the crowd. The bouquet-tossing deal would be over in seconds.

'Hey, Amanda,' Sephy suddenly heard Luke pipe up as he walked back towards the table, 'Don't be throwing your bouquet yet, Sephy hasn't made it into position.'

The crowd of female guests automatically parted down the middle and Sephy went hot all over as the spotlight of interest beamed brightly down on her.

Turning her head, she offered Luke her most impressive death glare. Unfortunately, and possibly after the way she had been avoiding him all day, Luke had no trouble acting like he had the upper hand and merely raised his eyebrow, daring her to say something in front of all these people.

Wow. Okay. This was obviously payback.

And even though she knew she deserved any punishment he meted out, she really, really didn't want to go up there onto that dance floor.

'Sephy?' Amanda chirped into the microphone she was holding, 'get on up here on the dance floor, please.'

'Yes, Sephy, duty calls,' Luke said and Sephy could happily have swung for him. It would be just her luck if she caught the stupid thing, she thought, rising reluctantly to her feet, and preparing to walk onto the dance floor.

'I tell you what,' Luke continued in good humour, 'I'll even escort her onto the floor for you.'

'Luke, what the hell are you doing?' she asked out of the side of her mouth.

'Can't have you, the sister of the groom, standing at the back, now, can we?'

'This is ridiculous.'

'Not ridiculous,' Luke said. 'Tradition. You don't want to make a show on your brother's big day, do you?'

'Look, I know you're angry with me and we need to talk, but it's kind of difficult when you're manhandling me onto a crowded dance floor.'

'You do this. Then we talk,' he steered her right to the front of the group of women, who were vying for prime position. 'Don't forget to smile when you catch it.'

'What makes you think I'm going to catch it?' she said, knowing full well she intended keeping her hands glued to her sides.

But it turned out that when a large object was hurtling towards one's nose, one's natural instinct was to reach up and either bat it away or catch it. Damn her hands and their reflexive need to catch.

Amongst all the cheering, Sephy made sure to keep the smile plastered on her face.

Don't tell me I'm next. Don't tell me, she silently pleaded.

'Yay,' she heard Amanda say, the microphone sounding more like a megaphone to Sephy, 'Nora next and then you.'

Sephy stared down at the bouquet and not for the first time today felt a lump form in her throat. She had thought she had everything she wanted – everything she knew she could get, at any rate. But here she was staring down into the beautiful cream roses, interspersed with pearls and crystals, and why, then, did it feel like this was one more thing she suddenly wanted.

She shook her head a little as if in doing so the thought would fall right out of her head and looked up to find Luke staring right back at her with an inscrutable expression on his face.

Panic made her look around, trying to find an exit.

This couldn't be happening to her. She couldn't be wanting Luke and marriage.

Between losing her father, letting Ryan back into Daisy's life, starting up Seraphic and the estate being put up for sale, Luke had consistently been there for her and had consistently snuck into her thoughts. He was her secret keeper whenever her parental fears spilled over. He was her voice of reason when she needed pulling back from full-on panic mode, and when she'd turned to him for help with her ad campaign he had put aside his own insecurity.

For her.

He'd championed her and he'd seduced her.

And she had fallen completely and utterly in love with him.

'Holy crap,' she silently mouthed.

Of course she was in love with Luke Jackson.

Hadn't that been exactly where she was headed every time she had flirted with the boundaries of their friendship?

She dragged in a breath, but her lungs refused to inflate properly. Why had it taken catching the bridal bouquet for the penny to drop? Because it wasn't as if she could navigate a relationship with him – not with her track record and not with how she felt about long-term relationships that might lead to marriage. She wouldn't be able to bear it if it *ever* looked to the world like she had married for financial gain or financial rescue.

Hysteria started to fizz along her nerve endings.

She knew her fear, left over from her father's last letter to her, wasn't watertight logical.

Did. Not. Make. Her. Feel. It. Any. Less.

And was it really so wrong to want to prove to her father, to herself, to all those gossip mongers who had clamoured to judge when Jared had left all those years ago, that she could make it in her own right?

Luke had made his own money doing what he loved and working every minute of the day those first years. She'd spent those same years focusing on the wrong things in life. Her mother had told her to try and forgive herself for that, but it was hard when her father's last words to her were that she needed to find her drive and make something of herself.

The walls of the room seemed to be creeping closer in on her, and as she stared down in panic at the wedding symbol she had caught, the roses blurred before her eyes and then, suddenly, she felt a hand grip her wrist and realised it belonged to Luke. Determinedly he pulled her off the dance floor to cheers. As if he had claimed her, or something. Honesty had her wanting to explain to everybody that it wasn't real. It couldn't be.

Her heart wasn't designed for that.

Her heart was designed for using her friend in the worst possible way and then not knowing any graceful way to stop wanting him.

Back at the table, Luke took the flowers out of Sephy's white-knuckled grip and passed them to Daisy. 'You think you can look after these for your mother?' he asked gently.

Daisy nodded her head, stroking her hand over the delicate flowers.

'Isobel,' Luke said, 'would you mind keeping an eye on Daisy for a while? Sephy and I need to have ourselves a little talk.'

Sephy looked at her mother and willed her to decline. But who ever declined Luke, especially when he asked so politely, flashing those dimples of his for good measure?

'Take all the time you need,' Isobel answered smoothly. 'Daisy and I will be fine here for a few hours yet.'

This was it, then.

Moment of truth time.

Once again, she felt herself being dragged through a room by Luke. She considered why on earth she was letting him and knew that it was because, one way or another, they had to have this conversation – she had sewn Luke into her heart and unpicking those stitches was going to hurt like hell, but it had to begin now.

CHAPTER SEVENTEEN

They ended up in some sort of small meeting room. Sephy looked around at the stacks of chairs and wooden-topped tables that were usually transformed by white linen tablecloths and fancy draped bows on the chairs.

'Alone at last,' Luke murmured, shoving his hands into his pockets and giving all the impressions of waiting patiently for whatever she had to say.

With racing heart, Sephy felt her defences shoot up to reach the ceiling. 'All right, yes, I should have made more of an effort to get you alone and apologise for last night.'

'Apologise?' Luke flashed a grin that didn't meet his eyes. 'Huh. Okay. Did not see that one coming.'

Sephy winced, the guilt of what she'd done nearly swallowing her whole.

'Come on, then,' Luke said his voice tight. 'Give it to me with both barrels – what's the deal?'

'I –' Lord, where did she start? How did she tell him what she was afraid she'd done? 'I shouldn't have done what I did last night.'

'Hmm.' Luke regarded her thoughtfully. 'I kind of thought it was more of a "we" thing, but, you're not feeling that?'

'We, then,' she capitulated. '*We* shouldn't have done what we did.'

Luke stood there staring at her and Sephy tried with all her might not to get distracted by how he filled out his tuxedo, or how she loved his gorgeous green eyes, or how generous his approach to life was and how much she admired the person he was.

'What you're telling me is that this morning you ran away?' he finally said, the green eyes she got so easily caught up in turning dull with disappointment.

'I'm so sorry, Luke.'

A hand came out of his pocket to swipe over his jaw as he turned his head away and then back to her. 'You said you didn't pity me.'

'I didn't. I don't.' She rushed out and as she looked down at the floor she knew she was going to have to say the words. Bracing herself, she whispered, 'I think I did something worse. I think I used you.'

She brought her head up in time to see him recoil slightly and her throat filled with remorse. She cleared her vocal cords because the very least he deserved was an explanation along with her apology.

'Last night I was so overwhelmed from finding out that Mum was definitely selling the estate, and truthfully? I actually couldn't believe Jared and Nora wouldn't even try to help me keep it in the family. I lashed out at them because it felt like another thing I wasn't getting – another thing I was losing, but also because I was tired of feeling so raw.' At the admission, her gaze flashed up to his. His focus on her was intense and unwavering. Reminding her of the way he had looked at her when he had made love to her the night before.

Her heart thundered in her chest and she deliberately turned away from him. They hadn't made love, she told herself. They'd had sex. Hot, hard and intense sex. Over and over again.

She threw him a look over her shoulder. 'You have this way of saying all the right things. You never ignore me. And then in the pool you made me feel so good and by the time we got to your room I wanted to feel that again and so I…put myself in front of you and I took.' *And took and took and took.*

'So, first I'm the guy who does all these things for you,' Luke ground out, 'and then I'm just a quick fuck at a wedding? I magically turned into Mr Any Man?'

Sephy closed her eyes because when he said it like that it made what she'd done sound even worse and then, suddenly, warm hands were clasping her shoulders and turning her around to face him and he was asking her, 'Did you ever think that maybe I was the one using you?'

Sephy inhaled sharply. No. He was too good. Too generous. He would never treat her so carelessly. He would never use her. She was the one who had form. This was her fault.

'Luke,' she forced herself to stare into his eyes so that he could see the ugly truth. 'I've behaved like that before,' she whispered. 'When I've found the future spinning out of my control, or,' she licked her lips, 'when I've wanted attention.'

She waited to see the realisation turn to disgust on his face. Waited for the harsh words she knew she deserved.

Instead he cupped her face in his hands and took a step closer to her.

The butterfly net inside her tore open and a swarm escaped to flit through her, careening off her insides and making her confused. 'Luke?'

Slowly he bent his head and laid his lips against first one eyelid and then the other. Tears instantly formed at the back of her eyes. She didn't understand. She'd just told him what she'd done and he was being tender with her? His lips moved to her forehead, the tip of her nose, under her cheekbone and her hands came up to grip his biceps and steady herself because he was making her dizzy.

His mouth slid to the corner of hers and everything changed as greed instantly took over. She tipped her head, desperately trying to capture his mouth, but he wouldn't let her, dropping a kiss to the sensitive point under her left ear instead. Goosebumps travelled from her scalp to her toes as he nuzzled the place he'd kissed and without warning bit down on her earlobe and then salved it with his tongue.

Lust, pure and simple and hot as molten fire had her hands driving into his hair so that she could hold him still long enough to get what she wanted, what she needed: his lips on hers.

Rising up onto tiptoes she laid her mouth over his and furiously kissed him with all the pent-up need he'd created in her. All she could think was that she had to appease this ache he was responsible for. She bit down hard on his bottom lip, heard his groan against her mouth and her tongue swept in to claim. Luke's arms came around her and she was being lifted off her feet and then set down on top of the first available table. She sighed when his hand found the side split in the fitted column of her dress. She trembled when his hand slid seductively up her thigh. Shuddered under him as his mouth left hers to lay a string of open-mouthed kisses along the swell of her breasts.

His mouth came back to hers, but even as she felt triumphant, even as the pleasure built, there was anger. Anger that he could make her want him like this.

That he could make her want him to the point she lost control scared her. Wrenching her mouth from his she lashed out with words. 'I can't have sex with you again.' As much as her body craved him, didn't he understand? She didn't want to hurt him. 'I'll hate myself, if I do.'

Luke reared away from her. Breathing hard, he took a couple of steps back. Sephy came up onto her elbows, trying to get her own breathing and racing heart back under control. 'I should check on Daisy,' she said hearing her voice shake and hating it.

'Your mother thought she'd be fine for hours.'

'But it's not up to you or my mother. It's up to me. I'm not in the habit of passing my daughter over to someone so I can disappear off to have sex.'

Luke's eyes narrowed. 'I was never under the impression that you did.'

Her heart jumped into her mouth. She hoped with all her heart that Claire Jackson had never done what she'd accused herself of doing to Daisy, but Luke had paled and from the way he shoved his hands back into his pockets, she wished his biological mother was alive so she could march right up to her and punch her out.

'You're a good mother, Sephy. Don't ever doubt that.'

His words had her wanting to cry. Again. God, she was a mess.

'Thank you for saying that,' she said softly, hopping off the table and smoothing down her dress. As always, he had this way of saying the loveliest of things to her, right when she needed to hear it most. While she? She mucked everything up. 'I'm so sorry for ruining everything between us,' she said, as she made to move past him.

Luke's hand shot out to wrap around hers and impede her progress. 'Damn it. No. We're not leaving it like this. Are you intending to be celibate for the rest of your life?' his hand squeezed against hers for an answer. When she couldn't give him one, he added, 'Or, is it that you're only intending for it not to mean anything? A release? Like you let loose with me. Time and time again, last night.'

She didn't respond. Couldn't.

'Shall I tell you what I think last night was really about, Sephy?'

Hadn't she just told him what last night was about for her? Every blessed word of it?

'I think,' he continued, 'that it's about we spent all year working up to last night and now, afterwards, you can't handle it.'

She tugged on her hand, but he wasn't letting go. Obviously she couldn't handle it. The weight of the guilt was crushing her.

'You're really going to have to get over this misnomer that you're the wild child – who's also the bad child,' Luke said and her chin tilted up stubbornly. Did he think she liked being reminded of who she had been? 'Jared told me today that one thing he's realised since coming back into your lives is that while he was gone, Nora adapted, but before you had Daisy you mostly got ignored. I know what it feels like to be ignored. But you and me…we don't seem able to ignore each other, do we?'

She stared down at their joined hands and, knowing he was imprinted on her heart, shook her head.

'Sephy, you partied for a couple of years. Acted irresponsibly for about five minutes. So what? If you're so bad and I'm so good, you tell me why the hell I would want to be with you?

She couldn't. She didn't understand why he would. Didn't get what she had to offer him. Couldn't trust that what she felt was real. More. And that she wouldn't ruin it all.

'No comeback?' he released her to rub a hand back and forth through his hair in a familiar gesture that meant he was trying to think his way through the problem.

She should be running to the door. Escaping. But she didn't. She was rooted to the spot.

'I must be a complete idiot,' he told her. 'I keep putting myself out there for you and you keep knocking me back. So this is the last time. I'm going to lay it all out for you.'

Now she did make a move. She couldn't let herself hear this. She needed to get out. She stepped around him, but in two strides he was back in front of her.

'Look at me, Seph,' he commanded in a voice that was so deep, so gruff, her gaze automatically swung up to meet his gorgeous green eyes. 'After last night, *before* last night and damn it, even now…I want in. I want all in with you.' He took her by the arms so she couldn't run. 'I think you do too, but you're too scared. I thought you had more guts than that.'

Sephy stared as his words penetrated. 'You don't know what you're saying,' she whispered.

'Don't I? How about if I tell you that I've been speaking to your mother about buying the estate?'

She couldn't breathe. 'Don't be silly. Why would you do that?'

'For you – for us. When I told your mother what you wanted

to do with the place, she incredibly graciously knocked a couple million off the asking price.'

Boiling-hot emotion started queuing up in her mouth, begging for release. 'Let me get this right. You've been negotiating with my mother?'

'You should have told her your plans for the estate, Seph. She was actually excited to hear them. Not that I was surprised. You sold your ideas to me and I one hundred percent know you could pull them off. So, us – if there's going to be an "us", now comes with the estate too.'

Sephy's heart hammered right out of her chest, fell on the floor and skidded between them to jackknife at Luke's feet. She had thought not getting married would prevent her from looking even remotely like she'd chosen to have someone bail her out. Chosen someone to get her what she wanted with no effort on her part. Never in her wildest dreams had she imagined Luke would simply wade in and throw his money down, effectively splitting open the cracks left behind by her father's letter.

This couldn't be happening. He couldn't be standing before her offering her all of him, together with the one thing that would potentially turn their whole relationship into being about money. How many times had she begged him not to offer her money? Buying the estate was a roundabout way of doing the same. It was too much. How did he not see that?

'Luke, I'm telling you right now that even if my mother sells to you you'll be living there alone because I will not be made to feel financially beholden to anyone.'

'Beholden? What the hell?' he stared aghast, as if she couldn't have insulted him more.

He didn't get it. On a breath of anger she hurled her most painful knowledge at him, 'It's why he took my money and gave it to Daisy.'

'Who did? Your father?'

She nodded, beyond humiliated that she was letting the words out. 'I'm supposed to do this on my own. I'm supposed to prove that I can provide for myself and for Daisy.'

'That's what this is about?' Luke's usual patience was now nonexistent. 'You can't set aside your stupid pride about doing everything yourself? You're prepared to cling to it even if it loses you something you didn't want to let go of?'

Sephy blanched. Was he talking about the estate or him? She heaved in oxygen to explain, but Luke was on a roll.

'You would have taken Jared and Nora's money last night,' he accused. 'You practically begged them to. What? My money isn't good enough? *I'm* not good enough?'

'I was panicking that I was losing the place I loved,' she hurled back, hating for even one second that he might ever feel he wasn't good enough. 'I'd only just found out. I'd had no time to let the news sink in and work out it was meant to be like this. And it's different when it's family.'

'Why is it?'

'Because it is,' she shot back, stubbornly. 'I can't owe you, Luke. I won't.'

'What if I told you I had plans for the estate, too?'

'What?'

'I want to open a resource centre for adoptive and foster parents.'

Immediately he said it, she could see it, and because it came from him, her response was honest and emotional when she whispered shakily, 'Okay. That's actually a wonderful idea that I can see working. But if that's what you really want, it should be completely separate from us.'

'I don't agree. I think that for you, the estate, marriage…us. It's all tied up together in your head and in your heart. When your father wrote you his letter and put your inheritance in Daisy's name, did you really think he was testing your ability to provide for yourself and your daughter?'

'Of course that's what he was doing. He was asking me to

choose between the life I had had before and what I could achieve for myself in the future.'

'But you already had chosen,' Luke insisted. 'You already had plans. Lots of them. You told me that you used to go to the lake and walk Daisy when she was a baby and dream about Seraphic and dream about what you wanted the estate to be in the future.'

'I –' she broke off, not trusting her voice as she ran damp palms down her sides, because hadn't she, for far too long now, felt the sting of anger that her father could think she didn't have plans for a better life for her daughter?

'Is the real reason you never wanted to get married because you thought if it looked like someone was able to provide more for you financially than you could for yourself that you had failed?'

Sephy sucked on her bottom lip, refusing to admit that to him.

'That wasn't *choosing not to get married ever*, Sephy. That was simply denying yourself a go at your dreams in case you failed.'

'What –' she stopped, appalled. 'No,' she denied automatically, but in her head doubt was making her question just how cowardly she might be. God, she knew the Kings didn't tend to do things they weren't convinced they'd be very good at, but…

'Sephy, don't you get why I want a shot at everything with you? Why it's all or nothing and I won't let myself settle for less? I want to be around your crazy-creative-caffeine-induced hyper-activity because I love it. I want to make a home with you because I believe that home would be welcoming and safe and nurturing and chaos – good chaos. I want to be a part of watching your incredible daughter grow up.'

When her shoulders slumped a little, he took a careful step towards her, reached out and ran his hand down the length of her hair. 'I want to see you open your eyes and lock straight onto mine in the mornings.' He moved his head to her ear and whis-pered, 'and God I want to hear more of the beautiful sighs you make when I'm moving inside you, because I know that it's me that makes you make those sounds – not any other man. We could have such an adventure together, Seph. Bend like the willow and choose me. Choose us. I love you, Seph.'

'Tears gathered and escaped and she felt him reach out with his thumb to gently brush them away.

'No guts, no glory,' he whispered, before stepping back. 'Remember that while you figure out what you want.'

God – he wanted her to make a decision now? Right after painting the canvas of her soul with a picture of just how good sharing a life with him could be? That was cunning, she thought. That was going to make it so much harder to apply logic.

'But Sephy, I want to be very clear on this,' Luke said, pausing before stepping out into the hallway, 'if you decide you can't risk it, then I'm going to insist you do me the greatest of favours and stay the hell away from me.'

CHAPTER EIGHTEEN

The door slammed behind him and Sephy's breath left her body in a rush. She bent over to try and release the pressure and drag more air into her lungs.

She didn't know what to do.

He didn't think she'd used him.

He said he wanted all in with her. That he was in love with her.

He was asking her for everything.

There was a soft knock at the door and then it opened and Nora poked her head around the gap.

'Luke thought you might need someone to brainstorm with.'

'Oh, you have to be kidding me,' she said, throwing her hands up in the air.

'Actually,' Nora stepped into the room, 'he asked me to make sure you were all right.'

Sephy looked at her sister and said in a voice that sounded as shocked as she felt, 'He wants me, Norsies. I mean, he wants a relationship with me.'

'Bastard.'

'No. Please. I can't do flippant right now.' She bent down again. 'Apparently I can barely do breathing.'

'Is it such a bad thing that he wants to be with you,' Nora asked carefully, 'I mean – if you want to be with him…?'

'I don't know. I mean he knows some of my baggage, but I basically just unpacked it all in front of him and you know what he did with it all?'

'What?'

'He declared it wasn't that bad.'

'I've always liked Luke.'

Sephy looked at Nora as if she was no help at all.

Nora grinned and added, 'I've always liked him for you.'

'But do you like *me* for him?' Sephy asked, desperate to hear the cold, hard truth. 'I mean, what if I can't transition from friends to lovers? What if I don't have the time to give him because of the business? I can't go back to being friends with him and pretend this hasn't happened. He won't let me. I'm basically all in – or I'm out of his life.'

The panic doubled. She didn't know how she would deal with not having him in her life.

'He's talking…' she swallowed. Felt the catch and release in her belly. 'Marriage.'

'What,' Nora shrieked with delight. 'He proposed?'

'Not exactly. At least, I don't think he did,' she answered, trying to let go of the image of a more romantic proposal coming out of Luke's mouth. 'He was just laying out the big picture for me.'

She felt the trembling start deep in the pit of her belly.

Luke had tried telling his foster parents that he didn't need to get married to be happy, but given his upbringing, it made total sense that deep down he would be kind of traditional and want marriage.

She registered more trembling going on inside of her, making her feel queasy.

Could she set aside her fears and marry Luke one day?

In denying her any option to pretend their connection wasn't deeper and more significant than any she had ever felt, Luke was basically telling her that he believed in her ability to be with him – that she wouldn't be taking one of those giant missteps she was always so worried about taking.

In his arms last night, consumed with his brand of tangible loving, his faith in her was impossible to avoid and made her feel fear-conquering and all-powerful. Could she, out of his arms, hold that knowledge and stand firm against her fears?

'Sephy?' Isobel poked her head through the door and when she spied both her daughters, stepped right into the room.

'Oh, good grief,' Sephy said, sniffing back tears and turning away to conceal them. With a hasty swipe of her hands over her cheeks, she muttered, 'Shouldn't at least one of us be representing the Kings at a King wedding?'

'Absolutely,' Isobel soothed, approaching cautiously, 'which is why I left Cousin Muriel on the dance floor. She's creating enough of a spectacle that I suspect, should Jared and Amanda work out where we are, we will suddenly have company.'

'Who's Cousin Muriel?' Sephy asked, momentarily distracted.

'You know,' Nora said, crossing her eyes, 'tomato-red dress, watermelon-pink hat and shoes.'

Sephy winced, remembering chatting to someone in an eye-watering colourful combination during the photos.

Isobel stepped closer and pursed her lips when she registered her daughter's tears. 'Oh, Sephy, what have you done? I was expecting to see you and Luke re-enter the wedding reception, well, together, at least. And when you did, I would have laid odds on you smiling from ear to ear as well.'

Sephy harrumphed, 'And why does it have to be my fault that I'm not?'

Isobel patted her arm. 'Because usually when a man tells a woman he's thinking of buying her a house and wants to make his home with her, less than an hour later they're still inseparable.'

'Even if one of them is worried that if she accepted it would look as if he manipulated her world to get her what she wanted?'

'Perhaps you put too much store in what others think,' Isobel stated quietly.

'Right,' Sephy answered, blowing out a breath. 'Because it's not as if this family hasn't had experience of how that screws things up, is it?'

Isobel reached out to pat her daughter's cheek. 'Sometimes I forget how young you were when Jared left. How it must have impacted on you harder. I know that neither your father nor I handled it in the best way we could have, but you know, people will always find something to talk about. If you're happy with your world, it hurts a lot less. Is there some reason you think you don't deserve to be happy?'

Slowly Sephy shook her head.

'Well, then,' Isobel said and watched closely for her daughter's reaction. 'Why, exactly, do you think Luke wants to buy the estate?'

'Because he can. Because he's super-generous with his money.'

Isobel sighed at the stubborn answer. 'I swear I don't understand why young people have to over-complicate everything, these days.'

'You wouldn't wait a while to sell the estate to me,' Sephy accused her mother softly. 'Why would you agree to sell it to Luke?' She stared at the floor thinking of how foster kids grew up sometimes not feeling good enough and how she knew Luke lavished money on those he cared about – on those he loved, as a way of showing them, because he didn't always feel comfortable using words.

Yet, he had used words with her. He had laid everything on the line, for her.

And now he was somewhere in that wedding reception, waiting.

Not knowing which way she would go.

And she hated that she was the person leaving him dangling when he deserved so much more. When he deserved everything.

'Sephy,' Isobel's tone was gentle, 'you would never have got a loan even if I had reduced the price to less than Luke offered on it.'

More tears slipped unheeded down Sephy's face because hadn't she worked that out for herself and wasn't she supposed to be getting busy coming to terms with that? So that she was baggage-free about the estate. And if she chose Luke and the estate came with it, would her mother really be happy? She had wanted to leave it, after all.

'Aside from the money' she pressed, 'why would you really consider selling to Luke?'

'Because he loves you and I think you love him,' Isobel answered matter-of-factly. 'And because he loves Daisy and Daisy loves him,' she added. 'He also made me see what the estate could be turned into in both of your names. Why didn't you ever tell me what you wanted to do with the place?'

'I thought it would all go to Jared.'

'I'm guessing you never told your father either, otherwise he would have left the whole estate to you.'

Sephy couldn't have been more shocked if the place *had* actually been left to her. Her father never would have done that. Would he? What did it matter now, anyway? 'It was all pipe dreams, Mum.'

'Well now it doesn't have to be a pipe dream. Now you can move forward with those dreams at a pace that's right for you and Luke.'

'I can't accept a gift that big from him.'

'Don't be ridiculous. Stop thinking it would be for you singular and start embracing what it could mean for both of you, together. Are you really going to sacrifice your dreams because it wasn't paid for with your money? Is that what you think your father would have done? Did you ever once see him sacrifice any of his dreams?'

'You don't understand,' she declared, flinging her arms out with the beginning of temper. 'Nobody understands. Dad wanted me to do all this on my own.'

'No, Sephy, it's you that doesn't understand,' Isobel said plainly, taking her daughter's hands in hers. 'Don't you see what we all see? Don't you know you already have been doing things on your own – since the minute you brought Daisy into the world?'

'He didn't see it,' she whispered, thinking about her father, her eyes brimming with fresh tears.

'He did.' Her mother's hands squeezed against hers. 'He wanted you to be able to see it for yourself.'

Sephy felt that last amorphous feeling that had been clouding her thinking for the past year slip silently free of her heart, leaving her lighter and more in sync with her world. Could it be true?

Had she taken this all too far?

All along, to help her family heal, she had insisted to them that she had understood why her father had done what he'd done.

But deep down, in all the ways that affected how she felt about herself, she hadn't, had she?

'Sephy,' Nora said, sliding off one of the tables to stand in front of her. 'Mum's right –you're making this all way too complicated.'

'I have to,' she answered. 'I have Daisy to consider.'

'Daisy is a five-year-old little girl who is more than capable of adapting to a new situation. Kids do, given the right framework. Look at the way she's dealing with Ryan being in her life. Don't you know she gets that from you? Don't you know how well you set that up for her? And don't you think Luke is capable of being just as careful and just as patient and just as loving as you are with her?'

'Yes, of course. He's more than capable and he's always been good with her.'

'Then forget about Daisy. Forget about Ryan. Forget about me and Jared and Mum and the estate and Dad and Seraphic and everything you keep putting in your way. What do *you* want?'

Sephy blew out a breath. 'I want Luke,' she said. 'I want him so much.' The release of finally admitting it out loud left her feeling giddy.

Nora nudged her in the ribs. 'Then don't you think you'd better go and get him?'

'I'm scared,' she said quietly.

'So?' Nora raised her eyebrow in challenge.

Sephy sighed. 'Well, thank you very much for sparing me no quarter.'

'You're welcome.' Nora grinned. 'Now go be fearless.' She made a shooing motion with her hand.

'He's sitting back at the table,' Isobel said helpfully.

Sephy smoothed down her dress. 'Do I look okay?'

'You look like a woman who knows what she wants,' Nora told her with a grin. 'What man can resist that?'

'Especially,' Isobel added, 'when he's just told you it's what he wants too.'

'Okay,' Sephy squared her shoulders, tipped her chin up defiantly, 'Okay, I'm going back out there now. To find Luke. You two…you two, please try and look subtle when you follow me back into the room.'

Back in the room where Jared and Amanda were holding their reception, Sephy headed for the table they'd all been seated at. She could do this. She didn't want to watch him walk out of her life. He had put himself and their friendship on the line, telling her he wanted to be with her and she was going to take his 'no guts no glory' approach and run with it. Straight towards him, so that she could give them the chance they deserved.

Some of her bravado deserted her the moment she realised Luke was not sitting at the table. Quietly she took her seat in the corner and waved at her cousin Muriel.

'Where's Daisy?' she asked.

Muriel smiled and pointed to the dance floor.

'Oh.' Sephy's hand came up to her heart. There in the middle of the crowded dance floor Luke was dancing with Daisy in his arms. Her daughter was shrieking with laughter every time a grinning Luke spun her around or did an exaggerated dip.

Sephy's heart swelled within her chest as all the stuff Nora had accused her of putting in her way simply melted away. Now all she had to do was tell him.

Glancing down at the table she looked at the gold confetti that had been scattered over the tables – little crowns in a tongue-in-cheek nod to the King name. Reaching out she scooped up some of the confetti and on the bit of table Luke had been seated at, she reformed the little crowns to say: I'm in.

She added an exclamation mark and instead of a dot, shaped the confetti into a heart. Then, she settled back into her chair and waited, those butterflies that had taken up residence inside her flitting about for all they were worth.

When Luke and Daisy came off the dance floor, Daisy skipped right over to her and jumped up on her lap for a cuddle. Sephy put her arms around her daughter and kissed the top of her head, but kept her eyes on Luke. He looked surprised to see her sitting there and with only a slight hesitation sat down in his seat, his attention taken up by Muriel's teasing about his natural dancing ability and how he might save the next dance for her.

'Did you see me?' Daisy asked Sephy.

'I did.' Sephy nodded. 'You looked like you were having the best fun.'

'I was. Luke twirled me around and around and my feet weren't even on the floor.'

Once again, Sephy gazed distractedly at Luke, wondering how much more patient she could be while he finished his good-natured bragging about his dance moves.

When she could stand it no more, she interrupted to tell Luke, 'I expect all that dancing has made you thirsty.'

Luke turned to look at her and she pushed his drink into the space where she'd written her answer and glanced pointedly down at the table.

Luke frowned at her and reached for his drink but she didn't let go until he looked down at what she'd written.

He went very still and his hand came out to rest on the table under the letters.

'Who's Imin?' he asked, his gaze meeting hers.

With a sharp intake of breath she said, 'What do you mean

who's Imin? It says,' and before she could finish the sentence she realised he was grinning from ear to ear and flashing those gorgeous dimples.

'Mummy? Who's Imin?' Daisy asked, copying Luke.

'No one, darling, Luke is having a little fun with me,' and feeling the laughter bubble up in her chest, she reached over in front of Daisy and everyone, grabbed him by the lapels of his jacket and pulled him in for a quick kiss on his mouth.

When she released him he was looking shocked she'd actually kissed him in front of everyone. Truth was, she was a little shocked herself. Especially when Daisy's eyes grew round and she gasped and put a hand to her mouth as a giggle escaped. Sephy put a hand to her own mouth and giggled too, to show Daisy it was all right, and Daisy grabbed Luke by the neck and kissed him on his cheek.

'Aren't you having the best time ever, Mummy?' she said as she slid from Sephy's lap to climb up on Luke's.

Sephy nodded enthusiastically. 'Best wedding ever, Daisy,' and looking at the man sat next to her, she shared a special smile.

EPILOGUE

Sephy stood in her father's study, staring up at his portrait.

'So I finally worked it out, Dad. Yes, it took more than one person to point it out to me. What can I say? I'm definitely not perfect. What I think I am, out of your three children, is probably the most like you. Passionate – but stubborn in the extreme. Why Luke loves me I guess is the same as why Mum loves you. And he does love me, Dad. He really does. And I'd be the biggest fool on the planet if I let that slip through my fingers.'

So I'm choosing not to do that.

The study door opened and Jared poked his head through. 'You about ready?'

Sephy's butterflies performed a perfectly choreographed loop-de-loop as her brother opened the door wider and stepped into the study.

'He came, then?' she asked, pressing a hand to her stomach.

Jared grinned. 'Of course he came. It's not every day a guy has trays of cupcakes delivered to his office, spelling out very specific instructions.'

'I guess the fact that he's here means they at least arrived in the correct order. The last time I spelled out something out for him, he –' she broke off, smiling. He'd known what she'd been saying when she'd spelled out 'I'm in' for him, with the King crown confetti at Jared and Amanda's wedding three months ago. He'd been teasing her. He had this incredible way of not letting her take herself too seriously.

He had this incredible way of loving her.

And she had worked out the most perfect way of showing him how much she treasured that and how much she loved him back.

'Jared,' Sephy said, 'thank you so much for flying back for this.'

'Are you kidding? As if I would miss this. Amanda has brought her camera, if you want some photographs taken.'

'I suppose it depends on how it goes.'

'You can count on her to know if it's going well or not.'

'So where *is* Luke? Is he already in position, because I need to check Nora's fixed the speakers and I ought to check on Daisy.'

'Relax. Ethan is looking after Luke. Something about counting grains of rice with him.'

That was weird enough to distract her from being nervous for about ten seconds and then Nora turned up.

'Hi,' her sister said, beaming. 'Everything is ready. Want me to go tell Ethan to take Luke down to the gazebo?'

'I guess. Wait, where's Daisy?'

'She's hopping up and down with excitement. Mum is containing her in the kitchen.'

'Okay. So – if this all goes horribly wrong you're both sticking around to help me get drunk, right?'

'Absolutely,' Jared nodded.

'Definitely,' declared Nora.

'Good. Do you think it's too much?' she asked in a worried voice. 'Be honest. I mean, Luke can be shy sometimes and I don't want to scare the hell out of him.'

Nora snorted. 'I didn't believe you the first time you told me Luke was shy with you, and I don't believe you now. Look at how he kept putting himself on the line for you. Have a little faith.'

The butterflies fluttering within Sephy's stomach settled at Nora's last words, making her smile. Nora couldn't have said anything more perfect if she'd tried.

'Okay,' she picked up the jeweller's box that had been sitting on her father's desk. 'Nora, give me five minutes to get to the gazebo and then tell Ethan I'm ready. And Jared, you can make sure the rest of the guests know where I need them to wait for my cue.'

With a last look up at her father's portrait, Sephy left the study.

As she walked over to the lake and gazebo, Sephy smiled again. Nora had done a good job; she could see the silk banners of her and Luke from the Seraphic ad campaign hanging from the sides. As she jogged up the three wooden steps she saw the microphone and speakers cable-tied into the corners of the roof.

All she had to do now was wait.

For Luke.

It was like that time in the ballroom when she'd been figuring out how on earth to ask him to model for her in her ad campaign, only with way more riding on it. She ran quick hands over her hair, smoothing it down and pushing it back behind her ears. Considering how much she had riding on this meeting between them, now that she was here, she wasn't as nervous as she'd feared.

And then she spotted him walking towards her, a frown forming over those gorgeous green eyes of his.

She waited until he walked up the gazebo steps to stand opposite her and then, feeling incredibly shy all of a sudden, she said, 'Hey you.'

Luke tipped his head in greeting. 'Hey you,' he answered back softly.

'So you got the cupcakes all right, then.'

'I did. The lads ate them up in record time. I had to work out the last part of the message from the 'G' cupcake and the 'O' cupcake.'

'Good job you're a genius, huh?'

Luke smiled and then took his gaze from hers to indicate the gilt-framed chairs that had been set up in front of the gazebo. 'Expecting an audience?'

Sephy licked her lips. 'Possibly.'

'Possibly?'

'It kind of depends.'

'On?'

'You. And then me getting my cue right.'

'Okay.' He took a cautious step towards her. 'And what's your cue?'

'It's a go.'

'Huh?'

'I said,' she repeated louder, 'It's. A. Go.'

A cheer went up in the air and Sephy rolled her eyes as Luke's head whipped around to see a crowd of people walk out from behind the bank of reeds at the lake towards the chairs in front of the gazebo.

'What the…?' Luke whispered.

'Oh, for the love of God. This is my fault. I forgot about the speakers.'

'Speakers?' Luke looked completely bemused, his attention now drawn to the fact that people he knew were sitting down in front of the gazebo with huge grins on their faces.

Sephy looked out and saw Nora and Ethan, Amanda, Steve and Lily Jackson, and Ryan and his new-old girlfriend, Michelle, and right at the edge of the lake she saw Isobel, Daisy and Jared waiting for her second cue.

Dragging in a breath, she spoke loud enough for the speakers to relay her words across the whole of the King estate. 'Okay, so, I was supposed to do this bit without an audience, but life doesn't always go according to plan, does it? Luke,' the man she loved turned around to face her, his gaze sweeping her from head to foot, taking in her white top covered in daisies and her white skinny jeans. His smile was gentle and that was all she needed to continue. 'A few months ago we were standing in a room in a hotel in New York. You wore your heart on your sleeve for me and in the most arrogant, most exasperating, most confusingly patient, way you asked me to choose you.'

She saw Luke's chest rise as he inhaled deep into his lungs, saw his hands go self-consciously to the back pockets of his jeans and, stepping forward, she grasped them in hers. As the warmth of his skin pulsed through her, she shook out a breath, looked deep into his eyes and said, 'It was the bravest, wisest, most generous thing anyone has ever done for me.'

'Seph,' said Luke and her name on his lips, spoken in that quiet, patient, but slightly gruff way of his, made her heart melt.

'I figured it out, you know – what you were trying to tell me,' she confessed. 'What everyone has been trying to tell me,' she said with half a smile before sobering. 'My father wasn't asking me to choose, was he?'

Luke's gaze never left hers as he shook his head.

'What he was doing was testing my faith. My faith in me.' Her smile wobbled a little and she blinked to steady herself. 'Because he knew I'd lose it without him there to spur me into believing in myself. And he knew once I chose more things in life I would need the courage to believe I deserved them.'

She felt the tug on their joined hands as Luke went to pull her in close to him, but she shook her head, disentangled her hands and took a step back.

'Wait, don't move.' Looking around her in panic, she spotted what she needed and grabbed the jeweller's box off the gazebo balustrade. 'Right. Ready,' she continued. 'Oh, hang on a minute,' she asked, and as gracefully as a woman could in stilettos and skinny jeans, she went down on bended knee.

'Seph – what are you doing?'

Holding the box out to him, she smiled. 'I'm choosing you, Luke Jackson. You've been my fake boyfriend and I've been your fake fiancée, but all the way through we've been best friends who could never ignore each other. I love you and I'm asking you if you will fake marry me today and then marry me for real as soon as we can organise it.'

In the stark silence and kneeling on the hard wooden floor, it felt to Sephy as if the small congregation leant forward on the edge of their seats to catch his answer, but as she stared up into his eyes, she wasn't worried.

She had faith in herself.

She had faith in them.

They'd been living together at the estate for six weeks and even with her spending lots of time on Seraphic and Luke dividing his time between working with the council to organise the resource centre and his new game Zero Hour, she knew that she had never been happier.

Like Luke's game, the two of them were about forging a new beginning.

A nanosecond later and Luke was pulling her to her feet and into his arms. 'Yes,' he laughed. 'Yes, I will fake marry you and yes, I will real marry you.'

His hands came out to cradle her head and his mouth crashed down onto hers.

She sighed as his lips tasted hers.

Their mouths couldn't fit together more perfectly if they'd been designed exactly for that purpose.

Maybe they had.

Haute couture for their hearts.

'We can invite all your brothers and sisters to the real wedding, but for now I need to give my second cue,' Sephy said, when his lips finally left hers.

'Wait. What's in the box?'

'Oh,' she ripped off the ribbon and opened it for him. 'It's a tiny platinum seraphim and daisy. I thought you could put them on your leather cord.'

When he remained staring down at the charms, his throat working, she felt the first stirrings of uncertainty. 'If they're too feminine, you don't have to wear them. It's a gift,' she added.

'I love them,' he whispered. 'Um, Ryan is okay with all of this, right? I mean he understands I love Daisy but that he's her father.'

'He wouldn't be here today if he didn't understand. And he's really happy she'll have two men laying down the law when boys start coming around. I spoke with Daisy, too. It's very simple in her world. She loves me and she loves you and she loves that we love each other. Speaking of Daisy, are you ready for the next part of the proceedings?'

He nodded, smiling down at her.

'Okay, then I need you to stand in front of the gazebo. I'm going to disappear for a minute, but I'll be right back. Here comes cue two,' and clearing her throat she said over the crowd, 'Calling Darth Daisy, we have a wedding ceremony for you to perform.'

Marching up the makeshift centre aisle between chairs came Daisy King dressed in the Darth Vader costume Luke had bought her and carrying her beloved lightsaber. When she reached the gazebo she walked up the three stairs.

'Back in a minute, then,' Sephy grinned and jogged down the centre aisle to stand beside Jared.

Amanda, who had been taking photographs from the beginning, grinned at Sephy and stood in the aisle to take a photograph of Sephy and her brother.

'Oops, hang on a moment,' Nora said, diving out of her chair. 'Before I get the music playing, I thought you might like this,' and from behind her back she presented Sephy with a small bouquet of roses and daisies, wrapped in Seraphic tissue paper. 'I had to improvise a little.'

'They're perfect. Thank you. Are you absolutely sure you don't mind Jared walking me down the aisle before he gets to do the same for you?'

'I'm sure. It'll be good practice. Right. Music,' and she walked round to hook up the MP3 player to the speakers.

'You ready for this, sis?' Jared asked.

Sephy beamed at her brother. 'Never been more ready for anything in my life.' She turned to look at the willow tree.

I love you, Dad.

As the theme tune to *Star Wars* started playing through the speakers, Sephy concentrated on her future. The one that was right in front of her as she walked with her brother down the makeshift aisle towards her daughter and her now very real fiancé.

When she was standing opposite him, Nora stopped the music and Daisy immediately said, 'That was for you, Luke. Mummy said you would prefer it to "Love is an Open Door".'

'Mummy was right, Daisy.'

'Okay.' Daisy turned her Darth Vader helmet towards her mother, 'Do I get to do my bit now?'

'Yes, darling. Remember to speak clearly so that everyone can hear you. Just like we practised, okay?'

'Okay. Luke, do you love my Mummy?'

'I do,' Luke said, smiling down into Sephy's face.

'Mummy, do you love my Luke?'

'I do,' Sephy said with an equally large smile on her face.

'Then, by the powers "vespered" in me by this lightsaber, I now pronounce you husband and wife.'

Laughter and applause broke out amongst the crowd as Daisy knighted Sephy and Luke with her lightsaber. Luke swept Daisy up into his arms, removed her Darth Vader helmet and gave her a big kiss on the cheek and then reached for Sephy and kissed her soundly on the mouth.

Isobel King wandered over to sit on the wooden bench in front of the willow tree they had all planted the month she lost her husband. Turning her head towards the gazebo she watched her son Jared throw back his head and laugh at something seemingly outrageous that his wife Amanda was saying to him. Her eyes followed movement and she watched as Ethan wrapped her daughter Nora up in his arms and twirled her around in the air, no doubt happy that it would be their wedding next. And then her eyes went to her daughter Sephy and her grand-daughter Daisy and the latest addition to the family, Luke Jackson. The trio were standing in a circle together holding hands. She had absolutely no doubt in her heart that they were all going to make each other happy and that in Sephy and Luke's hands, this estate was going to thrive. She would visit from time to time and when she did she would always come to this spot and talk to the willow tree.

She smiled softly as the willow tree bent in the breeze. He had done it. He had started making amends before it was too late and in doing so he'd opened up the path for each of their children to find their brightest futures.

Family.

Love.

You couldn't change the past, but you could change the future.

I love you. She told him.

And the whispering on the wind came back to her.

I love you, too.

The End

Also by Eve Devon

The Love List

Her Best Laid Plans